To Kevin

Hope you enjoy it

WHEN FATE COMES CALLING

Sean Doyle

Sean Doyle

Book Guild Publishing
Sussex, England

First published in Great Britain in 2009 by
The Book Guild
Pavilion View
19 New Road
Brighton, BN1 1UF

Typesetting in Baskerville by
Keyboard Services, Luton, Bedfordshire

Printed in Great Britain by
CPI Antony Rowe

A catalogue record for this book is available from
The British Library

ISBN 978 1 84624 316 5

To Katherine, Lucy and Liam –
my reason and my inspiration

Chapter 1

With the benefit of hindsight, I wonder what I might have done differently. At what stage might I have chosen another option, one that wouldn't have ended in hopeless despair, in lives being torn apart – one that wouldn't have ended in the spilling of innocent blood?

Was it fate? Was it just meant to happen? Did I miss the flight for a reason? Did I glance up at just the wrong time ... or was it the right time? A single innocuous decision, a fleeting glance that would change my life for ever, and not just mine, others' as well. But, of course, life doesn't come with hindsight; it doesn't come with warning signs. We make choices based on what we know, but it's what we don't know that matters; it's what we don't know that would change our minds and make us act differently. But even if I had known what would I have done differently? I would still have walked into that bar.

As I walked into the hotel reception, I succumbed to the desire for a drink – it had, after all, been a bad day. I hesitated: lounge or bedroom mini bar? The latter would provide me with the solitude I craved, but as I glanced into the lounge I caught a brief glimpse of a pair of slender tanned legs, crossed and pulled tightly together. I couldn't see the woman's face, but I wondered whether the rest of her would match up to those legs. Suddenly the bar seemed an intriguingly more attractive option ... and the die had been irrevocably cast.

She was hidden behind a pillar and as I walked through

the lounge I avoided being too obvious, resisting the temptation to look to my left and see what she was really like. I got to the bar and pulled out one of the steel-backed chairs, sat down and ordered a gin and tonic. I glanced at my watch, only six o'clock, a bit early perhaps, but it had been a frustrating few hours and I needed something to help me relax.

I tried to see her through the mirrors at the back of the bar, but from my angle all I could see was the alcove, where three men, dressed in Western suits but Middle Eastern in appearance, were huddled together over cocktails.

I had positioned myself at an angle to the bar, so that I could turn and survey the scene, look at her without being too blatant. Would I be disappointed, or would she be as beautiful as my imagination speculated? I casually turned and looked up, and as I did, my heart missed a beat. She was already there – waiting for me; she wasn't just beautiful, she was absolutely stunning! I had intended to glance up and subtly move on before she caught me looking, but her eyes trapped me and I found myself unable to look away. I sensed a surge of adrenalin run through my body, my breathing quickened – temptation mischievously tiptoed across my mind.

She was no more than twenty feet away. Highlighted coppery fair hair reached down to her shoulders, surrounding a pretty, no, a beautiful face; high distinct cheekbones; a sultry look matching a southern European complexion. Despite her obvious beauty, the feature that took my breath away, even from this distance, was her eyes. Azure eyeshadow and long dark lashes both contrived to lure me seductively towards their centres. I stared into their depths and was unwittingly drawn in, albeit if not unwillingly. There was something strangely surreal about them, as if they emitted some kind of radiance, some kind of force that left me breathless.

We seemed to stare at each other for ages, neither prepared to look away, as if it had become a challenge; survival of the fittest – Darwin would have been proud. I wanted to hold her gaze, but then I slipped up. I started to think about it, started to wonder what the hell was going on, started to feel self-conscious! It was fatal and I knew that I wouldn't be able to do it; it would be me, not her who would look away first. I gave in, turned away, looked back towards the bar, disappointed with myself, but also slightly exhilarated. I turned slightly to my left and caught her reflection through the wooden slats on the mirrored pillar – she really was quite beautiful, early thirties, slightly older perhaps; I wasn't sure.

Why was she there waiting for me? How had we found ourselves in a private battle to hold each other's gaze? I looked up at the bar to see the perfect symmetry of the bottles of orange and lemon liqueurs, positioned equally either side, like two armies facing each other – just like the two of us. Who would make the next move? Which of us would be the victor, which the vanquished?

There was something familiar about her. A memory stirred but I couldn't place her. Perhaps she was famous, but no names came to mind. My mind ran through a range of emotions – curiosity, intrigue, fear – but they all led back to one thing, and try as I did to put it off I couldn't avoid it forever – I had to look again. There was no pretence this time, no effort to scan the room, no casual glance. I raised my eyes as I looked to my left – there she was again, just waiting for me to make my move. My heartbeat resonated against the hotel walls – surely she would hear it.

She was wearing a light khaki-coloured skirt and open jacket, a white blouse beneath, taut across her breasts, revealing little, but leaving a lot more to the imagination. Her slender neck was decorated with a subtle gold chain, from which a simple cross hovered tantalisingly over her cleavage.

Once again I became lost in her mysterious eyes. It was as if they were covered by an invisible veil that hid her true thoughts, but still revealed enough for me to recognise the deep emotions running through her. I was drawn in, slowly seduced by their magical quality, a quality that enticed one to look further, deeper, searching into their depths for the answer to an unknown question. A sense of déjà-vu – I'd been here before, I'd seen her before, but where and who was she?

She had a slight air of arrogance about her; she knew just how beautiful she was, how powerful she was when it came to men. But what was her game? Why was she investing so much time in looking at me? As high an opinion as I have of myself, I knew I wasn't that good looking. Perhaps on a good day, but let's not get carried away! I held her stare for a few more seconds before negative thoughts started to buzz through my brain. I was going to fail – again! I fought desperately with myself, but I couldn't do it, and reluctantly I dropped my eyes.

I ordered another gin and tonic; I needed strength for this. 'Better make it a double actually, not too much tonic,' I pleaded with the barman. My drink arrived and I took a large gulp. It was nice and strong, and instantly I felt a pleasant burning sensation as the gin worked its way through me. I tried to slow down my breathing, taking deeper breaths, calming myself down.

I casually looked up, as if indifferent, but as I did, so did she, listing her head slightly to the right, brushing her hair deliberately back to reveal more of her beautiful face. A sparkling flash as the light caught on a golden hooped earring. We looked into each other's eyes, again that recognition. There was something about those deep blue eyes that enticed me to keep looking; they begged me to continue, not to look away, for fear of what I might miss. That feeling of familiarity flirted with me again and I wondered where I had seen her before. I held her stare. The gin was doing its job and encouraging me, but like all drugs its effects were temporary and I started to feel the anxiety creeping back. Just as I was ready to give in, to reluctantly capitulate, she raised the stakes and unexpectedly smiled. I was caught completely off guard and smiled back weakly, but then immediately turned away, embarrassed and humiliated.

I was confused, smiling was an unexpected move on her part, it took the game to a new level, a level inviting participation, where I could no longer get away with holding her sultry look. I knew I couldn't ignore her, I had to continue the game, but what was my next move going to be, or would she make another surprise play?

Before I even had time to think, in the periphery of my vision I saw her get up. My heart beat louder, a surge of panic swept through me; either she was coming over or leaving – neither was an attractive scenario. Too quickly I realised she was coming to the bar; I felt like a teenage boy embarrassed when the school's most beautiful girl innocently says good morning. Calm down, I told myself, she's only a woman, a beautiful woman admittedly; OK, the most beautiful woman I've ever seen, but still only a woman ... and anyway I'm married so why the hell am I so nervous? I was desperately trying to look calm and cool, but inside I was anything but. I didn't dare look up, hoping in vain that she might have chosen to ignore me.

As she moved closer, I took a large swig of my G&T – and looked up. Our eyes met and again she smiled, but this time more determinedly, not a casual throw-away kind of a smile but one that said, 'Hi, how are you?' I smiled weakly, feeling my heart soar, not in joy, but in panic as it headed inexorably higher. What should I do? What should I say? My mind went blank – I have an IQ of 145, those fools at MENSA think I'm a genius, yet I couldn't think of a single word to say.

As she approached, the depth of her blue eyes became clearer, a blue that is only seen in the deepest oceans, full of beauty and danger. They drew me in, unable to resist the temptation and as the curtains to her world were drawn back, I realised where I'd seen her before. I felt my whole body shake, then weaken as I sensed the blood drain from my face, my windpipe constricting as I struggled to breathe. A momentary sense of panic flooded through me, unable to quite believe that she was standing before me, after all these years.

Then her hair had been much longer, much darker, and her face had looked so much younger, but then that had been eighteen years ago – she had been no more than a girl, not the woman she had clearly become. Her beauty had not been diminished by time; if anything it had become enhanced by the intervening years. But it was her eyes that hadn't changed at all. Eyes so blue, they had enshrined themselves in my memory...

Yet the memory was not a happy one, it was not of our love for each other, nor of her stunning blue eyes, instead it was of the tears that had clouded them, the pain and anguish on her face, the look of someone who had been betrayed by the one person she believed in – and it was a memory that had scarred my heart so fiercely that I thought it would never heal until the day I died.

But here she was, the woman who had taken my heart and kept it – here she was right in front of me again, as beautiful as ever, and perhaps this was my second chance, my chance to change things – to right the wrong I had done.

Chapter 2

Jack handed over the pesetas and placed the jar of mixed peppercorns in his shirt pocket – not ideal, but with pocket-less swimming shorts, the only safe place available. A vital ingredient if tonight's meal was going to be slightly more appetising than those he'd had the previous three nights. Since his arrival at the weekend his German hosts could not have been faulted on their hospitality, but when it came to culinary skills there was a distinct lack of imagination. They appeared to think that adding HP sauce was adventurous, while the suggestion of using some fresh herbs was greeted with total bewilderment.

Pulling his Ray-Bans over his eyes, Jack jumped onto the moped. As he inserted the key, he thought for a second about putting on the helmet. Common sense said yes, but bright orange, wide-brimmed, it wasn't exactly a fashion statement! Vanity won the day; after all, it was only a five-minute journey.

The engine caught, Jack turned the accelerator and headed off down the narrow Sant Pere Boix towards the beach front, weaving his way round the numerous potholes. It was late afternoon and the streets were quiet; a few stragglers were heading home from the beach, but most were already back in their hotel rooms soothing their sunburnt skin with layers of calamine lotion and tarting themselves up for the tacky delights that Rosas had to offer at night.

As he approached the beach, Jack slowed and looked to his right but the front was virtually empty. He turned left and headed out of town – the warm sun caressed the bare skin of his arms and legs, the breeze flowed through his hair. He couldn't help but smile – four weeks in Rosas with Heike, a German friend of his, her parents and brother Peter. No studying, no working, just relaxing, enjoying himself; lots of beer, hopefully some decent food and perhaps, just perhaps, a bit of romance – there was that rather nice Dutch girl he had met last night.

The moped slowed as it started to climb the hill heading north out of Rosas, the 50cc engine struggling on the steep incline. Ahead of him, Jack noticed a bright-white poodle, freshly bleached by the look of it, yapping away, pulling at its leash, its woman owner trying to hold it back. As he reached them, the poodle, in what was presumably a suicide bid, jumped into the road, right into Jack's path. Instinctively he swung the handle bars to the right, but it was too late and the moped started to fall away underneath him. He stuck out his leg to break the fall but, as he did so, caught the poodle in its mid-rift, sending it flying backwards. As the moped crashed to the ground, Jack found himself flying through the air now regretting his decision not to wear the helmet. He passed over the upside-down poodle, before going into a roll, and ending up sitting on his backside, a bit battered and bruised, but at least in one piece. Miraculously, his Ray-Bans remained in place, allowing him to retain at least a shred of dignity.

The same could not be said of the poodle, which was whimpering and lying on its back, its legs floundering aimlessly in the air, or more importantly of the moped, which was, to put it bluntly, buggered.

Jack didn't move for a few seconds, as he struggled to regain his breath. He looked up to see the woman approaching him. She was wearing a skimpy white top and flouncy white skirt that showed her nice long legs.

Her dark hair was pulled tightly back into a ponytail and she was wearing ridiculously large round mirror sunglasses, which gave her a slightly Martian appearance. Rather foolishly Jack assumed she was going to apologise, but instead she unleashed a torrent of abuse, most of which Jack didn't understand. He did, however, pick up enough to realise she wasn't a local. French – that would explain the bleached poodle, he thought.

Jack gingerly picked himself up and brushed himself down. At full height, he was only slightly taller than her. As he tried to look imposingly down at her, all he could see, rather disconcertingly, was his own image in each of the reflective lenses.

'*Espèce d'imbécile!*' she shouted as she checked the poodle for damage.

'Why am I the imbecile?' Jack asked, to himself as much as her.

'Huh, English eh!' she puffed, switching easily to Jack's native tongue. 'I should have guessed – look what you have done to the poor dog, you idiot.' She crouched down to pick up the poodle, cradling it in her arms and gently stroking it.

'So you keep telling me, but how exactly was it my fault? It was your bloody dog that tried to attack me,' Jack retorted.

'It is not my dog,' she replied.

'Not your dog,' Jack repeated, momentarily bemused. After a moment's hesitation, Jack continued the case for the defence.

'I don't care if it's your dog or not, you are responsible for it and that dog attacked me and caused me to fall off the moped, which is now damaged.'

'You were riding carelessly and now you've injured the poor dog!' she said more aggressively.

'No I wasn't. Your stupid dog jumped into the road

9

straight into my path.' Jack's voice rose as bemusement started to turn to exasperation. 'If you had proper control of your dog in the first place, it wouldn't be hurt... '

'It's not *my* dog; I already told you!' she interrupted.

'Whoever's bloody dog it is,' Jack shouted, '*you* were in charge, *you* were responsible for it. It was *your* fault the dog got hurt, *your* fault I fell off the moped...'

The woman stared back at him. Was she about to apologise, or was this the calm before the storm? It turned out to be neither. She spoke very calmly, almost softly, but not without a hint of venom.

'Listen, mister arrogant Englishman, you are the irresponsible idiot; it was your fault! You were on the wrong side of the road. If you had been on the right, you would have been nowhere near us and we would not be having this conversation now. Instead you decide to ride on the left. It's just a shame it was a dog and not a lorry that you hit.' A sarcastic smile emanated from her lips. Case for the prosecution closed.

Jack was taken aback, realising to his horror that she was right. OK, so he wasn't completely innocent, but the dog still attacked him. He recovered his composure, but she had delivered more than a flesh wound.

'So what if I was on the wrong side of the road?' Jack countered. 'Your dog didn't know that, or being a French dog is it so bloody clever that it knows the English drive on the left?'

'It doesn't have to know. If you were on the right, this wouldn't have happened!' she shouted back. 'Imbecile!'

Jack realised they were just going round in circles. He shrugged, and shook his head, then turned towards the moped. With its front forks bent at such an unnatural angle, it wasn't going to be taking him anywhere.

Behind him, Jack could hear the Frenchwoman as she continued to soothe the poodle and occasionally cast yet another 'imbecile' in his direction. Forlornly Jack began the trek home, pushing the bike up the hill. He was worried about the damage to the bike, and felt slightly guilty, too, about hurting the dog. He could feel the sweat trickling down his back and face. How was he going to explain this to Peter? Ahead of him he could see the twin white apartment blocks, five storeys high, looking out to sea and back towards Rosas. Heike's parents' flat was on the second floor of the right-hand block with views over the bay from the front and to the side, where the pool and gardens separated the two blocks. It was a generously proportioned three-bedroom apartment, which the Webers had bought when it was built a decade earlier. They spent most of their summers in Rosas, driving down from Germany in two cars, the four of them plus the dog. Heike's dad was an architect, a very successful one apparently, and was able to afford the best part of six weeks off in the summer, so every July they departed en masse to Rosas.

Much to Jack's surprise, Peter didn't seem bothered about the damage to the bike.

'Don't be worried, we fix it tomorrow.' His English was good, but not perfect. Peter was much more excited by his discovery than Jack's misadventure. His usual afternoon routine was a search-and-interrogate mission, and today's had proved rewarding. From the apartment balcony, Peter would roam the poolside area with his binoculars, searching out new arrivals, or at least the female ones, zooming in on them and studying their anatomy. It was slightly too voyeuristic for Jack's liking, but it kept Peter entertained. Today apparently he had hit the jackpot.

'Jack, she's gorgeous – tall, flowing red hair, and she has a beautiful friend, too. We are meeting them at eight tonight.'

Peter had a great chat-up line; it seemed so naff, but

11

it always got him into a conversation and from there, there was no stopping him. 'Do you speak English?' That was it. So simple, but so effective, or perhaps it was the self-confidence and boyish good looks that went with it. Peter was only seventeen, but six foot three, powerfully built and with a body girls loved. Typical German bone structure, head held high, dark hair and brown eyes. It was going to be an interesting month.

'So just how beautiful is her friend?' Jack asked, as nonchalantly as he could.

'Very beautiful,' Peter replied confidently, before adding more quietly, 'Apparently.'

'What do you mean, "apparently"?' Jack asked, a frown creasing his brow.

'Well, I haven't actually seen her, but Simone says she is and she should know.' Jack's heart dipped; he had a feeling that perhaps this was a set-up. Still, with the day he had had, could it get much worse?

Supper wasn't quite what it was meant to be. The peppercorn sauce that Jack had offered to make lacked one vital ingredient – peppercorns. Sadly they hadn't made it back to the apartment and were presumably lying in the gutter, along with a bruised ego and some bloodied poodle hair. It therefore became what was fast becoming the normal fare – overcooked steak, undercooked chips and a very bland sauce.

The meal followed the now familiar pattern of a short period of silence as everybody gorged on the tasteless food, followed by a debate between Heike and her father that gradually rose in tempo and aggression as each raised their voice to outdo the other. As the volume was turned up, Heike's father, Herr Weber, would start to spit out his words, accompanied by bits of meat that hadn't made it down to his oversized belly. This was the cue for Peter and his mother to join in at full voice. By the end the whole family was shouting, no one was listening and Jack was left just sitting there, not understanding a word and oblivious to the whys and wherefores that had caused such a ferocious debate. Initially he had felt very uncomfortable, but now he knew the format and right on time, the whole thing ended, as abruptly as it had started – the result, as always, a high-scoring draw.

Chapter 3

Jack had decided to make a bit of an effort that night and had a shave and shower, gelled back his spiky hair and splashed on some aftershave. Tapes and stereo in hand, shades in place, Jack, Peter and Heike went down the steps to the sea. Heike looked good tonight, tight jeans and a skimpy top doing ample justice to her more than ample bosom. Nothing had ever gone on between Jack and her, though sometimes he wondered why. She was good looking in an unconventional way, pretty eyes, stocky build, but attractive. She had a tomboyish streak about her, but when she wanted she could be very feminine.

'You look really nice tonight,' Jack found himself saying and then wondered for whose benefit he had said it.

Heike turned to him and smiled. 'Why thank you! You don't look too bad yourself.' She'd spent a summer in Louisiana when she was younger, so her fluent English often had a Southern lilt to it.

Much to Jack's disappointment, some of the others, friends and hangers-on, were down on the beach as well. Eric the Belgian for one, to whom Jack had taken an instant dislike. Much to Jack's satisfaction Eric turned out to be a smug and arrogant pain in the arse, with an absurdly high opinion of himself. His short blond hair and slightly oversized glasses, along with his rather ungainly and stilted movement, reminded Jack of an SS officer dressed up as Joe 90.

Apart from Eric, there were the French twins, Jean-Pierre and Jean-Paul, along with their very attractive little sister. Not that little physically, but at only fifteen, Marie-Claire was a bit on the young side. Their parents' penchant for double-barrelled Christian names also extended to their youngest sister, Marie-Christine. All four of the Clements had copious amounts of black curly hair. Both boys wore it down to their necks, like shaggy manes, where it met with more of the stuff coming up their backs. The girls were fortunately not so hirsute, but both had a mass of curls and ringlets cascading down their backs. They were all relatively small, but the boys made up for their lack of height with generous builds and very broad shoulders. They were all a good laugh and Jack got on particularly well with the twins, though they were also competition.

Sebastian, the token Spaniard or Catalonian, as he would prefer, completed the group. Very tall, at least six four Jack reckoned, but very thin; always hunched like he was embarrassed by his height. Mousy-brown hair, pale skin and small pigeon-like eyes, always darting around as if he was looking out for something. He was an intellectual of sorts and spoke lots of languages, which made Jack feel very inadequate, though he couldn't help liking the guy.

Jack put in the Alphaville tape and the opening cords of 'Big in Japan' drifted across the beach and out to the Mediterranean. There was a light breeze, and the temperature, too hot earlier in the day, was now pleasant. It was a romantic setting, but at the moment Jack was with five other blokes, one girl who was too young and another who was 'just' a good friend.

He wondered whether Peter's finds would turn up. What would the beautiful friend really be like? Would anything come of it? The mood was boisterous but suddenly silence descended and Jack felt a nervous shudder flow through him.

The redhead led the way, followed closely by her

companion – Jack's date, or so he hoped. Peter and the redhead immediately took control. In English she introduced herself as Simone. Her friend was Abrielle. She hadn't been lying – Abrielle was beautiful – Jack smiled to himself. Simone wasn't too bad either, although a bit too thin for Jack's liking.

As Abrielle was introduced, she remained silent and expressionless. She even looked bored by the proceedings. She had long dark wavy hair that rested on her shoulders, before continuing down her body, curving around her breasts. When they were finally introduced, Jack looked into her eyes ... his heart missed a beat. For a moment, he felt the world around them had ceased to exist. Her eyes were the deepest, strangest blue he had ever seen. For a second, perhaps two, they held each other's stare. He felt his heart racing. It wasn't just him, his imagination, he was sure she felt it too – some kind of electricity that flowed between them.

Suddenly Abrielle's eyes blazed. 'So the imbecile has a name!' and with that she turned away and stormed off to an outcrop of rocks a few yards away where she sat down and looked out to sea.

Jack was open-mouthed. How could this beautiful girl be the same as that loud and arrogant Frenchwoman he had encountered earlier?

Everybody else was equally perplexed, so Jack explained what had happened. He went for the slightly biased version and dressed it up a bit. Better to get in first, he thought, although he was careful not to criticise her too much. Jean-Pierre thought the story was wonderful, particularly the bit about the flying poodle. Jack felt uncomfortable and quickly changed the subject.

Abrielle's beauty and aloofness were a clear challenge to each of them, men or boys – time would tell which. Joe 90 was first up, and Jack felt a jealous pang as the

16

Belgian went to sit next to the gorgeous Frenchgirl; he had burnt his bridges already. To Jack's delight, Joe 90 spent just five minutes with her. It was painful to watch. She barely said a word to him, hardly even looked at him. In fact, Jack was sure she was looking at him! Was the fire in her eyes perhaps slightly less hostile? He couldn't take his eyes off her, trying to fathom her out. Was she going to forgive him? Was there hope for him after all?

Joe 90 gave up and walked sheepishly back, tail between his legs. Jean-Pierre, the elder twin, by a mere eight minutes apparently, was next. JP1, as he had become known, swaggered over to Abrielle, trying to look cool and laid back, but his bravado lacked conviction and his nervous smile betrayed him. No hope, Jack thought. He didn't last two minutes. Abrielle spent the whole time staring at Jack and he spent most of it staring back at her.

Jack wanted to go and speak to her, but after seeing the way Joe 90 and JP1 had been humiliated, not to mention his uncertainty about how she felt towards him, he didn't want to suffer the same experience. If only he had a little more self-confidence, he thought. There was definitely some weird chemistry going on and in a rather masochistic way he was enjoying it ... but if he made a move now it might break the spell.

Sebastian took the plunge next. He had spent the evening talking to Heike; they had known each other for a few years, but only saw each other when she was down in Rosas in the summer. Jack thought that Heike had a soft spot for him, and he for her, but it looked like he had been seduced by Abrielle's beauty as well.

Abrielle did actually pay him more attention than the others, but when she glanced up, Jack was waiting for her. He kept his cool and held her stare, but inside he was on fire. His body felt taut, mixed emotions of elation

17

and bewilderment fighting for control. He was used to flirtatious situations, but with girls on Tube trains or in a darkened student bar, but they rarely lasted for more than a few seconds. This was lasting forever. As the sun edged closer to the horizon its rays bounced off the calm Mediterranean and Jack would have sworn he could see the sparkling reflection of the light dancing off the water in Abrielle's eyes.

Finally, Seb too, gave up and walked the now familiar walk of dejection back to the group. Heike was seemingly amused by the whole affair, teasing each boy as he returned broken-hearted.

Jack was suddenly drawn out of his trance by a nudge from JP2. 'Your turn, you're the one she wants!' Jack hadn't realised the others had been so aware of what was going on, but perhaps it was obvious. Jack smiled and suggested that JP2 should have a go. But before JP2 had a chance to move, Joe 90 decided to go back for some more. Jack felt a sadistic grin spread across his face as he watched the Belgian's attempt to engage Abrielle. This time she contemptuously ignored him, turning away and shifting her body angle more towards Jack, and raising her eyes to meet his. With the sunset, her eyes had taken on a darker shade, a smouldering, smoky blue.

Eric returned looking even more humiliated and dejected than after his first attempt. For a split second, Jack almost had some sympathy for him, but then remembered what a prick he was and how much he disliked him. Serves the arrogant bastard right, he thought.

JP2 now decided to go for it and boldly strode over to Abrielle. Despite his initial self-assurance, he too faltered as he drew near and came face to face with her steely indifference. As Jack looked at JP2 trying to talk to Abrielle, she looked back at him. He was conscious that the endgame was approaching – only he wasn't sure how to play it. Up to now, he had played it very cool, by doing absolutely bugger all, except holding her stare, but what next? He could just go up to her and start talking to her, but that would be too obvious; that's what each of the others had done and she might be disappointed at his lack of originality. He had no intention of suffering the same fate as the rest of them! In any case what would he say? He certainly didn't want to apologise for earlier. No way!

JP2 had decided enough was enough and tried to make his way back as inconspicuously as he could. Silence descended upon the group as eyes turned towards Jack in expectation. He was unsure what to do and felt a surge of panic. He decided not to move, justifying his stance by playing the arrogant and aloof role, but if he was honest with himself, cowardice won the day.

Once the group's attention had turned elsewhere, however, he manoeuvred himself to face Abrielle straight on. His boldest move so far.

They stared at each other for he didn't know how long – three, four, maybe five, even ten, minutes – just stared into each other's eyes, trying to read the other's thoughts, trying to anticipate the next move. No smiling, just staring; it was completely surreal.

Then all of a sudden the spell was broken – not by Jack though, but by Abrielle. She stood up and started to move towards him, closing the twelve-foot gap between the two of them. Jack sensed his heart quicken and the adrenalin flow again. Was she coming to him or was she, God forbid, going to walk straight past him?

Outwardly he desperately tried to remain cool and almost indifferent, holding her stare as she walked towards him. Eight feet and closing fast – his brain was becoming a mass of conflicting thoughts. What would he say if she joined him, worse what would he do if she carried on? Four feet... His heart was pounding heavily – surely she

19

could hear it, surely she wouldn't abandon it now! Or had she been toying with him all along? Was it just a game to her ... was this her revenge?

Jack held her stare right up to two feet, when her eyes disappeared as she walked straight past him. The tiny element of relief at not having to talk to her was completely overwhelmed by the gut-wrenching disappointment he felt, not to mention the humiliation.

Chapter 4

Jack felt a hand rest gently on his shoulder as Abrielle steadied herself to sit on his other side. He offered up a silent prayer of thanks and turned to his left and looked into those eyes for the first time at close quarters, and was met by a radiant smile.

'I think in English you have an expression "to get off on the wrong ankle".' Her voice was sexy, not at all like the shrill tirade she'd launched at him earlier that afternoon.

Jack smiled. 'Foot! The expression is wrong foot.'

She smiled again. She was less than two feet away; he could nearly touch her – probably could have if he put his hand out – she might even have taken it. But no, he'd played it slow so far, and it seemed to be working. She was so beautiful and Jack had the feeling that he had just fallen in love for the first time in his life. While he might have used the words once or twice before, that had seemed like duty in the throes of lust – this was completely different. This was the real thing; he had never felt like this before.

The real thing! Who was he kidding?

Jack was not going to bring up the flying poodle incident, and Abrielle didn't seem inclined either. Instead they just talked about themselves. The talk flowed smoothly, like a lazy river meandering through a meadow on a warm summer's afternoon. No uncomfortable moments, both happy to listen to the other. Jack was so close to her now he was breathing her scent, her smell, feeling the heat of her body.

Abrielle explained to Jack that she was in Rosas with Simone and Simone's mother, who was a bit of a bitch apparently. She lived in Paris with her parents, but they had gone on safari and she had opted for a month in the sun with Simone instead. (A month! Jack's heart leapt. Oh God, this was too good to be true.) Simone's mother was a landscape artist and, according to Abrielle, was a particularly bad one. She had rented the apartment as there was some good scenery in the mountains north of Rosas and invited the girls along. (Thank you, Simone's mother, you sound like a wonderful woman to me, Jack thought.)

'So Jack, Mister Englishman, what are you doing here with a bunch of Germans. I thought the English hated the Germans even more than the French?'

Jack smiled, not taking the bait. 'It's a long story, so I'll give you the abbreviated version;' he began. 'A couple of years ago, a friend and I decided to cycle around Europe. It seemed a good idea at the time, but unfortunately what neither of us realised was just how much we hated cycling. We ended up trying to sell the bikes; we even left them un-padlocked but no one would even steal them. In the end, we cheated and caught the train from city to city and just used them to cycle around wherever we were staying.'

'We ended up near Heidelberg, where we bumped into Heike and some friends in a bar and just got talking. My friend Bill decided to fall in love with her and so we hung around for a while. It didn't last, but she and I got on really well and kept in contact. She came over to London last year and stayed with me for a few days and when she asked if I wanted to spend a month in Rosas at her parents' apartment, it was too good an opportunity to turn down.'

Abrielle gave Jack a look he hadn't seen before. 'So what's gone on between you and Heike?' she asked.

'Nothing! We're good friends, but that's it.'

Abrielle looked reassured, or was his imagination just running wild?

Jack listened to her talk about her life in Paris, her father, a judge, her mother the dutiful wife, but the power behind the throne. She was an only child, a welcome surprise for her parents who had all but given up after ten years of trying, a series of miscarriages eating away at the hope that they would one day have a child. Her mother was forty by the time Abrielle was born, her father already into his fifties.

'A bit too old to go on safari, but they think they're younger than they are,' she added. Abrielle looked older than her seventeen years. She was mature both physically and intellectually. She knew what she wanted; she also knew how beautiful she was, though she couldn't possibly know the effect she was having on Jack. He was playing it as cool as he could, but with every movement, every smile, every glance, every word, he knew he was becoming infatuated.

Jack had a feeling that he was walking on dangerous ground, but he also knew that the desire, which was not purely physical, was too strong to resist.

Then she said something that surprised him.

For someone who was still too young to vote, she held strong political views. She despised President Mitterand and admired Jean-Marie Le Pen. This was where the next argument nearly began.

'Jean-Marie Le Pen, but isn't he that fascist bastard who stood for President, when he should be languishing in jail for inciting racial hatred and intolerance?'

Abrielle gave Jack an icy stare. He immediately regretted being quite so forthright.

'Perhaps we should tread as carefully around politics as we do poodles,' she said with a little smirk.

Jack smiled back, relieved that he hadn't ruined things by his comment. Still, this was a conversation they would have to have at some time.

'How are the bruises?' she finally asked, seemingly more out of curiosity than concern.

Jack smiled. 'I'm picking up quite a collection actually. I seem to be getting into the rather bad habit of flying through the air at the moment.'

'Really?' asked Abrielle, pausing before adding, 'Are you going to tell me more?'

'It's a bit embarrassing really,' Jack began. 'Last Saturday when I arrived, I flew to Barcelona and then caught the train up to Figueras. I managed to fall asleep on the train and when I opened my eyes we were moving really slowly and I saw a sign saying Figueras. The train was pulling out of the station and I was about to miss my stop.'

'*Non,*' said Abrielle, her eyes sparkling in anticipation.

'Fortunately, there was a door right next to me, so I threw it open, chucked my bag out and then jumped.'

'But wasn't that dangerous?' Abrielle asked excitedly.

'Well, the train was going pretty slowly. At least I thought it was, because when I landed, the momentum carried me on and I went flying, much as I did earlier today...'

'But you made it,' said Abrielle.

'I did, but sadly my bag didn't, at least not in one piece. It split open and my clothes went everywhere, especially my pants!'

Abrielle laughed. 'Ah, so that's why it was embarrassing.'

'No, the embarrassing bit came when the train stopped and everyone else got off.'

'*Non!*' Abrielle cried.

Jack nodded. 'Everyone was giving me very funny looks. I hoped I'd got away with it but Heike and Peter saw me, and they're still teasing me about it.'

They exchanged broad grins.

Their private world was rudely interrupted with a rather dramatic scream from Simone.

Abrielle looked at her watch. *'Mon Dieu!'* she exclaimed and explained to Jack that they should have been back by 10 o'clock and it was now 10.15. She had to go.

Meanwhile Simone and Peter had decided to consummate their relationship with a passionate and very sloppy French kiss. Jack suspected it wasn't the most romantic moment they could have had, not with the other four guys standing around, trying not to stare. He would like to have kissed Abrielle, but not like this; it was too tacky for a start and he didn't particularly like the idea of being surrounded by a group of voyeurs – it was much too personal for that.

Abrielle dragged Simone off Peter's face and flashed Jack a final smile goodnight. As the two girls climbed the path back to the apartments, Jack could hear them giggling to each other as they disappeared into the darkness. Peter had a big grin on his face, but the others all turned to Jack.

'How the hell did you do that?' Jean-Pierre asked, with a slightly envious smirk across his face.

'Do what?' Jack asked in mock innocence, for which he got a gentle punch in the ribs from Jean-Paul.

'You know exactly what he means,' said Heike, 'She's gorgeous-looking and she couldn't take her eyes off you.'

Jack didn't really know what to say; he didn't want to appear arrogant.

'She is quite pretty, isn't she?' he admitted.

'Shame about her poor eyesight though,' quipped JP1.

Jack didn't mind the banter; it was all good-humoured stuff. He noticed, though, that Joe 90 wasn't joining in. He looked furious and spent the rest of the evening with a vengeful look on his face.

* * *

Jack hardly slept that night. He lay on his back in the dark, Peter snoring away in the other bed. Even without the snorts, he didn't think he would have slept; there were too many conflicting thoughts running around his head. How did she feel about him? Did she feel the same chemistry he felt? Was it possible that she, too, was lying in bed, unable to get to sleep, because *she* was thinking about him, wondering how he felt about her?

Jack knew that he had completely fallen for her.

Chapter 5

The sun crept through a gap where the curtains didn't quite meet. Jack felt the warm glow and stirred, a smile spreading across his face as he remembered the beautiful Abrielle.

'Morning, lover boy!' Jack opened his eyes.

'Me! What about you, Peter? You were the one playing tonsil tennis for the crowd.'

Peter smiled guiltily. 'OK, fair point. They're both rather nice though, aren't they?'

'That they are,' admitted Jack, though secretly he believed he had made far the better deal.

It was 10.30 by the time Jack and Peter made their way down to the pool. The twins and Joe 90 were already there, showing off their already bronzed limbs. Jack thought of his own pale white skin which was just beginning to turn a little pink. He threw on the factor six and decided to go for a swim.

The pool glistened. Jack stood on the edge looking at the shallow end 25 metres away. He still hadn't managed to swim the length of it underwater, although each day he was getting closer and closer. It was always his first attempt of the day that was his best and perhaps today he would make it. If he succeeded, perhaps that would be a good omen for the day; if he failed ... well, he'd rather not think of the consequences.

He took a deep breath and dived in. The coolness of

the water surprised him. He straightened out as the blurred bottom appeared below him, then made slow determined breast strokes through the water. Halfway there – he could do it! Gradually he started to rise and, as he hit the surface, he switched to front crawl. His lungs were beginning to ache, and his muscles tired as the oxygen supply dried up. The fear of failure began to take hold as his lungs started to scream at him and his head started to ache; he knew he wasn't going to make it. Why oh why had he tempted fate? Idiot, he thought. He lifted his head above the water and gulped in the fresh air, his lungs gratefully accepting the gift of oxygen. He was less than four feet from the wall.

Out of breath, Jack climbed out and wrapped himself in his blue-and-red towel, with 'CRICKET' emblazoned at the top of it. Once he had thought it rather cool, but now he wasn't so sure; naff more like. Suddenly he became aware that the conversation around him had dropped into hushed tones. He looked up, and saw Peter and Joe 90 jumping up to welcome the girls, just as if they were royalty. Peter took Simone's towel off her and laid it next to his. Meanwhile, Joe 90 moved over to Abrielle and offered to lay out her towel for her. She seemed amused and gave Joe 90 a smile as she let him take her towel.

Bollocks, thought Jack to himself, why was she giving him a smile? Last night she wouldn't have given him the time of day. This was not a good start.

Abrielle looked stunning. Her long brown legs reached up to her two-tone swimsuit, red and navy waves stretching up her sculpted, toned body. Her hair was tied up, though not as tightly as when they had first met, but in a more relaxed fashion, leaving an unobstructed view of her face, in all its radiant beauty.

Abrielle turned to Jack and smiled, '*Bonjour*!'

Jack responded in kind, but there was no lingering

28

gaze, no special acknowledgement for him. The magic of last night seemed to have gone. Joe 90, it seemed, was right back in the frame and making all the moves. Jack felt like getting up and hitting him.

Jack watched as Joe 90 chatted away to Abrielle in French, a language Jack knew that he couldn't keep up with. Jack had no idea what they were discussing, but disconcertingly Abrielle seemed to be amused. He knew he couldn't just watch; he had to do something.

Jack moved over and knelt in front of her. 'Would you like a drink?'

She looked up and smiled, 'I'll have a cold chocolate please.'

'Me, too, if you don't mind, Jack,' Joe 90 said insincerely. Jack really wanted to hit him now and he certainly didn't want to get him a drink.

Sod off, get your own! Jack thought. 'Yeh, no problem, Eric,' he muttered. A refusal would have looked petty and he wasn't going to give the idiot any ammunition.

Jack walked over to the bar, trying desperately to look happy and confident, despite feeling neither. He ordered three cold chocolates and briefly thought about doing something nasty to Joe 90's, but commonsense prevailed. On his return, he decided to sit with Joe 90 and Abrielle; hopefully it would make it harder for Joe 90 to exclude him from the conversation.

'Are you coming in for a swim?' he asked Abrielle, pointedly ignoring Joe 90.

'No, not yet. Perhaps later, once I've finished my drink,' she replied, and before Jack had a chance to come up with something else, Joe 90 was in there again, speaking in French.

Jack tried to follow, but quickly became lost. He tried to look interested, as if he understood, but he knew it was all going horribly wrong. Uncomfortably he watched

29

her listen to Joe 90, watched her smile, watched her wrinkle her little button nose when she laughed, flick her hair back as a stray lock fell over her eyes. Every now and again she would catch his eye and smile…

Jack was wondering how long he could carry on sitting there, like the proverbial gooseberry, when there was a sudden shout.

'Magnus, no!'

Everyone stopped and turned around. Little blond Magnus was standing at the end of the diving board in nothing but his arm bands, proudly holding on to his manhood as he readied himself to pee into the pool. His mother rushed over, but it was too late. During this time an oblivious Jean-Pierre had been swimming lengths, trying to impress any girl who was interested, and now as he surfaced he was met with a stream of pee. Initially he didn't realise what was happening, but the raucous laughter coming from his brother and Peter, not to mention the apologies from Magnus's mother were all that were needed to enlighten him. Furious, he went off to take a shower and remove any lingering evidence.

Unsurprisingly the pool had emptied after Magnus's intervention, but this gave Jack an idea.

'Hey, how do you fancy a swim in the sea, seeing as the pool is well … you know?' he asked Abrielle.

Much to his delight, she jumped up. 'OK, that would be nice. I'm getting a bit hot.'

Jack's despondent soul leapt. At last, something is going right. The ray of hope disappeared as fast as it had arrived.

'Are you coming, Eric?' she asked.

NO! screamed Jack inside, that wasn't part of the plan. Why oh why would you ask him?

'That's a good idea,' said Joe 90.

His heart fell again. There was nothing he could do.

They strode down the path to the rocks, down to where they had been last night, to where Jack had first seen her, where his heart had first jumped at the sight of her. This time, though, things were very different; he had a battle on his hands and he felt he was losing it.

Jack was determined not to let it show. He climbed nimbly over the rocks, jumping down like a mountain goat, taking Abrielle's hand and helping her, while Joe 90 struggled to keep up. Soon they reached the spot known as the diving board, a rock that jutted out like a natural board, only without the springiness.

Now here was an opportunity to impress. He was, after all, a good diver. He took two steps forward before launching himself into the air, gracefully flying through the sky before cleanly entering the water ten feet below.

As he broke the surface, he saw Abrielle ready to follow. Being the slight chauvinist he was, Jack expected her to hesitate before jumping in, but she followed him without a moment's thought and with a dive as good as, if not better than, his. He was impressed and swam towards her. For a second it was just the two of them and as he looked into her eyes, he thought he saw that spark again between them. There was a strangled cry from above and Joe 90 came flying towards them, entering the water with an elephant-sized splash, arms and legs flailing in all directions.

Abrielle thought his ungainly entry hilarious. Jack on the other hand had lost his sense of humour and just wanted to kill Eric, preferably with the use of some gratuitous violence. To make matters worse, Joe 90 was taking control again, suggesting in French of course that they swim around the rocks towards Rosas. It was at least a 300-yard swim before they would reach rocks low enough to clamber out and Jack wasn't sure he fancied it. On the other hand, there was no way he was going to let this bastard have her to himself.

Jack was a better diver than swimmer and, although he managed to keep up, he felt more and more excluded. The other two were not only strong swimmers, but they spoke continuously in French, laughing and smiling away, and Jack started to wonder what the hell he was doing – he was following her around like a lapdog. Jesus, he thought, if he'd seen this happening to one of his friends, he would have been the first to tell him what he thought: get a grip and start acting like a man.

Jack stopped. He was going to tell them he was going back, but he guessed they wouldn't even care. How could he have been so stupid? How could he have fallen for this girl who clearly enjoyed toying with boys' egos. Was it some kind of revenge? He didn't think so. Last night seemed genuine, but this morning the magic had gone; he didn't know why, but he had to face the facts. Enough was enough.

He turned and slowly swam back past the diving board, before reaching the low rocks. He despondently clambered up them and onto the path. He hadn't felt this sorry for himself in a long time; in fact he couldn't remember ever feeling quite this way. He'd loved and lost in sixteen hours flat. Was that possible? To go through the full gambit of emotions in such a short period. He could sense the self-pity beginning to take hold of him. Only one thing for it – time for a San Miguel or two.

Chapter 6

At lunch Jack looked at the Weber family around him. Two relatively good-looking children and two definitely unattractive parents; he wondered if they'd both been adopted. Both parents were considerably overweight, which of course didn't help, but even if they hadn't been, there were no redeeming features that Jack thought could be considered attractive. Both had greying hair flecked with some original browns. Franz Weber had big eyes, set deeply into his skull, which looked slightly too large for his round face, hardly complimenting a squashed nose and wide mouth. Sophie Weber, on the other hand, had a small head which looked out of place on her very large body. She had small eyes, a small mouth, and a permanent hollow, slightly scared look on her face. There was something about Edvard Munch's *Scream* about her.

After six San Miguels, on a mostly empty stomach, Jack was beginning to feel the effects. Herr Weber had got through the best part of a bottle of red wine and this usually meant that he would start to speak directly to Jack in German. It wasn't a case of forgetting Jack didn't speak the language, more that if he said things often enough, loud enough, the language barrier might miraculously disappear. Normally Jack would happily smile away but today, the San Miguel emboldened him to take Herr Weber into his confidence and tell him all about this stupid French girl who was messing around with his feelings. Herr Weber seemed particularly sensitive and made lots of sympathetic comments – at least Jack liked

33

to think he did, as of course he couldn't have understood a word; it was the thought that counts. Their afternoon 'chat' was only brought to a close when Heike suggested in both languages that the two of them should go and sleep off their impending hangovers.

A two-hour kip didn't do much for Jack's mental state, nor did it do much for the headache he now had. He needed to clear his head and decided to take Heinrich the *Hund* for a walk. Heinrich was a daft floppy-eared spaniel who liked nothing more than chasing rabbits around the fields outside Heidelberg. He wasn't so impressed with Rosas – too many other dogs and no rabbits. He was happy to accompany Jack for a walk down into Rosas though, no doubt hoping to be let loose on the beach, which Jack had no intention of doing. Once unleashed, Heinrich would go temporally deaf until he was knackered and only then would he rediscover his hearing. Jack had made this mistake once before when he had been staying with Heike in Heidelberg and spent two hours trying to get the *Hund* to return to him, getting drenched by a storm in the process.

Jack decided that, having already shared his thoughts with Herr Weber, perhaps Heinrich would make a good listener, too, and poured out his heart to him. Heinrich, however, was more interested in smelling the groins of passers-by, which proved rather embarrassing, and Jack started to regret his decision to take him along.

The beach was emptying out when they arrived and Heinrich was desperately trying to get into the water, but Jack kept a tight leash on him. Though he would never admit it, Jack at heart was a bit of an old softy, and eventually Heinrich's large pleading eyes got the better of him and he let him off the leash. It was a decision he suspected he would regret, but what the hell, why not let the dog enjoy himself? – he didn't often get the chance.

Jack sat on the beach watching the waves gently roll in, while Heinrich chased them as they rolled back again, only to do a sharp turnaround when the next one came in. He was like a little child, not getting bored by the repetitiveness of it all – each wave a new experience. Oh, how nice it would be not to have a care in the world. Jack sighed. Why oh why had this girl entered his life? His mother always told him that there were plenty more fish in the sea. Unfortunately, though, that was irrelevant – the fish he wanted no longer appeared to want him.

Heinrich eventually got bored and padded back to Jack of his own accord. As he sat there, the silly dog gave Jack a big sloppy lick on his face.

'Get off!' yelled Jack, but it still felt nice to be loved, if only by a dumb dog.

By the time he returned, supper was ready. Peter was absent; he was taking Simone for a meal in Rosas. Lucky bastard. The meal was slightly more muted than normal; no doubt the lunchtime excesses were taking their toll. After the washing-up was done, Heike told Jack to get ready; they were meeting some of the others down by the bar and he was coming whether he liked it or not. She was a good friend, she might not know exactly how sorry for himself he felt, but she had no intention of letting him wallow in his own self-pity.

Sebastian and the twins were already down at the bar, there was no sign of Joe 90 or Abrielle. As much as he disliked Joe 90, he would have loved to have seen him there because that would mean he wouldn't have been with her. No such luck. He downed a cold San Miguel and immediately felt better. Another followed in quick succession. Fortunately everyone steered clear of mentioning Abrielle and he listened to the others chat away – thankfully all in English, the language they all understood.

Unfortunately for Jack, however, the conversation turned

to the matter of boy and girlfriends. The inevitable question came – had Jack ever been in love?

'No!' said Jack, a bit too firmly. 'I'm only twenty for God's sake!' he added for good measure. 'I was going out with a girl from college last term, but she ended it just before I came away. It wasn't going anywhere though – three months and I start to get bored.'

'But what about Abrielle? How do you feel about her?' Jean-Pierre persisted.

Thank you, Jean-Pierre, thought Jack. Just what I needed.

The beer was now running through his veins and, although he hadn't wanted to talk about her, now the opportunity had arrived, the words just came out. The alcohol seemed to make things clearer, more coherent … or was that just the way his intoxicated brain saw it?

'OK, if I am going to be honest, there was a moment last night when I thought she was kinda nice. She, it must be said has got wonderful blue eyes which … which …' Jack struggled to find the right words. '… Which draw you in and take you into a different world, a world of their own, they make you feel special.' He knew he was letting his guard down, but he didn't care.

'But that was last night. Today, well, she's nothing special. I mean she's gorgeous to look at and' – he grinned at the twins – 'she does have a lovely body, doesn't she?' They both nodded back enthusiastically. 'But, well, what the hell, if she finds that Belgian pillock good-looking or amusing, that's her lookout. Good riddance, stupid bitch.' Jack's disjointed monologue ended and an uncomfortable silence followed.

'Come on, time for bed, Jack,' said Heike. It was an instruction not an invitation. Jack was in no mood to argue; he'd lost count of the number of beers he'd had, but it was into double figures and he knew he was going to suffer for it in the morning.

36

As they got up to go, Peter and Simone arrived back. After another sloppy kiss in front of everyone, they went their separate ways and Peter joined them. He told them what a great time he'd had and volunteered the information that Abrielle had decided to stay in that evening with Simone's mother – which meant she wasn't with Joe 90 after all. Perhaps there was a ray of hope. Just perhaps.

Chapter 7

'Jesus, I'm never touching another beer,' Jack muttered to himself. A headache hitting him the moment he woke up.

'You were completely out of it last night,' laughed Peter.

Jack put his hands up to his face and rubbed his eyes, trying to clear the haze in front of them.

'Was I? Did I make a fool of myself?' he asked sheepishly.

'No, just mouthed off about a certain "French bitch" apparently.'

Jack grimaced and struggled to get out of bed. He sat on the edge of the bed contemplating whether or not he should try and stand up or just fall down onto the bed again.

'God, it's 10.30! Where did the morning go?'

Peter smiled. 'Tell you what, let's have a game of tennis; that will clear your hangover.'

'You're bloody mad! Play tennis in this state; I'm not sure if I can stand up, let alone run around a tennis court!'

Peter looked down at him with a stern look. 'Seriously, Jack, it will cure your hangover quicker than anything else, or are you scared I'll beat you?'

'You *are* serious,' said Jack. 'Oh, why not? It might teach me a lesson.'

Jack managed to get his shorts and a top on, but doing up the laces on his trainers was more of a struggle. He downed a couple of pints of water followed by three black coffees and then they were off.

Jack was hoping for a gentle run-around, but Peter was too competitive for that; it was Germany v England all over again. After a quick knock-up, that was it, gloves off; a bit too serious for Jack's liking, but he couldn't let his country down. His heart wasn't in it though and within a few minutes he was three games to one down and heading for defeat. As he trudged back from the net, the heat of the sun weighing heavily on him, Jack noticed behind the court, partly hidden by the shade from the trees, that they had an audience. Only an audience of one, but a very significant one. Jack couldn't see Abrielle's face, but he knew it was her. As he turned to serve, he concentrated slightly harder, thought a little more about what he was going to do with the ball, and tried to think ahead. An ace straight down the middle whistled out of Peter's reach. That's better, thought Jack, nothing to do with her. The game went to love and suddenly Jack felt more confident; Peter knew he had a game on his hands.

The next game was tight, before Peter eventually produced an ace of his own to take a 4–2 lead. The quality of tennis had jumped dramatically in the last two games and Jack knew he still had a chance – he was only a break down. The next three games went with service, but at 5–4 and serving for the match the pressure was on Peter. A nervy double fault to start and Jack knew this was his chance. He tried to concentrate on the tennis, but every now and again he would glance up and check she was still watching. Not that it mattered of course he tried to convince himself.

A series of forehands down the line brought Jack the break he needed and now he knew the match was his. He served confidently to take a 6–5 lead and now just had to break Peter again; he didn't want a tiebreak. Peter started with an ace, not what Jack had planned, and followed up with another first serve, this time rearing up and catching Jack off guard at the amount of top spin. All he could manage was a return into the net.

'Come on, got to dig deep,' Jack said to himself.

Peter hit another strong first serve, but this time to Jack's favoured backhand and he sent a reply flashing over the net deep into court, catching Peter wrong-footed. A double fault followed and Jack knew it was now or never; this was what she was waiting for, surely she was only there to see him. A weak second serve was put away with ease and suddenly it was match point.

Jack stood motionless deep behind the baseline, concentrating, breathing deeply, sweat dripping into his eyes, the hot sun on the back of his neck. Peter wasn't one to give in easily and the serve was as Jack expected, deep to his forehand, but he was ready for it. He hit it back aggressively, hard and low, plenty of top spin. Peter was already at the net, but only just managed to get his racket down in time to volley back to where Jack was standing. With a little more time to think, Jack motioned to play it across court, before unleashing a forehand straight down the line. Peter read it though and tried to kill it dead; it was a good drop shot but not good enough. Jack raced forward and lifted the ball up over Peter's head, but there was too much height on it and Peter had time to get back to the baseline and send the ball flying back. Jack had reached the net, but realised it was going to be out of his reach.

This was it. Perhaps this was the moment she had come to see. Could this be the defining moment? he wondered. In much the same way as Boris Becker had thrown himself around the tennis courts of Wimbledon a couple of weeks earlier, Jack threw himself to his left and yet again found himself flying through the air – a too common occurrence these days. He managed to get his racket to the ball, but his motion carried him on twisting backwards as he fell to the ground. As he rolled over he saw the ball gently loop up and then, as if in slow motion, it landed on the top of the net, thought for a moment about which way it was going to fall, before rolling over and coming down the other side, leaving Peter stranded.

Jack didn't get up – he hadn't the energy – and he realised his headache which had taken a back seat for the last hour had returned with a vengeance. In the distance he heard gentle applause from their sole spectator. It brought a smile to his face, but he didn't look up. Eventually he mustered the strength to get up and shake Peter's hand. He wanted to go over and speak to her, but he decided it was up to her to make the moves.

Jack made straight for the pool and decided that this was his opportunity, his one chance. He stripped down to his shorts and taking a deep breath dived into the pool. Rather than try and swim he glided effortlessly through the water, kicking his feet gently, but saving as much oxygen as he could.

As he reached the surface, he started the front crawl and this time felt he had the required reserves to reach the far wall. Keeping his head down, he tried not to swim too fast, but rather maintain a rhythmic stroke. He could feel the lactic acid starting to build in his muscles as they began to ache. Come on, nearly there! His lungs began to hurt as well, but the wall was there, just in front of him. As he broke the surface and took in a lungful of air, his hand touched the wall, but he knew it hadn't been simultaneous, he'd touched the wall fractionally late.

Jack closed his eyes and sat in the shallow end trying to regain his breath. Nearly! He had so nearly made it. Did that also mean she was nearly his, but not yet?

'Oh shut up!' he told himself.

Jack saw little Magnus in his birthday suit wandering mischievously around the pool's edge and thought it prudent to get out of the water. He looked up and there she was sitting between Simone and Joe 90, but seemingly ignoring the pillock. She was looking at him, straight at him.

Jack walked over, not quite sure where to place his towel. He was damned if it was going to be next to Joe 90, which meant the other side of Peter, two down from Abrielle, but that was OK; that was near, but not too near. He didn't want to seem keen; in fact, he wanted to appear indifferent; that way he could retain his pride, but keep the door open, just in case.

'We'll have to have a rematch you know,' Peter said.

'Hey, let me just bask in another English victory against Germany, would you? It's a bit too early to start thinking about revenge,' Jack said with a big smirk on his face.

'English victory?' Peter remarked with a surprised look on his face. 'But surely it wasn't 'til the French cavalry arrived that the English started to win,' he added provocatively.

'OK, thank you very much, Peter,' said Jack, who didn't want this conversation going any further. Fortunately he was saved by Magnus.

'Oh Magnus, stop it!' came a screeched plea from his mother.

There he was again, standing at the end of the diving board peeing away, pointing it this way then that. His mother came running over, her bikini briefs the only difference in the clothing they wore. She looked slightly embarrassed, but her husband thought it hilarious, laughing away in his equally tight Speedos. She grabbed Magnus from behind and picked him up, but, unfortunately for her, Magnus wasn't finished. As she held him in front of her to avoid getting peed on, she made the mistake of passing too close to a rather large middle-aged woman, who was surely old enough and large enough to know the dangers of going topless. Whether Magnus aimed accurately or was just lucky, he caught the woman with a final gush across her vast bosom. A brief row ensued, partly in French, partly Swedish, which ended with the very unamused Frenchwoman storming off.

Jack smiled at the commotion, lay down on his front and turned his head to his left. Peter and Simone were sitting up, which gave him a clear view of Abrielle. Joe 90 was chatting away to her, but she had that 'I'm really not interested' look on her face. She turned her back to Joe 90 and onto her front, then lay down, her lithe tanned body stretched out on the towel, like a contented lioness in the warmth of a Serengeti sun. Slowly she turned her head to look in Jack's direction.

His heart fluttered slightly as he looked into those eyes once more, holding that stare. For how long, he wondered, how long could he hold her gaze, get lost in those blue eyes. With a warm wind blowing gently over him, he felt protected in his own little world, taking in everything she offered – every flicker of an eyelid, every pupil movement. What they were saying, he had no idea, but he was enjoying it; they were back playing the game. It was just the two of them, searching each other's thoughts – a silent conversation that brought them closer and closer.

Their private sanctuary was shattered when Peter announced it was lunchtime at the Weber household. Reluctantly Jack got up, but he didn't take his eyes off her as he picked up his towel and racket. Eventually he turned away and only when she couldn't see, he smiled to himself.

Jack slept after lunch; the excesses of the previous night still needed to be purged from his system. When he woke it was nearly four and the flat was silent. He went out onto the balcony, from where he could see the pool. He could see most of the usual suspects sunbathing, Peter and Simone together and Joe 90 chatting to Abrielle. He felt a pang of jealously.

Jack grabbed Peter's binoculars and scanned the group, before focusing in on Abrielle. She was sitting up, legs stretched out, leaning backwards, arms behind her taking the weight, her head raised to face the sun. She was wearing a plain-blue swimsuit; always a swimsuit, never a bikini, why not? The binoculars had a zoom function, which Jack twisted until she filled the lens.

He watched each little movement, as she flicked back her hair, as she wrinkled her nose. She took out some suncream and dabbed it onto each of her arms, then gently rubbed it in, caressing it into her soft skin. She suddenly turned to Joe 90. He must have said something to her, probably offered to rub in the sun cream, judging by the look she gave him. She didn't seem particularly happy at his comment.

Jack couldn't just sit and watch. He grabbed his shades and his towel and made his way down the two flights of stairs and then out into the manicured gardens, making his way through the greenery and down the steps. As he emerged, he felt nervous, uncertain as to why; he certainly had no intention of speaking to her. Perhaps it was just the thought of being in her presence again. He wondered which Abrielle would have turned up this afternoon.

The answer appeared to be neither. In the minute or two she was out of his sight, Abrielle had left. Jack's heart sank a little. The others had seen him now and he couldn't turn back.

'So when's the return game?' ventured Simone. It was the first time she had actually spoken directly to him. 'I gather from Abrielle that you're rather good.'

'She's obviously a good judge of talent then.' Jack hadn't meant to sound arrogant; the words had just kind of come out.

'Oh yes, she's a very good tennis player, school champion last year,' Simone said proudly. 'Perhaps you should play her.'

'That could be interesting,' Jack ventured.

'If you want a proper game, I'll show you how to play,' a voice behind Jack said very coldly.

He turned to see the unsmiling face of Joe 90. Another person who'd hardly ever spoken to him directly before. Twice in five minutes! Must be his lucky day.

'Yeh, you and whose army, Joe 90!' Jack retorted.

'What did you call me?' Eric asked aggressively.

Jack realised his mistake; the nickname wasn't one for general consumption.

He turned to Joe 90, his dark shades hiding his eyes, and calmly said, 'I don't think I called you anything,' before adding pointedly, 'Eric.' Jack didn't do mean and nasty very well, and as much as he disliked Eric, he had no desire to humiliate him.

Jack turned back to the others, his cheeks burning slightly, conscious of the tension that he had created. Perhaps not everyone disliked Eric as much as he did, but then perhaps not everyone saw him as competition.

Jack turned to look at the pool as suddenly Abrielle emerged from the depths. First her head, then her torso and finally her legs, pulled up tightly, as she cleared the water and her feet landed on the edge. It was quite a feat, to pull herself out from the deep end of a pool in one clean movement.

He had been conscious of someone swimming lengths in the pool, but hadn't realised it was her. Now she was walking gracefully towards him, slightly side to side, displaying her long brown legs. Jack raised his eyes, briefly settled on her breasts, before continuing the ascent of her body and coming to rest at her face. The radiance of her beauty took his breath away. Jack had his shades

45

on, but consciously removed them as she picked up her towel to dry herself. As her head emerged from under the towel, he caught her gaze, and she held it for a few seconds before settling down on her towel.

Jack lay on his back, absorbing the sun, wondering where all this was going. He knew where he wanted it to go, but he knew he was going to have to do something about it, and therein lay the problem: what? how? when?

His eyes gradually closed and, although he tried to keep focused, his body slowly became overwhelmed by the desire to sleep. The daydreams began – just the two of them, lying together, side by side; it felt great.

Jack was awakened from his sleep by Heike shaking him. 'Come on, sleepy head, we're off out soon.' Jack came to and was surprised to see Abrielle was gone; in fact everyone was gone except Peter and Heike. The heat of the sun had been replaced by a cool late-afternoon breeze.

'What time is it?' Jack enquired.

'It's gone six; you've been out for over an hour,' Heike responded. 'Come on, the restaurant's booked for seven.'

Awake, his thoughts returned to Abrielle. What was it about her? What was it that was so tantalising, so irresistible? He knew he was heading down a dangerous road, gradually falling for her; he was being seduced by her beauty and a little bell kept ringing in his head, warning him, but he was choosing to ignore it – the masochism of desire.

Chapter 8

Jack stood on the edge of the pool. This is it, he thought. Today is the day. He took a deep breath, then another, and then dived into the pool. A shallow dive and he quickly came to the surface, the initial shock of the cold disappearing to be replaced with an even colder determination. He smoothly moved into a front crawl – a steady motion, repetitive, but consistent. The far wall slowly came into focus and although his lungs were beginning to complain and muscles weaken, he knew he had made it. He touched the wall and surfaced slowly, as if to prove there was still something left in him. Today is the day, he thought.

As Jack dried himself down, Peter arrived with the twins. It had only just gone ten and much too early for the French girls, but not apparently for the Dutch girls, who had mysteriously been absent for the last couple of days and were looking fair game until Simone and Abrielle had upset the apple cart. This could be interesting!

Astrid and Maria arrived in their tight bikinis and the joyous look on Peter's face was something to behold. Jack knew what was coming up next as Astrid and Maria left even less to the imagination and removed their tops.

Peter had invented a game for the pool a few days earlier which consisted of one person sitting on another's shoulders and then trying to push over another couple. Jack wasn't quite sure of the merits of the game, apart from Peter's obvious desire to get closer or, if his luck was in, to make contact with female anatomy.

The only thing that confused Jack was the teams. Peter had suggested that each of the girls sat atop a twin, while Jack sat on Peter's shoulders. This left Peter grappling with a twin, while Jack ended up fighting one of the girls. This was where Jack found the game slightly difficult. A normal method of attack would have been to push the opponent in the chest, but he knew that to do so would inevitably mean pushing, touching naked breast. Even if the girls wouldn't have minded, somehow it just didn't seem quite right. Consequently, he ended up grabbing arms and miserably failing to overcome them. They weren't the most successful team and Jack knew why.

Jack took a breather and let Eric, who had just arrived, take over. That's proof that I'm not always nasty to him, Jack thought. As he sat in the shallow end watching the commotion, he could see Simone and Abrielle coming down the path. An unamused look on their faces, particularly Simone's. Was it what was going on, or – more likely Jack suspected – the threat of competition?

When they had first met, Jack had quite liked Astrid – petite, cute, blonde, but just not Abrielle, in fact not in her league. It was like being offered a burger when you were used to fillet steak, not that he'd actually had any fillet steak recently.

When Peter became aware of Simone's arrival, he quickly ended his participation in the game, which unfortunately brought Joe 90's to an end as well, although Jack felt he was no longer a threat. This left the twins to the Dutch girls, which they all seemed very happy with.

Jack found himself the normal two doors down from Abrielle, which he kind of liked – close, but not too close. Joe 90 had placed himself the other side of Abrielle, but if he hadn't got the message now, he was never going to get it. She ignored him the whole morning.

Straight after lunch, Jack was down to the pool again.

He swam a few lengths, then thought about what he was going to do that afternoon. What about asking her for a walk – just the two of them, no distractions? He knew he had to do something and it was going to be today, this afternoon. No more delaying.

The others slowly turned up, the French girls as usual the last to arrive. Joe 90 had made sure that no one had moved Abrielle's towel or taken her place. Jack watched her arrive, his shades were on, but he knew she knew he was looking at her. She picked up her towel, skirted around the outside of the group, placed her towel on the grass next to him and lay down on her front. Game on, thought Jack.

He turned to lie on his front as well and removed his shades. From a couple of feet away, her eyes took on a different complexion; they seemed brighter, lighter, deeper. Jack felt his breathing quicken and knew they were reaching a climax of some kind.

It may have been an hour, half or double that time, he had no idea. They stared into each other's eyes and he was aware that he was no longer conscious of time. Every now and again a shriek, a scream from the pool would try and interrupt their world, but failed and disappeared into the background.

All of a sudden Abrielle jumped up and picked up her towel. She walked off towards the path that led up to the steps and her flat. Shit! Jack thought. Had she given up on him, just as he had finally plucked up the courage to do something? Then, rather than going up the steps, she turned onto the path that headed down to the rocks and onto Rosas. Just before she disappeared out of view, she turned to look at him, before vanishing. An invitation? It had to be.

Peter looked at him. 'Jack, what's wrong with you? Just kiss her for God's sake, for all our sakes.'

49

'Is it that obvious?' Jack asked.

'Yes! What the hell are you waiting for?' Peter said firmly, a look of exasperation on his face

Jack followed the path she had taken, gradually descending, twisting through the rocks until it straightened up. As he approached the 'diving board', he could see she wasn't ahead of him on the way to Rosas as he had expected. She must have clambered onto the rocks, where they had first met – well, at least first met properly. Perhaps she thought that might help.

When he arrived, there was no sign of her. Surely she couldn't have dived into the sea – her towel would be lying around. Where the hell had she gone? It didn't make sense. A shiver ran through him as he contemplated the posibility that she might have fallen in, but he quickly dismissed the idea.

Jack slowly made his way back up the path towards the pool, mystified. She seemed to have simply vanished. Then just before the bend that led back to the pool, he suddenly noticed a slight gap between the shoulder-high rocks. Funny how he'd never noticed it before, despite walking past it dozens of times. He peered round the back, still not expecting anything, but to his surprise found what looked like the beginning of a very narrow path. He eagerly moved forward and found that it twisted through the rocks for a few feet before dropping sharply. The rock face was surprisingly cool to the touch. He followed it down, his heart racing. Surely she must be here.

The path was steep and sandy, but holding onto the rocks for balance, he made it to the bottom without falling. It opened onto a tiny cove, with a small beach, no more than fifteen or twenty feet across, a similar depth. It was spotless, golden, beautiful and empty, except for one sole sunbather lying on her side on a towel, propping up her head as she stared across at him.

50

He walked slowly over to her, his heartbeat intensifying, his breathing quickening. He put his towel next to hers and lay down on his side, propping his head up just like hers. They formed a perfect symmetry. He looked into her eyes, but this time from just a foot away – he had never been so close to her.

Jack brushed a stray lock of her hair from over her left eye, pushing it back behind her ear. He kept his hand there, caressing the smooth skin of her left cheek, following her high cheekbones, gradually down past her mouth, to her chin. For a second he held her chin in his palm before tracing up the other side of her face with the back of his hand. He never took his eyes off hers and she held his stare, leaning her head slightly to the right to increase the contact with his hand.

He moved his hand slowly back down her face, his fingers running across the edge of her lips before returning to her chin. This time he cupped it in his thumb and forefingers and gently pulled her towards him. The gap between them closed, inch by inch, everything in slow motion – he wanted to take it all in, remember this moment.

He leant slightly forward and their lips met, just – their first taste of each other. They moved slightly closer and he felt a thrill of electricity run gently through his body. They kissed again, softly, delicately, effortlessly. He resisted the desire to kiss her more passionately; he wanted this to go slowly.

They broke for a second, leant back, a few inches away, looking into each other's eyes, before the need to kiss took over again. They both closed their eyes now as their tongues touched for the first time. It was like an electrical current running through them, connecting them. Jack moved his hand onto her arm and gently brought her even closer, her breasts touching his chest. He felt like he had never felt before. This feeling, this moment was presumably what love was all about.

He pulled away from her and looked into those deep blue eyes, still holding her close.

'I thought you were never coming,' she said gently.

'I couldn't find you. I thought you'd disappeared, but now I've found you I'm never letting go.' Jack was trying to be romantic but as the words came out he realised they sounded crass. Abrielle simply smiled, moving towards him to kiss him again.

Chapter 9

To look at it now, one would never believe what it had been through, unrecognisable from the battle scarred days of a decade ago. The bullet ridden walls carefully restored to ensure that no clues to its infamous past remained. No evidence of the lobby shoot outs or the room to room hand grenade clashes, which eventually saw it become just another casualty in an endless list of death and destruction.

Today, the Meridien Commodore stands proud and arrogant, situated just off the bustling Rue Hamra, with its designer stores and exchange bureaux, integrated with tiny jewellery shops and the inevitable fast food outlets. Tacky vases and false icons appeal to ignorant tourists alongside pretentious book shops, while the wonderfully named Wild Willy entices visitors only to disappoint with nothing racier than a child's Scaletrix set.

Residing in what used to be known in the Civil War as Muslim West Beirut, but now in a more cosmopolitan era, in a more forgiving Beirut, finds itself in the less inflammatory area known simply as Hamra. The intensity and buzz are still there, but these days it's the incessant noise of horns and whistles, rather than bullets and shells that dominate the decibel scales.

The car horn rules in Beirut, but in Hamra, with its narrow streets crisscrossing each other like a claustrophobic spider's web, the horn is not just king, it's also queen, knave and ace. A high pitched toot can be friendly and say hi or do you want a lift, a taxi touting for business or Stop, do you fancy a chat? A deep aggressive blast;

get out of my way, go faster or look out I'm going to cut you up! The horn has replaced the indicator, why signal left when it's easier to just hit the horn, and so what if I'm in the right hand lane, I tooted my horn; surely you knew what that meant!

Red lights, unlike most places in the world, mean different things to different drivers in Beirut. Admittedly, some do stop, but for most, it's slow down a little or speed up a lot, either way a quick prayer comes in handy, *Inshallah*. But for the battle hardened, for those who survived the onslaught, those who avoided the bullets, who never knew when they went to sleep if they would see another sunrise, for those who flirted with death and emerged victorious, the red light is a challenge, a challenge to get the adrenalin flowing once again, to try and cheat death one more time. A red light is a signal, not to stop, but to close one's eyes, foot down hard on the accelerator, then pray, pray hard and get that living on the edge buzz once again.

The incessant cacophony of noise is intense and for the uninitiated, it can be claustrophobic, but like many Capitals, Beirut has that buzz, that feeling that you're somewhere special, somewhere where things happen. A city that can go through what Beirut did and come out the other side smiling, is infectious, it begs forgiveness for its failings and rewards with its warmth, its beauty and its spirit.

I'd fallen in love with Beirut when I first visited, the war still fresh in the memories, but Beirut was determined to put history behind it and look forward. It had a romance to it and now here I'd found myself, unexpectedly face to face with a romance that I thought would never see the light of day again. But here she was right in front of me, as beautiful as when I last saw her, a blurred image through tears of torment, shattered innocent lives torn apart by fate.

I don't know how long I stared, open-mouthed, astonishment no doubt etched across my face. I couldn't believe what I was seeing, who I was seeing, after so, so long. It was a lifetime away. Spain 1986, a summer of love, a summer that promised so much, yet in the end delivered nothing more than agony and anguish. I'd often wondered how she'd coped, what had happened to her, but here she was, as stunning as the image embedded in my memory.

'Jesus – Abrielle!' I managed at last. 'I ... I don't know why I didn't recognise you immediately,' I stammered. 'I guess I just didn't expect to see you.'

'No, nor me you,' she said, waiting a second before adding, 'It may have been nearly eighteen years, Jack, but the moment you walked into the bar I knew it was you. You haven't fared too badly, your hair isn't receding, no surplus weight ... a few extra lines perhaps!' A warm smile emanated from her face, her blue eyes sparkling. A shudder went through me – there are some things time just can't change.

'Sorry!' I felt the need to say. 'Your hair's a bit shorter, a bit blonder, but otherwise you haven't changed that much either.'

'Oh I have, Jack. I'm a grown woman now, not a little girl anymore,' she said with a mischievous smile. It was a familiar look. 'I was just seventeen when you last saw me, thirty-four now – half a lifetime away.'

I still felt dumbstruck. I'd given up expecting to see her again long ago and suddenly, out of the blue, here she was, right in front of me, as beautiful as ever.

'Summer of '86, nearly eighteen years. My God, was it really that long ago?' I asked rhetorically. It was still so fresh in the memory; the pain might have been diminished by time, but I could still feel it. I wondered if she did too. 'Well, how are you? What have you been up to? What are you doing here in Beirut...?'

'Hey, one question at a time,' she interrupted. 'I'm here

on work, for *Le Monde*. They wanted me to come here and do an article on the presence of Syrian troops in Lebanon. The UN's debating whether or not to pass a resolution condemning them and the French Government is pushing hard. I've some old contacts here, so I thought I'd find out the Lebanese view, both official and unofficial.'

'So you fulfilled your dream. You always wanted to be a journalist.'

'I guess I did. After school, I started on a local Parisian weekly and worked my way up. Then I joined *Le Monde* and started climbing the ladder again and now I'm Foreign Affairs Editor.'

'No university first, I thought that was the plan?' I was surprised; she had been so determined to study journalism.

'Plans change Jack.' She spoke firmly, as if warning me not to push further.

'You've done well,' I said, feeling strangely proud.

'What about you then? If I remember correctly, you were going to make a fortune in the financial world.'

'I've done OK. I spent a few years in investment banks trying to make money, but found I was better at the IT side than trading, so I concentrated on that. Turned out to be perfect timing. PCs were just taking over from mainframes and banks couldn't get enough new technology. Seven years ago a colleague and I decided to go it alone, and now we've got twenty people working for us. The last few years haven't been so easy though, what with the end of the dot.com boom, but we have our own niche and we do all right.'

'So what are you doing in Beirut?' she asked, a lock of hair falling over her left eye. She flicked it back – a gesture I hadn't seen in a long time.

I frowned. 'It's a bit of long story actually ... I won't bore you with the details. Suffice to say I shouldn't be here. I had been visiting some clients here before heading off to Yemen, but on the way to the airport my lunatic taxi driver crashed his cab and a pedantic traffic cop insisted on taking all my details. The result is I missed my flight and am sitting here with you.'

I offered up a silent prayer of thanks for the taxi driver's incompetence and the policeman's officiousness.

I didn't want to talk about me. I wanted to listen to her voice, learn what she had been doing all these years. What had happened to the girl I'd fallen in love with? As I looked at her face, her beauty as intoxicating as it had been the last time my eyes had rested upon her, it hit home what I had lost. If only I'd acted differently. What would have been the outcome? Would our relationship have lasted? A slight foreboding came over me. She was probably happily married with lots of kids. Married – I didn't like the sound of that, somehow it didn't seem right. I'd always thought of her as mine, but a four-week relationship doesn't give you an option for life. After all I'd got married, but I guess that was irrelevant; I had no desire to be rational.

'Married, lots of kids then?' I blurted out a bit too quickly, almost demandingly.

She looked me back in the eye and there was an uncomfortable silence before she responded. 'No. No husband, no kids.'

'What, you've never been married?' I was staggered. 'But surely every man in Paris must have been queuing up for you?' I was quietly pleased, but nonetheless surprised.

She smiled, but there was a slightly sad look on her face. 'No. Never married. Guess I never met the right man.' There was a curious look in her eyes which I couldn't interpret. 'Too much of a career woman I suppose,' she added. She wasn't giving anything away.

'What about you? I see you've got a wedding ring.' she asked.

'Yep, married, two sons, nine and seven, my pride and joy,' I smiled.

'What about your wife?' she asked.

I suddenly felt uncomfortable. 'Susan, she's called Susan. We've been married for just over ten years.' I didn't want to start discussing my marriage. Given our history, it just didn't seem right.

Perhaps she sensed it to and chose to move on. 'Do you know, I wanted to stay at the Commodore because in the Civil War, this was where all the foreign journalists stayed. There was a circular bar called the News Bar, which became infamous as the place where the militias mixed with politicians, with reporters, the UN peacekeepers, all getting drunk together. I thought it would be great to come and see where some of my predecessors drank, where they risked their lives, but they've got rid of it!'

'I remember it,' I said. 'I was here a few years ago and it was still here. They had an old camera and typewriter on the wall, a huge carpet with prints of newspaper front pages. It's a shame it's gone, I remember sitting at the bar thinking this is where Yasser Arafat's henchmen used to drink, where drunken guerrillas would roll hand grenades under the bar stools just for a laugh. There was a real feeling of history about the place. It was through there,' I pointed to my right – 'where the Cuchina Restaurant is now.'

She looked to where I was pointing, momentarily lost in thought, before turning back to me. 'There used to be a parrot, Coco I think it was called. Apparently it used to do an excellent impersonation of incoming shells and everyone would dive for cover. Poor thing got kidnapped, never to be seen again.'

'How come you know so much about this place?' I asked, rather bemused.

She frowned. 'It's my job to find out – I'm a journalist.

If you're going to do a story properly, you have to do your research and you pick up little snippets of information along the way.'

Suddenly the lights went out and the place dissolved into darkness. I felt a hand on my arm.

'What's happening?' her soft voice whispered with a hint of trepidation.

Before I had time to answer, the lights came back on. 'Not sure,' I said. I looked around. The bar staff and guests continued as if nothing had happened. 'Perhaps it's just power problems; no one seems too bothered'. Her hand lingered, slightly longer than necessary.

'I think perhaps tonight is a night for déjà-vu,' I said. 'The last time I was here was May 2000, you remember when the Israelis were finally withdrawing from southern Lebanon.' She nodded. 'Hezbollah were firing rockets at them as they withdrew, and the Israelis said that if the Lebanese government didn't stop Hezbollah, they would attack the power stations outside Beirut.' She looked back into my eyes as I spoke, radiating warmth. A connection made.

'I was lying in bed watching CNN late at night and they were saying that, although the Israelis had threatened to attack, as yet they hadn't. I remember thinking that's rather unlike them – they usually act first and ask questions later. Suddenly the TV went blank, the air conditioning died and the lights went off. Then there was the sound of a distant explosion. But it was incredible – within a few seconds the generators kicked in and on came the lights. I looked out of the window, and initially it was pretty black, but gradually little pockets of light started to appear and these grew and grew until everything seemed back to normal again.'

'Was it scary?' Abrielle asked, seemingly excited by the idea of being a bit closer to the action.

'Not scary,' I said. 'I didn't think the Israelis were going to attack Beirut itself, but it did feel a bit weird, a bit too close for comfort.'

'Let's hope this time it's only a power problem,' she said with a reassuring smile that lit up her face. It was that innocent but seductive look I remembered so well. A look that seemed so fresh, so recent and yet which seemed to belong to another time.

Chapter 10

'San Miguels all round?' Jack asked. Peter and Heike nodded and Jack went off to the bar. By the time he had returned, Heike had already got Peter talking about Simone.

'She's good fun, very sexy, but I'm on holiday, just having a good time. Nothing serious, not like Jack here,' Peter said with a smirk.

'What's that meant to mean?' Jack asked rather defensively.

'You know perfectly well, Jack,' Heike interjected. 'Let's face it, your relationship seems to have taken on a slightly deeper meaning.'

Peter saved him from further interrogation. 'Anyway, as you know, Jack, they're going off to Madrid for a week, so I need to keep a look-out for other women.' Simone's mother wanted to see an exhibition of the Impressionists as well as visit some other galleries.

'What about you, Heike? Who's the man of your dreams?' Jack asked, determined to keep the conversation away from him.

'Oh, you know, the stereotypical male – tall, dark and handsome. The problem is he's got to be intelligent as well.'

'You mean someone a bit like Sebastian?' Jack asked.

Heike hesitated before smiling. 'Someone a bit like him, perhaps, but not so serious.' A good answer, Jack thought. Noncommittal, but leaving the possibility out there.

'Why do they want to go to Madrid for God's sake? I don't think Simone can stand her mother and I don't think Abrielle can either?' Peter complained.

'I don't think they were given a choice,' Jack commented. 'When Simone's mother asks if they want to go out for dinner, it's an instruction, not a question.'

'Time for another beer,' announced Peter. 'My round – same again?'

The others nodded, then Heike turned to Jack and gave him one of those serious looks.

'What?' Jack eventually asked.

'Are you OK?' she said.

'Course I'm OK. Why wouldn't I be?'

'Jack, I've known you a few years now and you mean a lot to me. I don't want to interfere, but be careful.'

'What do you mean "be careful"?' he asked.

'You know exactly what I mean, Jack. Stop pretending. I've seen the way that you look at her, the way you just disappear into your own world, just the two of you. Surely you're not going to deny it?'

'Is it that obvious?' Jack asked, feeling slightly embarrassed.

'It is to me, but then perhaps I know you better than most,' she said. 'You've got love written all over you.'

Jack knew she wouldn't tease him. She cared for him; he could afford to be truthful with her without being ridiculed. He sighed.

'You know, I've gone out with a few girls before; some were semi-serious, but I always felt in control. Now I meet this French girl, three years younger than me, almost *too* young, but she has woken feelings in me, feelings that I didn't know I had. I just feel so alive when I'm with her, when I listen to her voice, look into her eyes, every little movement – I just want to be with her, touch her, hold her and not let go. I've never felt anything like this before, never even knew that I could feel like I do.'

'Jesus, Jack, you are seriously infatuated, aren't you?' Heike had a smile on her face, but it was tempered by

62

concern. 'Jack, be careful! She's very beautiful, but she knows it as well. I don't want to see you get hurt.'

'What do I do though? I can't deny the way I feel; I'm not going to pretend that she means nothing to me.'

'Have you told her how you feel?' Heike asked.

'God no! I only kissed her for the first time this afternoon; it's a bit early to declare my undying love for her!' Jack responded. 'Not that I feel that way of course,' he added unconvincingly.

'Do you know how she feels?' Heike asked.

Jack shook his head. 'No, when we look into each other's eyes, when we, as you put it, go into our own little world, then I hope she feels the same way as I do, but I don't know. There's a chemistry, almost a symmetry in everything we do; we just seem to connect. I must mean something to her for that to happen, but what goes on inside that head of hers, I don't know.'

'Jack, I hope you know what you're doing. This has trouble written all over it.'

'I can't help it. All I know is that I have never ever felt this way about a girl before. She's just ... she's just so beautiful, so gorgeous, so ... I just want to hold her, be with her.'

Heike stared at Jack for a few seconds. 'Jack, just don't say I didn't warn you. A woman's intuition is rarely wrong, trust me.'

Peter arrived back with three bottles of San Miguel in each hand, a big smirk on his face. 'I thought it would save lost drinking time if I bought two rounds at once.'

'To gorgeous French girls!' Peter announced, raising his bottle.

To one in particular, Jack thought.

As the sun moved slowly towards the horizon, a light breeze came up and the temperature cooled. The leaves in the trees around the bar began to rustle.

'Hi everybody!' came a voice from behind Jack.

'Hey, Seb, where have you been?' asked Peter. Not much had been seen of him in the last few days, but his arrival had brought a smile out of Heike.

'I have to try and get my thesis finished before the end of the holidays,' explained Sebastian.

'Fancy a beer, Seb? We seem to have a few extra ones lying around.' Jack offered him a San Miguel.

'Oh thanks, Jack,' he said gratefully.

'So what's your thesis on then, the emergence of Catalonia as a global superpower?' Jack asked teasingly.

'Well, almost. It's about how dictatorships hold countries together, but once democracy returns it's inevitable that eventually the country will disintegrate into its various parts along regional and cultural lines. In twenty years Spain won't exist as it does today. The Basque region and Catalonia will be separate countries with their own governments,' Sebastian stated very matter-of-factly.

'Do you really believe that?' Jack asked, not sure if Sebastian was being totally serious.

'Of course.'

Jack was intrigued now. 'Why? Because it suits your theory or because you genuinely believe that it will happen?'

'It *will* happen. Since Franco died ten years ago Catalonia has already become more autonomous and that will continue until we have full independence.'

'But why should it be inevitable? The government in Madrid isn't just going to sit back and watch as the Basques and Catalans go their own way.'

'They'll have no choice. Look at what's happening in Yugoslavia. President Tito ruled with an iron fist; now he's dead and gradually ethnic tensions are rising, the regions are pushing for more and more autonomy from Belgrade and in the next few years Yugoslavia will disappear.' Sebastian was getting more and more animated as he spoke; this was obviously something close to his heart.

'But Yugoslavia is different, Seb. At the end of the Second World War, Tito brought together six republics and forced them to unite. They speak different languages, and have different ethnic backgrounds and different religions. For Yugoslavia, it's just a matter of time before blood is shed and they go their separate ways, but Spain is different. You share the same religion, the same culture and pretty much the same language. I can't see Spain going the same way,' Jack stated.

'Why not? The principle's the same.' Sebastian responded.

'But it's not, Seb,' Jack said. He wasn't trying to destroy his thesis, but he couldn't agree with it. 'Spain has been a country for hundreds of years; Yugoslavia was forced together forty years ago.'

Jack was enjoying the debate now, but it would have to continue some other time. Raised voices were heard coming up the steps from the car park behind the apartments. French voices.

'*Quinze minutes!*' a hoarse voice said sternly. Madame Arnaux came into view at the top of the steps – a tall, gaunt-looking woman with short red hair, gothically dressed in a flowing black dress and ebony beads round her long neck. Simone and Abrielle were just behind her. Madame Arnaux glared at the group of friends in the bar, an unsmiling bitter-looking expression on her small-featured face. Jack felt a chill run through him. Definitely not someone to mess with, he thought. She turned and disappeared into the shadows, the clink of shoes on concrete steps the only proof that, ghostlike, she hadn't just evaporated into the ether.

'We only have fifteen minutes,' announced Simone, 'then we must go – time for one drink then.'

'I'll get them. What would you like Abrielle?' Peter asked.

65

'Nothing for me thanks, Peter.' Turning to Jack, she said more quietly, 'I need to have a word. Can we go somewhere quieter, just the two of us? I don't want Simone's mother to see us. She doesn't approve of men!' She had a serious look on her face and immediately Jack felt slightly uneasy.

'Course we can,' said Jack, finishing his beer. He jumped up and they walked round the pool and towards the steps down towards the rocks. 'Is everything OK?' he asked. She didn't answer.

At the bottom of the steps, out of sight of the others, she whispered, 'Let's just sit here, Jack.'

Jack could feel his heart beating loudly, thumping him from within, a sinking feeling in his gut. They sat next to each other, facing one another.

'Jack, I've been thinking. I don't know how to say this and I'm not sure how you're going to react.' Surely she wasn't going to dump him on the day they had finally kissed for the first time.

She kept looking straight into his eyes. 'Jack, please try and understand, but I need to do this.'

He looked into those lovely eyes and felt reality beginning to slip away, the sadness on his face betraying his feelings.

'Jack...' she hesitated, 'I just have to kiss you again.'

'What?' Jack asked.

A big smile broke out on her face. 'I just have to kiss you again, that's all.' She burst out laughing.

'Jesus!' Hook, line and sinker, Jack thought. He smiled, more out of relief than anything else.

'Well?' she asked. 'Are you going to kiss me or not?'

'After pulling that stunt, you think you deserve a kiss, I think a punishment would be more appropriate.' Jack felt his heart slowing down, the relief was over-whelming.

'Let's see, perhaps you are ticklish,' Jack said as he gently dug his fingers under her ribs.

'Stop it!' Abrielle shrieked, squirming as she tried to stop him, pushing his hands away, but laughing at the same time. He was determined to get his revenge.

'Please, Jack, I'm sorry,' Abrielle pleaded.

Jack stopped, held her arms in his hands and looked into her smiling face. 'You must promise never to do that again,' he said firmly.

'I'll promise, but only if you kiss me right now.'

Jack smiled. He didn't need another invitation.

The following day Jack suggested to Abrielle that they go down to Rosas for a coffee, although he really just wanted to get away from the pool area and the others. 'You can drive if you want,' he suggested.

'Drive what?' she asked with a quizzical look. 'I haven't passed my test yet.'

'The Beetle,' Jack said, pointing towards a lurid orange VW at the back of the small car park.

'That thing! Lovely colour,' she said sarcastically. 'Whose is it?'

'Heike's. It's dual-controlled,' said Jack. 'She and Peter drove down from Germany in it.'

'Dual-controlled, what's that?' Abrielle asked.

'It's for learner drivers. There are two sets of pedals so the instructor can take over if necessary.'

Abrielle looked at the car suspiciously. 'So let me get this right, I steer and you can brake or accelerate – sounds a bit dangerous to me.'

'I'm not going to touch anything unless we're about to crash,' said Jack. 'Though if you drive too slowly, I might be forced to put my foot down on the accelerator!' he added mischievously.

'You touch the brake or accelerator and I'll kill you!' she retorted with a smile, though underneath there was a warning not to interfere.

'You do know how to drive don't you?' asked Jack, uncertain if it had been such a good idea after all.

Abrielle looked at him with that condescending look she sometimes employed. 'Of course I do.'

Jack got the keys from Heike and off they went. Abrielle was a little hesitant at first, but clearly knew what she was doing. Her gear changes were smooth, even if she did keep her foot on the clutch a bit too long. Jack began to relax as they headed down the hill, the steep cliffs on their right, a small barrier to the left offering little protection to the careless.

As they headed towards the final bend on the coastal road entering Rosas, a gleaming black Porsche came flying round the corner towards them, but on the wrong side of the road as it recklessly overtook an open-topped bright-red VW Golf. Blood red, Jack instantly thought.

'Jesus, brake!' shouted Jack as he slammed his foot towards the floor automatically, forgetting that there was actually a brake there. Abrielle let out a piercing scream as the Porsche roared towards them. They were heading for a collision. The gap between the two cars closed rapidly, even as the Beetle slowed. As the moment of impact approached, Abrielle turned the wheel slightly to the right, bringing the Beetle tight up against the rock face. Jack pulled his elbow sharply in from the open window where it had been casually resting seconds earlier. Any closer and they would have hit the rock wall.

The Porsche meanwhile, swung back suddenly to the right side of the road, cutting up the Golf but more importantly narrowly missing them. A smudge of blond hair and a blurred face flashed by. The Golf driver blasted his horn, and the Porsche responded with a mocking toot-toot. Bastard, thought Jack to himself, furious at the driver's stupidity, but relieved that the two of them were unhurt.

'You OK?' Jack asked Abrielle gently.

'No, I'm not OK!' she screamed back at him. 'Some idiot nearly killed me – and you ask if I'm OK!'

Jack decided it wasn't the time to point out that the same idiot had nearly killed him as well. He could feel his heart pounding. 'Hey, you did well, Abrielle. It's thanks to you we didn't have a very nasty accident,' he said reassuringly.

She looked over at him sullenly. Jack could see she was holding back the tears. He put his arms around her and pulled her close to him, her head on his chest, just holding her, feeling very protective.

'Come on, let's go and have that drink, perhaps something a bit stronger than a coffee. You OK to drive?'

'No, would you mind? I'm a bit shaken up.'

Jack squeezed out and walked around the other side of the Beetle, while Abrielle moved across into the passenger seat. Jack got in and pulled away from the rock face onto the now deserted road. In Rosas they walked hand in hand to the nearest bar, Toro, which advertised itself to the world with a giant plastic bull standing arrogantly on the roof. They sat under the awning, overlooking the packed, sun-baked beach.

Abrielle ordered a brandy. Jack went for a cold San Miguel and raised a toast to her. 'To survival in the face of adversity,' he proffered. 'You know one day he'll kill himself and probably someone else as well.'

'How do you know it was a he?' Abrielle asked.

'I saw him – short blond hair, glasses. There was something familiar about him as well, perhaps it's someone I've seen around.'

69

Abrielle looked at Jack. 'Eric was telling me that his father has a black Porsche. Perhaps he borrowed it.'

The penny dropped. 'Eric! Of course, I knew he was familiar.' He felt a surge of anger. 'I'll kill him when we get back.' There was a moment of silence.

'It looks like we are going to Madrid next weekend for a week or so,' Abrielle said, changing the subject. 'Will you still be here for me when I get back?'

Jack looked back at her before answering. Every now and again she showed signs of vulnerability, of insecurity. He liked that – it made him feel wanted, needed. He smiled. 'Course I will. I'll be waiting for you. But...' He hesitated.

'But what?' asked Abrielle.

'We do have to change something about you.' Jack stood up and grabbed her hand. 'Come on, this way.'

'Where are you taking me?' she asked as Jack led her down one of the side streets.

'Here, have a look at these?' said Jack, stopping in front of a shop window.

'Sunglasses, what do I want with a new pair of sunglasses? I've a perfectly good pair,' she answered.

'No, you don't, you have a very scary pair that remind me of a very frightening encounter I once had.'

'Really? I quite like them. I think they're quite trendy,' Abrielle said defensively.

'No, they're not, they're last year's model,' said Jack, trying to sound convincing when he really hadn't got a clue; fashion and him moved in different circles. 'Come on, I'll buy you a new pair,' he added.

'What about these? Tortoiseshell, that's the new trend for '86,' Jack said without a clue whether he was remotely close to the truth or not.

'They are quite nice. Are you sure, they're a thousand pesetas?' asked Abrielle.

'As long as you promise never to wear the others again, it will be worth it,' said Jack.

Abrielle wore the glasses out of the shop. Definite improvement, thought Jack. She turned and gave him a big kiss on the lips. 'Thank you, Jack.'

'A pleasure!' He smiled, thinking that he'd done it more for him than her.

Chapter 11

'Are you ready to order sir?' the waiter asked. He was an Indian, one of many migrant workers who came to the Middle East to improve their lot, and looked uncomfortable dressed up in his tight bright-red jacket, with its brass buttons done up down the middle.

'We are, thanks.' I turned to Abrielle. 'What would you like? The wild mushroom risotto perhaps?' I suggested, remembering that she had been an ardent vegetarian. It seemed like only yesterday that she was trying to persuade me of the virtues of not eating meat, though the more she had gone on about it, the less convincing she had become.

'I'll have the veal please,' she said, looking up into my eyes, waiting for a reaction. I held her stare before turning to the waiter.

'I'll have the same. A selection of vegetables as well, please,' I added before turning to Abrielle and trying to keep a straight face. 'You *do* eat vegetables?'

She gave me a sarcastic smile.

'And to drink, sir?'

'You OK with red?' She nodded back. 'We'll have a bottle of the Ksara please.'

'Have you had Lebanese wine before?' I asked Abrielle. She shook her head. 'It comes from the Bekaa Valley; it's good, both the red and the white.' I hoped I didn't sound like a pompous connoisseur, but it didn't stop me. 'There's another red called Château Musar, also from the Bekaa, which is even better.' I paused but couldn't resist the little anecdote I had picked up from a waiter the previous night. 'Do you know that throughout the Civil War, they managed to carry on producing it, even when the front line went through the vineyards.'

'Really, how did they manage that?' Abrielle asked, but I could tell she was trying to be polite; I sensed her mind was elsewhere.

'Apparently they smuggled the bottles out in ambulances! The bottles smelt of antiseptic, though there was nothing wrong with the wine...'

I looked at her as she listened absent-mindedly. Her deep-blue eyes had lost none of their allure, they still had that ability to captivate me, to take me to a different place.

'So, veal?' I ventured. 'What happened to France's sole convert to the world of vegetarianism?'

Abrielle smiled that gorgeous smile and I felt a thrill run through me. 'I missed the taste of meat too much. I kept it up for a year, but in the end just got bored with fish – found it all too bland.'

I smiled back at her. 'It's true, you can never beat a bloody good steak.'

She smiled back, but didn't respond.

'So how long are you in Beirut for?' I asked.

'Just a couple of days. I fly back Thursday afternoon, once I've done all my interviews, met everyone I need to.'

She paused for a moment, then asked, 'What are you going to do now?'

It wasn't concern, more intrigue.

I hesitated before answering. 'I'm not quite sure actually. The meeting in Sana'a was a presentation to the bank's regional managers who were getting together for tomorrow only, so there's no point getting there a day late. And I'm not due back in the office until next week...'

73

She gave me a funny questioning look. 'Don't you just want to get home to see your wife and children? I'm sure I would,' she suggested.

Yes and no, I thought, or rather no and yes. 'I do, but I've always wanted to see more of Lebanon, go to the Bekaa Valley and see Baalbek.' I was conscious of a manufactured smile appearing on my face as I enthused about places I knew little about. 'So I thought I might spend a couple of days seeing the sights.'

The lie flowed like it had been well rehearsed, not the spontaneous falsehood it was. I was surprised at how easily it had come, how without even thinking about it I had already decided I would stay longer. No consideration, no thought about practicalities, about appropriateness, about morals, about responsibilities or even implications, the decision had already been taken – just to spend more time in her company.

'What's in Baalbek?' Abrielle asked.

Did she buy the lie? I wondered. Was it plausible?

'Roman ruins, not just ruins actually; there are some temples, one of which is still pretty much intact apart from the roof. I think they're the largest outside of Italy.' I paused before adding nonchalantly, 'Apparently there are fifty-metre tall pillars which are still upright; quite a feat to build them 2,000 years ago.' That was about as much as I had gleaned from a guidebook I'd read earlier.

Abrielle seemed to be listening to what I was saying, nodding so to speak in all the right places, but I felt that she was merely going through the motions and wasn't taking in what I was saying.

'The other great place to go to is the Jeita grotto, just along the coast from Beirut; there are a couple of caves with spectacular stalagmites and stalactites... It's meant to be very romantic,' I added and immediately wondered why.

Abrielle ignored the comment. 'Sadly I won't have time for sight seeing. I have meetings all day tomorrow – the official view, the government's view, and the Syrian view … though that's entirely predicable,' she said contemptuously. 'Thursday should be more interesting. There are some local journalists and also I'm meeting up with a Druze MP who I'm sure will give a very different view to that of the government.'

'You already seem to know what they're going to say. If that's the case, is there any point meeting them?'

'There is. If I'm going to be objective, I need to get both sides, even if I know what the official view is going to be. It hasn't changed in a decade, so it's unlikely to now.'

'Why bother though?' I smiled then added, 'Why don't you come along with me?' As soon as the words came out of my mouth, I regretted them, but they were out there and I couldn't reel them back in.

'Jack, you can't be serious!' A look of exasperation came over her face. 'I've flown all the way to Beirut to do these interviews. I'm meeting up with some senior members of the government. Very senior!' she emphasised. I could see the annoyance in her face, in her eyes. 'It wouldn't be very professional, would it? You think that I'm going to drop everything just because *you* happen to walk back into my life,' she snapped indignantly. 'Same old arrogant selfish Jack, always thinking of yourself!'

'Sorry!' I said bashfully, 'It was just wishful thinking. I thought it might be nice to spend a bit of time together and catch up.'

'Catch up, isn't that exactly what we're doing now?' she asked, leaving the question up there for me to decide.

'Sorry, you're right; I hadn't thought it through.' I sunk the last of the gin and tonic as the waiter brought the Ksara over. I felt embarrassed, the tension between us

75

obvious. He tried to open the wine as quickly as he could, realising that he'd interrupted something. Silence prevailed as he removed the cork, waiting for me to approve, then poured modest amounts into large round glasses, the size of bowls.

I felt like an idiot, like a child who had just been caught stealing chocolates, scolded by his mother, cheeks burning, head hung low to hide the shame.

'Jack,' she said slightly more softly, 'tomorrow I'm meeting a member of the Cabinet. It's not easy to arrange something like that. Some of my old contacts from the Lebanese Embassy in Paris managed to organise it. It's not something you cancel to spend the day with an old boyfriend.'

'OK, point made, I'm sorry.' I changed the subject. 'Who are you meeting, someone I've heard of?'

She smiled again; a sliver of relief crept through me. 'Might have done, you'll just have to wait till tomorrow night. I'll let you know at dinner.'

I smiled, my heart doing a little leap of joy. Dinner tomorrow night would do fine. I chose to ignore the fact that now she was the one being presumptuous; perhaps she was just trying to show that she was still in control.

The veal arrived, covered in a white wine, cream and mushroom sauce. I smiled. 'Do you eat foie gras as well?'

'No, I put my foot down there,' she laughed. 'I know I shouldn't eat veal, but I just love the taste; I don't have it very often.'

As the Ksara flowed, Abrielle began to talk more about her job in Paris. It seemed that her whole life centred around *Le Monde* and journalism; most of her friends were reporters. She talked about assignments, famous people she'd interviewed, even awards she'd won. But the more she spoke, the less I realised I was learning. It all seemed to be at a superficial level, a professional level;

76

she was talking about what she did, but she revealed very little. Was she hiding something? Or was that just the way she was, reluctant to reveal anything meaningful about herself?

'So tell me about your wife – Susan, isn't it?' she asked. Having revealed absolutely nothing about herself, I was now expected to reveal all. I knew that I had to be careful, the combination of the gin and wine had combined nicely and I could feel the beginning of tomorrow's headache.

'Well, we met New Year's Eve 1990 dancing and drinking in Trafalgar Square. We started going out immediately, moved in together a year later and got married in '94. She was a teacher, a very good one actually, primary school, but she's a mother and housewife now. She's a very patient person, which is probably why she is so good with kids, probably why she's still with me come to think of it.' I said it jokingly, but it made me think for a second.

'What about your boys?' Abrielle asked.

A pang of guilt went through me. Here I was having a meal with a former girlfriend, not their mother, more than a former girlfriend, a girl whom I had once loved so much that I would have done anything for her...

'Liam and Paul. They're good kids, though at times they are a bloody nightmare. But they behave at school and they seem to enjoy it; I haven't been summoned to see the headmaster yet. They're both sports mad, especially football. They get that from me I guess. They spend all their time outside kicking a ball, riding their bikes, climbing trees – you know, the normal boy things.'

She looked me back in the eye before responding. 'Not really, I didn't have any brothers. I went out with a guy once who had a little boy; he just seemed to whine and cry the whole time. I don't suppose all boys are like that though.'

A flicker of sadness appeared across her face, before

77

disappearing again just as quickly. It was a look, a brief glimpse perhaps of who she really was.

'Time for bed!' she announced. It wasn't an offer and I refrained from turning it into one; she might not appreciate the joke. 'It's gone midnight and I have to be up in just over six hours. What time do you want to meet for dinner tomorrow?'

'Don't mind really, whatever time suits you?'

'How about seven?'

It was earlier than I would have normally eaten, but yet again, my heart was plotting, the earlier we met, the longer we spent together.

'Seven's fine,' I said.

'Let's meet in the bar again. Leave me to book somewhere.'

'Sounds like you already have somewhere in mind.'

'Perhaps I have – you'll just have to wait and see.'

We made our way to the lifts, and at this late hour, even with only a few people in the bar, I felt heads turn – she still had that ability to make men – and women too, stop in their tracks. This woman with me, but not mine, not any longer; that was a long, long time ago.

As she entered the lift I could only but admire her, her shape, her stature, everything about her. She caught me looking through the reflection in the mirror at the back, but I'm not sure what my expression had revealed.

She turned to me, that seductive look on her face once more. 'What floor?'

'Eighth, please... Room 807,' I added rather un-necessarily.

'Oh I'm in 907, right on top of you.' It was said innocently enough, but I couldn't help smiling to myself, my mind drifting back to the first time we made love, Abrielle on top, in complete charge.

'What?' she challenged me.

'What do you mean, what?' I respond playing for time.

'You have got that little smirk on your face, I remember it well,' she said, that infectious smile spreading across her face.

'It was nothing, just a thought of something that happened a long time ago, that's all.'

The lift reached the eighth floor infuriatingly quickly and as the doors opened I wasn't quite sure how to say goodnight. A handshake was far too formal; we were lovers once for heaven's sake. She didn't seem to know quite what to do either.

I decided to take charge. I took hold of either hand, relishing the contact once more and kissed her on each cheek, French style. For God's sake, Jack, you're married, I thought.

'It was good to see you again, Abrielle,' I said as the lift doors began to close.

'You too!' she said. 'Tomorrow at seven in the lobby.' Then she'd gone and I was left staring at a set of closed lift doors, my warped reflection staring grotesquely back at me.

Chapter 12

Jack stared out the window, watching the cornfields flash by, the stalks waving frantically in the vortex created by the speeding train. The crop was planted tightly up against the track; there was no fence or barbed wire to ward off foolhardy kids from playing chicken with approaching trains – perhaps the youth of Spain weren't quite as stupid as some of their English counterparts.

Peter sat opposite fast asleep, while the two girls chatted away in French, much too fast for Jack to follow. He could feel the warmth of Abrielle's hand resting on his thigh and it felt good, reassuring, his own on top of hers, holding on, just in case she should think of removing it. He could feel the warmth of the early-morning sun on his face, and the colours of the rainbow danced on the plastic table that separated the two couples.

His thoughts turned to Barcelona, still over an hour away. Jack had seen little of the city, except for the railway station where he'd arrived a little over a week earlier, but he knew its heritage, its long history, the pride of its people, Catalans not Spaniards; Sebastian had been careful to explain all that.

The trip to Barcelona had been a spontaneous decision made over drinks the previous night; no organisation, no planning, not the kind of trip the highly organised Heike approved of. Jack suspected her refusal to come along had more to do with not wanting to be a rather large gooseberry.

'Who fancies Gaudí first?' asked Peter.

'Is he good-looking?' Simone answered, to giggles from Abrielle.

Peter gave her a slightly patronising smile, not particularly impressed by her attempt at humour. 'I doubt it; he's been dead for sixty years!'

'Yeh, come on; I'd like to see Casa Batlló,' said Jack. He'd learnt a little about Gaudí from his flatmate at university who was studying architecture. A 'genius', Steve had called him.

An hour later they were standing outside the genius's elaborate masterpiece. Jack stared at the building in awe. It was weird and beautiful, almost alien. So out of place in the middle of a city. The inside was no less impressive, a master lesson in how to utilise natural light to its fullest – wooden floors, spiral staircases, stained glass windows; grand but not gaudy, very Gaudí.

'I didn't know architecture could be so interesting,' remarked Abrielle as they left the building, 'but now it's time for shopping!' With that she grabbed Jack's hand to walk up to Plaça de Catalunya and to Las Ramblas. 'Come on, let's go, it's time to go and spend some pesetas.' A childish grin on her face, she pulled Jack reluctantly along.

Shopping didn't appeal to Jack, but somehow it seemed so much more acceptable when walking hand in hand with the most beautiful girl in the world. There was a pleasant breeze blowing, keeping the temperature bearable, the leaves rustling gently in the tree-lined street.

'It's our second anniversary – what are you going to buy me to celebrate it?' The childish grin had turned into a mischievous smirk.

'Second anniversary?' asked Jack, raising an eyebrow.

'Yes, on our first, you bought me a new pair of sunglasses.

81

Today is our second – what are you going to buy me?'
She maintained the smile, leaving Jack unsure if she was
serious or not.

'You think I should buy you something each day to
celebrate another day of us going out together?' Jack
wanted to believe she was teasing him, but inside he was
unsure. Was it a wind-up, or was she going to prove to
be very high-maintenance.

'Don't you think I'm worth it?' she queried innocently.

Jack felt a surge of panic as she continued to drag him
towards the expensive shops of Las Ramblas. 'I'm a poor
impoverished student, I'm not sure if I could afford to
keep you in daily presents.'

'Ah, but I insist! I'm not just any girl you know!'

God, she's serious, thought Jack, I need to put a stop
to this.

'Well, if you can't afford me, I have a difficult decision
to make!'

'I suppose,' she said thoughtfully, 'we could
compromise...' She paused for dramatic effect. 'I do *quite*
like you, so perhaps a present every other day would be
acceptable.' The smile remained intact and Jack was none
the wiser. Common sense said this was a wind-up, but
common sense had flown out the window five days ago
when this stunning gorgeous girl had walked into his life
and calmly turned it upside down.

Jack decided to play a straight bat. 'Not sure I could
afford a present every other day either; you might have
to settle for just me!'

Abrielle shook her head, the smile disappearing into a
solemn disappointed look. Jack momentarily felt a pang
of guilt at her sadness, before he told himself to stop
being so stupid. He lifted her chin and looked back into
those eyes, holding her sad stare, which gradually turned
into an excited smile.

'I know! Instead of buying me a present everyday, how about *giving* me a present every day?' she suggested.

'Giving?' asked Jack suspiciously. 'What exactly did you have in mind?'

'I know what I would like, and it wouldn't cost you anything...'

'What?' said Jack.

They had reached the entrance to Las Ramblas and she suddenly stopped. Peter and Simone were a few yards ahead wrapped up in their own conversation. Abrielle turned to Jack and put her arms around his neck and pulled his face to hers, their lips touching, teasing, tasting, but no more. Romantic, but decorum and dignity retained. She broke away and pulled his head to the side of hers, her hot breath caressing his earlobe. 'I want just that, *everyday!*' she whispered, 'You *must* promise.'

She pulled away and Jack looked into those dark-blue serious eyes, his heart pounding. 'I promise!' He pulled her close, holding her tight, wanting to hold onto the moment for as long as he could.

The moment was broken by a slow handclap. Peter stood a few yards ahead, sarcastically applauding, while Simone stood hands on hips. 'Come on you two. Can't you behave in public?'

'That's a bit rich coming from you!' Jack retorted, taking Abrielle's hand and walking towards the others. She squeezed his hand tight and he responded in kind. Another step forwards, he thought, not sure where though.

'Hey, let's try in here, I want to buy a new bag,' suggested Abrielle, ushering them into an already overcrowded shop that sold what looked like very expensive leather bags, all with designer labels.

'What do you think of this?' Abrielle asked, turning to show Jack a small light-brown handbag, with a long leather strap, and some brassy designer label that he couldn't read. He didn't think anything. To Jack, it was a handbag – nothing more, nothing less.

'It's lovely!' he lied. 'A bit expensive though?' he added, having seen the 5,000-peseta price tag.

'You think *that's* expensive?' Wait till you see the price of some of the more famous designers' bags.'

As Peter and Jack followed the two girls around the store, the prices began rising. As the bags got weirder and gaudier, the prices climbed ever higher, but Abrielle and Simone seemed entranced.

'Do you think they're actually going to buy anything, or is this what women do?' asked Peter.

'It's a female thing, Peter, just go with it. Agree when you're meant to agree, disagree when you're meant to disagree, and show approval at the right time.'

Peter looked confused. 'But how do you know when's the right time?'

'You have to learn to read the signals, look at what the eyes are telling you, not what the mouth is saying.' Peter looked perplexed. 'Peter, have you *ever* gone out with a girl for any length of time?'

'Well, not really, most of my girlfriends have been, err ... more short-term,' Peter replied, slightly embarrassed.

Jack smiled. For all his outward confidence, Peter wasn't quite so sure about women. While not an expert himself, a relationship of a whole year and two more girlfriends who had lasted over six months made Jack feel he was more than a novice.

'It's not something you can teach Peter. It's something you learn, learn through the painful experience of getting it wrong, horribly wrong; suffering the consequences and making sure you don't make the same mistake again.'

'Really?' was all that Peter could manage.

'Yup, unfortunately when it comes to women, they're a different species, and what I have learnt is that you can't rationalise with them. You try to, but you just end up getting exasperated when they refuse to see your point of view,' Jack said reflectively. 'What you have to do,' he added, trying to be helpful, 'is accept they're different and just go with your gut feeling.'

Peter nodded. 'And if your gut feeling's wrong, then what?'

'Tears!' said Jack starkly.

'Tears?' Peter repeated.

'Yes, and usually lots of them. It depends on how badly you've misread the signals.'

'I hadn't realised how complicated relationships were.' Peter's face was now a picture of despondency.

'And then, of course, after the tears come the apologies, lots of them as well.' The sadist in Jack was thoroughly enjoying Peter's discomfort.

'Why do we go out with them?' Peter asked, to himself as much as to Jack.

Jack smiled. 'Peter, we're men, hunter-gatherers. It's survival, Darwin's theory of evolution...' He knew he was rambling on, but Peter had taken the bait and Jack was slowly reeling him in.

'Right, I'm having this one,' announced Abrielle suddenly. It looked distinctly like the first bag she had picked up, but Jack was more concerned about whether she expected him to pay for it or not. For all his spiel to Peter, he still wasn't sure whether he'd read the signals correctly or not.

Abrielle smiled at Jack, placing the bag over her head, and dropping it onto her shoulder.

'Very nice, it suits you,' Jack said, sounding as genuine as he could.

The smile widened. Right answer, thought Jack. Thank God! Out came her purse and off she went to pay. Thank God, thought Jack again.

After a leisurely lunch and a stroll in the Park Güell – another of Gaudí's fabulous creations – where Peter was distinctly quieter than usual, they wound their way back towards the railway station via a couple of designer clothes shops. They stopped outside a jeweller's, and Simone, bless her, pointed out to Abrielle a thin gold ring with a small ruby on it.

'That's my birthstone, Jack! Isn't it beautiful?' Abrielle said, as her eyes became transfixed by the little ring.

Jack looked down at the innocent little ring, with its slightly less innocent price tag, but he had to admit, there was a certain beauty to it.

'Did you know that when you wear a ruby, if you wear it with gold, it's meant to absorb the sun's energy and rejuvenate the body?' Abrielle told them. Jack didn't know, but he could see how much she liked it. He wasn't often one for spontaneity, but he had an overwhelming and irrational urge to buy it for her. Twenty thousand pesetas, nearly a hundred pounds, it had taken a while to save that sort of money up, but what the hell, he thought, you only live once. He smiled. He'd brought a credit card on holiday, to be used in emergencies. Only this wasn't quite the emergency he had been thinking about.

'Would you like to try it on?' he asked.

Abrielle gave one of her slightly patronising looks. 'I don't think that would be a good idea. I probably wouldn't want to take it off.'

'No, I mean it; I'd like to buy it for you,' Jack said seriously.

Abrielle laughed. 'Don't be silly, Jack! You can't possibly buy me that!'

'Why can't I? I'd like to.'

'Jack, I was only kidding earlier about buying me a present every day, and I'm certainly not going to let you spend so much money on me.' Abrielle looked determined, but Jack was even more so.

86

'I know you were teasing,' said Jack, relieved that at least one issue had been cleared up, 'but I'd really like to buy it for you.'

'Really?' asked Abrielle, her face lighting up.

Jack nodded. 'Why don't you see if it fits?'

They entered the shop as Peter and Simone stood outside gobsmacked. 'Don't worry, Peter, Jack's mad; I don't expect you to be so stupid,' Simone reassured him. Peter wasn't going to argue.

Chapter 13

On the train back Jack felt happier than he could ever remember. He lay back in the slightly reclined seat, the rays of the setting sun making him squint. Abrielle slept, her head on his chest; he could feel rather than hear her breathing. Her right hand clasped his shoulder, and he could see her new ruby ring shining brightly. Jack breathed a deep breath, almost a sigh. I guess this is what falling in love is, he thought. Wonderful, if a bit expensive.

A little after nine the train arrived in Figueras. The sun had disappeared, but it was still light. Jack offered to drive and Peter was happy for him to do so. As they approached Rosas, Jack noticed flashing lights ahead. As he slowed the Beetle, a policeman beckoned him to stop.

"What do you think's going on?' asked Peter.

'Not sure,' said Jack, feeling slightly nervous, although he wasn't quite sure why. Something about uniforms and authority perhaps.

Jack wound down the window and a tall, imposing, unsmiling Spanish policeman bent down to peer in at them, after walking around the car.

'*Alemán?*' He asked having presumably seen the 'D' on the back of the car.

'*Inglés,*' Jack responded before pointing to Peter. '*Alemán.*'

'Passports!' The policeman demanded in an unnecessarily aggressive manner.

Jack dug his rather battered and torn passport out from his pocket, and offered it to the policeman. Peter did the same. He took them, flicked through them and then gave both Jack and Peter a long stare as he appeared to decide whether they matched their pictures before handing them back. Then he snapped his fingers at the girls, and they handed their passports over. Jack heard Abrielle muttering '*Imbécile*' under her breath.

Peter also heard. 'I'd be careful what you say,' he said firmly. 'You might not have noticed, but there's a policeman with a gun pointing straight at Jack's head. Probably best not to upset them.'

Only Peter had noticed that standing behind the little Fiat police car was an officer with a rifle resting on the car's roof, ready to fire. Jack took in a deep breath, the barrel of the gun seeming to grow as it emerged out of the dark.

The policeman grudgingly handed the girls' passports back, but ushered Jack out of the car and to the back of the Beetle. Jack moved slowly, beginning to feel more and more uncomfortable. Knowing that they had done nothing wrong and were perfectly innocent was doing little to calm his nerves. The policeman motioned Jack towards the Beetle's rear and ordered him to open the boot. Jack gave him a surprised questioning look, but the policeman took this as reluctance to open it and drew his gun, pointing at the boot. He obviously had little knowledge of how a Beetle was designed, thought Jack.

Jack moved slowly, not wanting to surprise the policeman. He was edgy enough and was in for a shock as it was. As Jack twisted the handle and heard the latch click, he sensed the policeman moving nervously round behind him. As the lid opened, Jack watched the policeman, wanting to see his eyes, the look of surprise on his face. As out of the dark the engine appeared, the policeman took a step back, confusion etched across his face. Jack smiled to himself – he had no idea!

Eventually his rather slow brain worked it out and he

motioned to Jack to go to the front of the car and lift the bonnet, or was it the boot lid? Jack opened what he decided was probably the boot and the policeman's torch scanned the almost empty boot before it picked out a heap at the back, a rag of some kind, covering something small. As he pulled away the rag, the policeman took a step back, revealing a box with wires hanging out. Jack felt a shudder run through him as he sensed the policeman's alarm. God! A bloody bomb – how on earth...?

Jack had never seen a home-made bomb before. Come to think about it, he'd never seen any kind of bomb except on TV or in films, but they didn't really count. Surely, there was some mistake. it must be something else.

The policeman, gun still in hand, looked at Jack coldly, trying to assess whether he had a terrorist in front of him or not. Or at least that's how Jack interpreted the look.

The policeman motioned to the box, and Jack shrugged his shoulders. He wasn't quite sure if the policeman was asking what it was or if he wanted him to open the box. He did know, though, that this was clearly not the time to make a mistake. This was a rather jittery, none too clever policeman who could, for all Jack knew, be rather trigger-happy.

The officer motioned to the box again, and Jack plumped for opening the box. Reluctantly and gently he lifted the cardboard flaps up and pulled the box towards him. Inside was a mass of wires and leads ... and that was it. Jack breathed a sigh of relief. The policeman lowered his gun and ushered Jack back to the car, forcefully closing the boot.

As Jack got back into the driver's seat, he was greeted by silence until he wound the window back up. Then, as if everyone had been holding their breath, a barrage of questions erupted, all clamouring to be heard above the others. But the voice that reached through was not the loudest, but the softest – Abrielle's.

'Are you all right?' she asked, a hint of concern in her voice.

Jack turned and smiled at her. 'I'm fine now, thanks.'

As they moved slowly forward, the Beetle's headlights picked out a battered little Peugeot halfway up the roundabout. A man was lying face down over the bonnet, hands behind his back, two policeman holding him there.

The silence returned until they reached the far side of the roundabout. Jack sensed a collective sigh of relief, the tension dissipating as they put distance between themselves and the police.

'What the hell was that all about?' asked Peter. 'Why did he want to look at the engine?'

Jack smiled. 'He didn't. He just didn't know that the engine was at the back!'

'What!' exclaimed Peter, mirth written across his face. 'But Beetles have been around for decades; everyone knows, don't they?'

'Apparently not everyone,' concluded Jack. 'He didn't seem the brightest and he didn't like that box of wires you've got in the boot. What on earth are they for?' he asked, deciding to keep his thoughts about home-made bombs to himself. It seemed rather silly now.

'Oh they're for the boat, for when we need to change some of the wiring.'

Jack turned to look at Peter quizzically. 'What boat?'

'Oh didn't you know? We've got a speedboat here, just a small one, but it goes quite fast, great for waterskiing,' said Peter nonchalantly, as if everyone had one.

Jack was impressed.

'That's cool! Can we have a go on it?' asked Simone excitedly, like the childish schoolgirl she actually was. An innocent smile lit up her face.

'I'll have to sort out the wires first, but once that's done, we should be able to take her out,' Peter answered.

'Ooh, can I have a go at waterskiing, I've never done it before?' Simone pleaded.

'Course you can,' said Peter, although none too enthusiastically.

It was quarter to ten by the time they got back. 'Time for one drink?' Peter asked, seeing Heike and Sebastian at the bar, deeply engrossed no doubt in some thought-provoking conversation. 'OK, my round, what are you all having?' You couldn't fault his generosity, thought Jack, always the first to put his hand in his pocket.

The orders went in, and Peter and Simone went to get the drinks, Abrielle started to relay the incident with the police to Heike and Sebastian. Jack watched as they listened; Seb seemed intrigued.

'Any idea what all that was about, Seb?' Jack asked.

'ETA,' stated Seb very matter of fact.

'ETA?' asked Jack.

'Yes, the Basque terrorist group – they want an independent homeland...'

'I know who they are, Seb,' interrupted Jack. 'Sadly, we all do. What is it exactly that they've threatened to do?'

'Bomb tourist resorts, put off holidaymakers, hurt the Spanish tourist industry and force the Madrid government to cede independence to the Basques.'

'And do they really expect it to work?' asked Jack indignantly. 'What government is going to give in to terrorism? The British will never give in to the IRA, and the Spanish will never give in to ETA.'

'You never know, Jack. ETA has a lot of support – you know, volunteers and sympathisers. If they damage the Spanish economy seriously enough, the government may be forced to negotiate.'

'Sorry, Seb, I don't buy it. I can't believe that there are

enough sick bastards who think it's acceptable to blow up innocent people in the fight for independence. Maybe a few hundred who've been brainwashed into believing that ends justify the means, but not sufficient numbers to make the government consider talking to an evil bunch of murderers.'

Before Sebastian could respond, they were interrupted by an unexpected yelp from Heike. It was a very un-Heike kind of yelp.

There was a look of shock on her face. Jack followed her gaze, but couldn't work out what she'd seen until Abrielle spoke.

'Oh, Jack bought it for me! Isn't it beautiful? I tried to stop him, but he insisted...' She smiled a big gorgeous smile, turning to Jack, her whole face lighting up. He smiled back. Her being happy made him happy. At the moment it was as simple as that.

'Come on, Abrielle, time to go, or we'll be in trouble,' urged Simone. As she got up, so did Peter, and on cue they both thrust their tongues down each other's throats. They were all used to it by now, but it still surprised Jack every time. No modesty, no decorum; not the German way, Jack imagined, just the Peter way.

Abrielle went over to Jack and leant her head forward, whispering into his ear, 'Thank you for a wonderful day and a wonderful present. You really are a lovely guy.' Jack smiled back and she delicately placed her lips on his, kissing him, before smiling back. Those blue eyes again, now darkened by the night.

'Goodnight, my...' She stopped herself, pausing while she looked for the right words. 'Goodnight, Jack – see you tomorrow,' she smiled.

Jack watched her disappear into the night and wondered what she had nearly said. Goodnight ... my love? – surely not. Not quite the same as 'I love you', but still the L word. Jack tried not to get carried away with the thought.

'Jack, what were you thinking of?' He was rudely awakened from his thoughts by Heike.

'Sorry?' asked Jack, not sure what she talking about.

'The ring! How much did that cost you?' She made no effort to hide her disapproval.

Jack smiled. 'It was on special offer, absolute bargain,' he lied.

'For God's sake, Jack, you met her less than a week ago! You hardly know the girl.' She was exasperated.

Jack just smiled. OK, he'd been rash, but on that Heike was wrong. He felt he knew Abrielle well. At least he *thought* he did – but only time would tell.

Chapter 14

The coach began the slow climb up Mount Lebanon, leaving behind the fertile red soils of the Bekaa Valley which provided the country with so much of its needs. I looked at my watch, the minute hand was closing in on the hour, while the hour hand was virtually at six. It was going to be tight, whether I made it back for seven or not. When I'd spoken to Nakhal, the tour company, they'd assured me I'd be back at 6.30 at the latest – that clearly wasn't going to happen now.

I'd woken this morning full of conflicting emotions, initially guilt and regret. Susan had been my first thought, at home looking after our house, our boys – an innocent party that I had betrayed without a moment's thought. As soon as I knew Abrielle was in Beirut for another couple of days I'd mentally delayed my departure so that I would be around to take advantage of any opportunity to see more of her. What's more, I'd done it without considering whether it was right or wrong, whether it was the appropriate thing a husband should do, or how Susan would feel if she knew. I hadn't questioned it at all. The moment I saw the opportunity, I'd gone for it, like a shark scenting blood, killing without thought. How selfish and callous I'd become. Or had I always been that way?

After the guilt came the excitement. Memories of last night came flooding back to me – the adrenalin rush that I'd felt when I'd realised it was her, her unique beauty, those incredible blue eyes. As we'd sat and talked for hours, my senses seemed to come alive again – as if they'd been in hibernation for eighteen years and she'd been the catalyst that had awoken them again. As the evening wore on, feelings I'd had all those years ago gradually began to resurface, to remind me of what I'd had, and what I'd lost and what ... what now? Surely I wasn't going to go down that path again.

The road up into the mountains was heavy with traffic, slowly meandering its way higher and higher towards the summit, heading back towards Beirut. As we started the downward trek, the stark reminder of how much Lebanon had suffered was evident, bullet-riddled buildings, empty towns – so much destruction still visible a decade on. My watch said 6.45. Time had dragged so slowly earlier in the day, but now it was racing. Still no signal on my phone. What would she do when I didn't turn up? How long would she wait? The minutes ticked faster and faster.

When my mobile eventually beeped to let me know it had picked up a signal, my rising panic subsided for a few seconds until I discovered that I didn't have the hotel's number. No key card, no bar invoice in my wallet, nothing that would let me contact her. Things weren't going well and let's face it, they hadn't been ever since Aanjar and the strange beggar woman who'd left me spooked.

We'd arrived at the ruins of Aanjar – our last stop – as the sun began its downward trek and as the heat of the day was replaced by a more pleasant springtime warmth. We'd made our way around the impressive remains, listening to Georgette, our lovely Lebanese guide, until we reached the Great Hall. It was there that I became aware of an old beggar woman who had followed us into the hall. She had short unkempt grey hair and waddled along, her overweight legs badly cut and bruised, and her arms weighed down by carrier bags – presumably the sum of her worldly possessions. Her clothes were dirty and torn, her shoes held together by string, toes poking out, soles ready to fall off. As she shuffled behind us talking to herself, dragging her bloated body with her, I wondered what cards life had dealt her to end her days walking the ruins of an ancient city.

As we left the Great Hall, I noticed Georgette reach into her purse and give some coins to the old woman. I pulled a 500-Lebanese pound note out of my wallet; it wouldn't do much, but it might buy her a meal. She took it gratefully and looked up at me, a hollow empty look, the look of someone who had suffered, someone whose spirit had died a long time ago, but whose body had yet to catch up.

I gave her a little smile, but as I did her face took on a look of horror. She grabbed my hand forcefully, letting out a babble of words in a language I didn't recognise. Then she started to sob. She pulled at my arm, banging on it with her other hand, before turning away, the tears streaming down her face, grabbing her bags, shuffling off towards the back of the temple before disappearing through a doorway.

I stood there perturbed. What had caused such a reaction I wondered? I looked up and the rest of the group had disappeared through the empty doorway, with the exception of Georgette who stood there staring at me, a look of shock upon her ashen face.

'What was all that about?' I asked, rather disconcerted.

She hesitated before she answered, as if she was choosing her words carefully, trying to regain her composure before she spoke.

'Don't worry about her. She's Armenian. She used to be a teacher, but she's seen too much...' She paused before continuing. 'Too much violence, too much persecution ... She was a little girl when she escaped the Armenian Genocide by the Turks in 1915. She escaped here but the Civil War ... was the final straw.'

97

Georgette looked sad, momentarily lost in her own world. 'She spends her days begging from tourists. What a way to end her life – amongst the ruins of a civilisation that died over a thousand years ago.' She smiled, a sad painful smile, one that epitomised the pain that so many Lebanese had gone through.

'Why that look on her face though, the tears? One second she was OK, and then she looked into my eyes and she changed.'

I could see Georgette's uncertainty, her hesitation. She had seen it too.

'You know what she said don't you?' I insisted. I could see the uncertainty on her face.

'Words, just words, she ... she didn't make any sense, she was just babbling...' Georgette looked away.

I wasn't prepared to give up. 'No please, tell me. What really spooked her? What did she say?'

'I'm not sure, she was confused, she...'

'Please, Georgette, I know you understood,' I pressed.

Her face was vexed with anxiety. She took in a deep breath. 'She used to be a fortune-teller, once her teaching days were over.' Georgette paused for a second. 'She saw something, something that upset her, I'm not sure what. I only understand a little Armenian.'

She was lying! She knew more. 'Georgette, please. That look on your face – you know exactly what she said, I can see it in your eyes. Please I *must* know.'

She raised her head to look into my eyes. The truth was about to emerge. 'She talked of suffering, someone suffering, someone close to you...' She paused, her eyes holding mine, before adding simply, 'And death!' She dropped her gaze, as if ashamed at having to reveal the truth.

'Death?' I repeated, trying to understand.

Georgette raised her head again, trying to regain her

composure. 'Listen, she's mad, senile, disturbed, call it what you want. It doesn't matter. Forget about her!'

But forget about her I couldn't, as much as I tried – I had seen that haunted look of horror on her face. As we went through the empty villages, burnt-out buildings, cars abandoned long ago, Beirut approaching, I began to wonder whether something had happened to Abrielle. My first thought had been Abrielle, not Susan, not the boys, but Abrielle. But then I dismissed the thought. It was me who'd lost my head!

The sun had disappeared, dipping below the Mediterranean horizon, by the time I jumped off the coach at the junction with Cairo Street. I jogged the few hundred yards to the hotel, dodging the throngs of pedestrians out for a casual evening stroll. No one was in a hurry, except me, breathing heavily, sweat trickling down my back, wondering whether she would still be there or whether she'd have given up on me.

At the end of a darkened Baalbek Street the lights of the Commodore shone eerily. As I entered the hotel, I glanced to my left, but the lounge was empty. Too early for diners, too late for afternoon tea. I turned right and, on the wall behind reception, the clocks of the world told me how late I was. Ironically most showed me in good time. London, still over an hour to go at 5.30. Paris getting close at 6.30. And New York, still only lunchtime. It was Beirut that mattered. And Beirut showed me 7.20 – bizarrely ten minutes behind the others, but late all the same. Was it *too* late though? Half an hour late and she was nowhere to be seen.

I checked with reception. One message ... my hopes rose momentarily but were dashed almost immediately. Air France, to confirm my return flight via Paris. Why? I asked myself. Was I trying to tempt fate once more?

I picked up the courtesy phone and called her room,

but after a few rings it went onto a message service. I turned back to reception. 'Are you sure there are no messages for me?' I could hear the desperation in my voice.

'No, sir, I'm sure. I'm sorry, I've checked twice,' he said firmly. 'I'm really sorry.'

I was despondent. Surely it couldn't end just like that, could it? She re-enters my life one day, re-awakens senses that have lain dormant for so long, and then I'm half an hour late and that's it – she's gone, out of my life as fleetingly as she came in.

'I hope you don't think that after waiting half a lifetime I'm going to let you off that easily?'

The voice sent an immediate tingle down my spine and I breathed out a silent breath of joyous relief. I resisted the urge to spin round and pick her up in my arms, twirl her around, tell her how pleased I was to see her. Instead it was a slow, deliberate movement, as cool as I could manage, but I suspect far from convincing.

'Let me off what?' I asked as nonchalantly as I could manage.

She smiled and another shiver ran through me. God, she's doing it again, I thought, having that effect and I can't help but just love it.

'I thought you might like to take me to a Japanese restaurant tonight. After all, you do owe me!' A teasing grin on her face.

'Japanese?' I asked rather nonplussed. I trawled quickly through last night's conversation, but nothing came to mind.

'You don't remember, do you?' she smiled. That hint of sadness again. 'Our last meal together ... was going to be at the new Japanese restaurant that had just opened in Rosas. Don't you remember?'

It rang the vaguest of bells, but I felt the need to be

slightly economical with the truth. 'Oh yes!' I lied, 'So we were!' But I didn't want to go on – we both knew why we had never made it to the restaurant.

Abrielle went for a subtle change of subject. 'Do you like sushi, because I know a great restaurant?'

'I love it. Where is it, Solidere?' Solidere was the new name for central Beirut, the first quarter to benefit from the reconstruction.

'No, there!' She said pointed directly behind me, to the Commodore's own Benihana Japanese restaurant, which I'd forgotten all about. 'But let me finish my drink first,' she added.

She turned and walked back to the alcove, the same one she'd been sitting in last night. I followed. 'You were sitting here all along?' I asked, wondering how I'd missed her.

'Have been for the last half-hour,' she said, smiling. 'I heard you rush in all excited, but the pillar blocked the view of reception, so I waited, but you never came!'

I smiled back. 'So you let me stew did you?'

'Ah but, Jack, you sounded so in control,' she said with a slight hint of sarcasm.

'I think I better have a G&T,' I said, trying to change the subject. 'Do you want another...' I looked down at her indeterminate drink – '...lemonade?'

'Nearly!' she said. 'Just make sure there's a healthy dose of vodka in it as well.'

The waiter was hovering and I gave him our order, before turning back to Abrielle. 'Seeing as I've kept you waiting half an hour, would you mind giving me another ten minutes?' She looked at me suspiciously. 'Trust me, it was hot out there today and I need a quick shower.'

'OK, but you only get ten minutes; otherwise I'll have to find some other dashing young man to tell my exciting news!' she said sternly, but with a hint of exhilaration in her voice.

101

'Really, what news?' I asked.

She looked at her watch. 'Nine minutes, fifty seconds!'

I didn't need telling twice. I ran to the lift, had the briefest of showers, threw on some deodorant, gel and aftershave, hopefully in all the right places, then chucked some chinos and a clean shirt on. The lift was thankfully waiting for me, and as it reached the ground floor I looked at my watch. Nine minutes had passed; undoubtedly a record for me, but then the adrenalin was flowing.

My G&T was waiting for me, as was this beautiful woman, dressed more casually than last night – tight dark-blue jeans, a pink blouse, her hair tied back in a loose ponytail, stray locks running down her cheeks. She really looked as stunning now as she had done in my dreams and nightmares of the last eighteen years, she still had that ability to ignite feelings in me that no other woman had managed, still made my heart race a little, my breathing heavier, my body tingle, but where was it going, where could it go?

I took a gulp of my drink and felt an instant warmth as the liquor slipped down my throat. Abrielle watched impatiently, obviously dying to tell me her news, but wanting me to invite her to do so. I was tempted to launch into my day playing the pitiful tourist, but thought better of it; she had been waiting a long time.

'OK then, what is it?'

Her face lit up, the excitement in her eyes like that of a little child who's just been given an unexpected surprise. That little girl look which I hadn't seen in a very long time.

'Guess who I met today?' she blurted out, finding it difficult to hold back.

I gave her my best bemused, slightly patronising look. 'I've no idea,' I said, 'who did you meet?'

'Oh come on, Jack, I told you last night I was hoping

to meet a member of the government. Have a guess?' she said, failing to hide the frustration in her voice.

I kept up my bemused stance, but turned to a confessional approach, 'Abrielle, I'm not an expert on Lebanese politics; you clearly are. I have to admit I don't know the names of any government ministers.'

'What, so if I said I met and interviewed Rafik Hariri, that wouldn't mean anything to you?' Her frustration was turning to slight annoyance – her great coup was being revealed to an ignoramus.

I sensed my bemused look morph into one of astonishment. I was lost for words at first, an incredulous smile, trying to digest what she had just told me. 'You met the Prime Minister?'

A smile of relief lit up her face. 'I did!' She moved closer to me, her hands resting on my arms as she fought to contain her excitement. There was obviously more to come, but what could be more impressive than meeting the great Hariri, the man who had done more for Lebanon than anyone else in the last twenty years. It was his company, Solidere, that was responsible for so much of the reconstruction.

'And guess what? I'd got him all wrong, I thought he was just another Syrian puppet, but he's not! He's not going to support them any more, he's going to fight against Lahoud and try and get the Syrians out – it's incredible!'

Her face was flushed with excitement, and my first thought was, not wow, this is incredible, but how sexy she's looking. Quick, Jack, get back to the conversation.

'Slow down a bit,' I said, buying myself some time. 'I'm just a novice here. Lahoud is President, right so why is Hariri fighting him? I thought they were on the same side.'

She shot me what looked distinctly like a patronising

glare, before taking a deep breath. 'OK, Lahoud is coming up to the end of his second term as President. He can't serve a third term, not unless they amend the constitution, and that's what the Syrians and Lahoud are trying to do. The Syrians are scared that a new president might not be so pro Damascus and Lahoud wants to hold onto power. Hariri is going to try and stop him, and he wants both the Syrians and Lahoud out!'

I tried to take it all in. I knew who Lahoud and Hariri were. I knew that the President had to be a Christian, the Prime Minister a Sunni Muslim, and the Speaker, a Shia Muslim, but that was it when it came to Lebanese politics.

'Hariri told you he was going to fight Lahoud and the Syrians?' I asked. It sounded like the right question, but it also sounded a little far fetched that Hariri would announce this to a foreign journalist, or perhaps he was just seduced into revealing more than he intended to by a stunningly beautiful Frenchwoman.

'Well, not quite in so many words, but he made it pretty clear that if they change the constitution so that Lahoud can get a third term, he'll resign and then openly fight the Syrian presence here. He certainly seems to support the French push for a resolution to kick out the Syrians.'

OK, so a little journalistic licence had been used, but fair enough, they're expected to elaborate. 'Is this what you call a bit of a journalistic coup?' I asked, feeling rather ignorant.

'It's relative, Jack,' Abrielle said, the patronising look returning. 'I don't think he's ever revealed as much before; I've certainly never seen anything like it. So on that basis, yes.'

A ridiculous feeling of pride swept over me, as if one of my boys had just won something at school... As if somehow she still belonged to me.

Chapter 15

Heike, her parents and Peter had gone down to Rosas to a restaurant which had been recommended by Sebastian, and Jack had persuaded Heike to ask her parents if he could stay at the flat and do a little entertaining of his own. Much to his surprise, they'd had no objection. He had thought it a bit cheeky to ask, but now here he was – subdued lights, candles, bit of Bob Seger on in the background, food prepared. All a bit clichéd perhaps, but what the hell – the only thing missing was the guest of honour.

Deceit was not something Jack normally encouraged, but Abrielle was adamant that Simone's mother would never let her come to the apartment if it was just her and Jack; a meal out together, perhaps, but that would be the limit. As Simone's mother had already suggested to the girls that they all go out for a meal in Rosas, it was just a case of feigning illness, not too serious of course, just before they left – that was the plan. Simone was persuaded to go along with it, albeit reluctantly.

Jack stepped out onto the balcony. The sun was beginning to make its way to the horizon, but heat still radiated from it. He looked across the calm empty pool, covered in shade, to the other apartment block, Abrielle's block. Her flat was on the second floor, same as the Webers', but it was on the far side facing the mountains, not the sea, and none of the windows were visible from the Webers'.

Jack took a step back into the shadows when he saw

Simone and her mother appear at the entrance, but they didn't look up, just made straight for the car park and a minute later, their car emerged from behind the building and headed off towards Rosas. He turned back towards the apartment entrance, and there was Abrielle, peering cautiously round the door to see if the coast was clear. He was going to shout out to let her know she was safe, but then thought otherwise; he'd just watch her instead. She didn't look up, but crept around the pool, tiptoeing until she was out of sight of the car park, before standing upright, head held high, walking confidently towards the Webers' apartment.

Jack watched her walk. Her long legs, the shape enhanced by the little heels she wore, went on and on until they reached a small denim miniskirt, with a simple red vest top, her long hair in a loose ponytail. She looked stunning, he thought. How on earth have I managed to land her?

She disappeared out of view and Jack went into the kitchen and poured two glasses of chilled champagne. He'd managed to find a half-bottle in one of Rosas' better supermarkets.

There was a gentle knock on the door and Jack realised he felt quite nervous. Was it the self-imposed pressure of cooking for her, or uncertainty over the next step in their relationship? When he opened the door, he was met with a glowing smile and the nerves evaporated instantly.

'Bonsoir mon ami,' she said in her sexy accent. Did that mean 'my friend' or 'my love' – Jack couldn't remember.

'A glass of champagne for the lady?' he asked.

Abrielle's face lit up. 'Champagne! How nice.'

They made their way into the kitchen and Jack raised a toast. 'To Rosas.'

She smiled before adding softly, 'And to us.'

Abrielle took a sip and then moved towards Jack and

kissed him on the lips, sending a little shiver through him.

'Thank you for this, it's a lovely idea,' she said, a little girl's look on her face.

'You might want to wait until you've eaten before thanking me; it might be horrible,' Jack suggested ruefully.

'I'm sure it will be delicious,' she said reassuringly.

Jack put a couple of carefully stuffed mushrooms under the grill. A moderate heat – he didn't want to burn the herbs. 'Starter in ten minutes OK?' he asked.

'Great, what's this music?'

'Bob Seger.'

'Bob who?' Abrielle asked, blank-faced.

'Bob Seger and the Silver Bullet Band. You've never heard of them?'

'*Non!*'

'"Hollywood Nights"?' Still nothing. '"We've Got Tonight",' he added. 'They were huge hits from seven or eight years ago.'

'Not in France they weren't. I've never heard of him,' Abrielle insisted.

Jack decided to try another angle of approach. 'Do you remember a film a couple of years ago called *Risky Business*; Tom Cruise and Rebecca De Mornay?'

Abrielle finally made the connection. 'Is that the one where he puts his father's Porsche in a lake?'

'That's right,' said Jack excitedly. 'OK, so you remember the part where Tom Cruise is just in his pants and a shirt, running around his parents' house pretending to sing?'

Abrielle flashed a wicked smile, her eyes lighting up. 'Yes, very sexy!'

'Really?' said Jack, slightly surprised, 'but he's so much smaller than you?'

'True, but he's very cute,' she said, before adding bashfully, 'A bit like you.' Her mischievous grin returned.

107

Sounds like a compliment, thought Jack.

'Right,' he continued, 'that scene in his pants, the song he was singing is called "Old Time Rock and Roll" – that's what's playing now, Bob Seger!'

Abrielle listened for a few seconds and then gave a nonplussed look. 'Don't remember it.'

'Oh well, this tape is the soundtrack from the film; some of it might come back to you.'

Jack gave up and smiled and took in her sweet face. He noticed her subtle blue eyeshadow, complimenting those deep blue eyes; a little rouge on her cheeks. Simple, but elegant. 'How did you find the time to put make-up on?'

Abrielle smiled. 'I pretended I was going out with them right until the last moment, then I said that I had...' She hesitated. 'What do you call it, pains in your stomach?'

'Cramps?' Jack suggested.

'Cramps, that's it!' she exclaimed. 'Don't think Simone's mother cared anyway; I don't think she likes me.'

Jack gave her a mocking grin. 'Why wouldn't she like you – doesn't everyone?'

Abrielle raised her eyebrows. 'No not everybody, not everyone seems to like the fact that I speak so frankly.'

Jack smiled. 'Or perhaps they don't always agree with your political views?'

A questioning look appeared on Abrielle's face. 'What's wrong with my politics?'

It was Jack's turn to raise an eyebrow. 'You told me the first night we met that you supported Jean-Marie Le Pen – he's a fascist, a racist – he's not a nice guy!' That was about as diplomatic as he could manage. He couldn't stand Le Pen and he hated everything he stood for. He didn't like the fact that Abrielle supported him.

She seemed a little taken back. 'He's not that bad, Jack. He's only trying to do his best for France – what's wrong with that?'

108

Jack gave her a slightly patronising look. 'Abrielle, don't be so naïve. He's not doing it for France, he's doing it for Jean-Marie Le Pen. He plays on the vulnerabilities of the weak-minded, the poor, the less fortunate and then blames all of France's economic and social problems on the weakest members of society – the immigrants, even second-third-generation, those who already have it hardest, and don't need a bastard like him encouraging racism and violence...'

Abrielle looked at him seriously. 'But, Jack, he just thinks he could solve unemployment and reduce social unrest. He's just being practical, I'm sure he's not really a racist...' Suddenly her voice seemed to be drained of conviction.

Jack clocked the hesitancy in her voice and decided to push home his advantage. 'Oh of course he is! He wants all non-whites to be repatriated for God's sake!' He paused for a second. 'And that won't solve unemployment, that's just a myth for his ignorant followers to lap up. I can't understand how a bright girl like you would like him. How does that tie in with the rest of your politics which seem so far left of Le Pen?'

Abrielle looked crestfallen. Perhaps I shouldn't have been quite so hard, thought Jack.

'I'm not a racist, Jack. I didn't realise he was that bad...' She dropped her head, a little shame-faced. 'We had a politics debate at school, and some of the boys talked about Le Pen, and well ... it sounded like he had a few good ideas. I'm sorry, I feel a bit stupid now.'

This wasn't how Jack had planned the evening. Romantic nights don't normally start off with a politics lecture; he needed to lighten the mood and cheer her up. He put his hand under her chin and tried to bring her head up, but she stubbornly refused to budge. Jack tried another tact and bent down, knees bent as far as they would go, until his head was under hers looking up. Her hair had fallen forward covering her eyes. Jack moved his head forward, looking up at her, a silly smile across his face. His stupid expression was eventually too much for her and she burst out laughing, throwing her head back.

Jack stood up and smiled too, and then his face turned to a look of horror as he realised that the burning smell that had just hit his nostrils was the mushrooms.

'Aagh!' Jack yelled as he turned and sped to the kitchen, grabbing a tea cloth and pulling the Pyrex dish from under the grill. Tinged a little, but not burnt. Jack breathed a sign of relief, until he felt the intense pain in the fingers of his right hand. The tea cloth had provided temporary but scant resistance to the scorching Pyrex dish. 'Jesus!' he exclaimed, trying to act as bravely as he could in front of Abrielle who had followed him into the kitchen.

'Ooh, you OK?' she asked with concern.

'Absolutely fine,' lied Jack, the false smile failing to hide the pain etched across his face.

'Cold water quickly!' commanded Abrielle, grabbing his hand and turning on the tap. The relief was immediate. 'Keep them there for a few minutes.'

Jack smiled at her as she took control of the situation, a role she seemed to enjoy.

'What?' she asked seeing the look on his face.

'Oh, I was just thinking how I planned this evening very carefully, but neither political speeches nor toasted fingers were on the menu; yet we've had both already and haven't even touched the starter!'

'Let's eat then, shall we?' she suggested. 'Shall I serve up?'

'Yeah, would you mind?' Jack asked, the cold water easing the pain as it ran over his fingers. 'But use the oven gloves, not the bloody tea cloth!'

'*Oui, monsieur*,' smiled Abrielle. Jack loved the way she

110

sometimes responded in little snippets of French. Very sexy.

Jack turned the tap off and dried his hand gently on the offending tea cloth.

Abrielle carried through the two plates and placed them on either side of the table, carefully avoiding the lit candles.

'A glass of Rioja?' asked Jack, picking up the bottle he had opened earlier.

'Yes, please,' Abrielle responded, that childish look of excitement on her face again, as if wine was a rare treat. In fact, as she explained to Jack, her parents, like many French parents, had given her watered-down wine as soon as she was a teenager and she had drunk a little most evenings for years.

'A word of warning,' said Jack cautiously, 'this is the first time I've cooked a vegetarian meal.'

'Don't worry,' said Abrielle, 'I'm sure it will be fine.'

She cut into the mushroom and delicately put it into her mouth. Jack watched her every move, the way her lips parted, revealing a set of neat white teeth, her tongue emerging to meet the slice of mushroom on its way in. He loved every little bit of it, every little move … it all seemed so fresh, so new – he wondered if he'd ever get bored just watching her.

The moment was broken when she spoke. 'Are you planning on watching me eat all night, or are you actually going to eat as well?'

Jack laughed. 'Might as well try it, I guess.'

'You should; it's actually very good!'

Jack took a bite. Bloody hell, he thought, that's lovely. 'That's OK, isn't it?' he said, out loud.

'It's very good, Jack, but you can stop looking for compliments now! You realise you've set a standard, which I now expect you to follow with each course?' she said

111

sternly. A mischievous grin escaped as she tried, but failed, to keep a straight face.

'Ve shall zee vhat ve can do,' said Jack in a poor Nazi accent, taking another bite and wondering quite where that had come from – perhaps his subconscious was still thinking about fascism. She smiled anyway, seemingly mildly amused; that was all that mattered.

Jack picked up the plates. 'It'll be five minutes before the next course, so if you want to join me . . .' He left the question open, hoping she would follow him into the kitchen. He'd had the sliced onions, peppers and more mushrooms gurgling away in some white wine for the last twenty minutes. He flicked on the gas and within a minute the water he'd boiled earlier began simmering again. Jack threw in the fresh pasta and then a dash of olive oil.

As Jack stirred the peppers and pasta, he felt two arms slip around him, caressing him gently as they worked their way from his back round to his chest before meeting, as Abrielle pulled them tightly together. Jack felt her body against him, her head resting against the back of his, a gentle kiss on his neck, then another as she kissed him again.

As Abrielle's fingers worked their way up his shirt, she undid the highest button and slipped her hand inside and fondled his chest, her lips continuing their slow trek round his neck. Jack tried to concentrate on the food in front of him, but his jeans were getting tighter. He emptied a small tub of crème fraîche into the colourful mixture, trying to stir it in with the bright red and yellow slices of pepper, but the sensations Abrielle was creating in his body were testing his concentration – the desire to stop what he was doing and turn around and kiss her was becoming overwhelming. He knew it was too much, but reckoned that he could spare one minute, but no longer.

112

Jack gave the two pans a final stir, then put the spoons down as Abrielle's lips continued to explore his neck. He turned around slowly as her mouth reached his Adam's apple where she lingered before her lips started to move up his neck, gently pushing his head upwards. Jack stared at the ceiling, taking in a deep breath, enjoying every little touch, every kiss, every stroke of her fingers. Her kisses reached his chin and then with both hands on the back of his head, she firmly pulled it down and her lips, having tantalised his neck for so long, now found their target. Their tongues clashed immediately, tasting each other, battling, stabbing, forwards then backwards, like gladiators fighting for supremacy.

The feeling was intoxicating and the more they kissed, the stronger the desire to continue. Jack didn't want this to stop – he was in heaven – but he was also determined not to mess up the main course.

'*Arrête maintenant!*' Jack commanded.

Abrielle opened her eyes, a look of surprise on her face. '*Pourquoi?*'

'You insisted on certain standards and I intend to meet them.' He smiled and reluctantly took Abrielle's hands from around his neck, kissed her on the forehead and then turned his attention back to the hob.

Back at the dining table they sat down and Jack watched as Abrielle pierced a red pepper, then a mushroom, twirled a piece of tagliatelle round her fork and then put it playfully in to her mouth. He sat pensively waiting for the verdict.

'*C'est bon!*' she said, a look of surprise on her face. 'I'm impressed.'

Jack dug his fork into the tagliatelle, twisted his fork around and raised it to his mouth. He could see Abrielle smiling at him, almost smirking. It's OK, he thought. Two down, one to go.

'So why would you want to eat meat when you can cook like this?' Abrielle asked accusingly.

'Because it's the only veggie dish I know,' Jack retorted, 'and I think I'd get bored with it after a while.'

'But there are so many other things you can cook,' she suggested.

'Abrielle,' Jack smiled, trying not to look patronising, 'I enjoy meat too much, you won't be able to convert me.'

'OK, I'll stop trying, as long as you can live with your guilty conscience.' She always liked to have the last word, thought Jack. The music interrupted his thoughts.

'Do you remember this song?' Jack asked.

Abrielle listened for a second, then shook her head.

'It's called "Love on a Real Train" by Tangerine Dream. You remember the scene where they make love on the subway train as it flashes through stations at night?'

'Oh I remember that,' said Abrielle, her eyes sparkling.

'Now that *was* sexy,' said Jack, remembering the scene in detail.

Abrielle smiled thoughtfully. 'Yes it was.'

Jack looked into those eyes of hers and wondered how long this road of seduction was. Every moment he spent with her, the more he wanted to be with her, just looking at her beautiful face, staring into those sublime eyes and craving the touch of her body.

'Another glass of wine?' he asked.

'Are you trying to get me drunk, Jack Duggan?' Abrielle suggested with a grin.

'Damn, you foiled my plan!' Jack said jokingly. 'Now how will I get to do all those terrible things to you?' he continued.

'You only have to ask nicely,' Abrielle replied. Her mischievous grin returning, her suggestive comment sending a pleasant shudder through Jack. '...But before you do,' she said, raising her eyebrows, 'is that it, or is there dessert as well?'

Dessert had been an afterthought when Jack had been shopping earlier in the afternoon. He had bought a couple of white-fleshed peaches and some raspberries. After cutting the peaches in half, removing the stone and skin, he had surrounded them with puréed raspberry with a single raspberry perched on the top of each. Jack removed the plates from the fridge and sprinkled a little icing sugar over each one. The white peach flesh and dark pinky maroon of the raspberry purée formed a nice contrast, very professional-looking, Jack thought.

He brought the two plates out of the kitchen.

'La pièce de résistance,' Jack announced as he placed the dessert down in front of her. 'I have called it *les Pêches d'Abrielle* or, *en Anglais*, Abrielle's Peaches.' As the words came out, Jack realised the sexual connotations this could have, and, looking down at the dessert, he saw that there was no doubting what they looked like!

Abrielle smiled at him. 'It looks lovely, though a little rude I think.' Her spoon dug into the soft peach flesh. 'Delicious!' she said, closing her eyes as she savoured the taste.

They finished the meal in silence, although their eyes continued their own private conversation.

Abrielle broke the silence. 'Thank you very much, that was a fantastic meal, Jack. All three courses were lovely and as for my peaches...' She hesitated, a wicked grin on her face. '...What can I say?'

'It was a pleasure!' Jack responded, smiling back.

'Hey, I know this song. What's it called?' Abrielle asked.

Jack smiled. ' "Hollywood Nights" – by some bloke called Bob Seger I believe.'

'Oh yeah, I remember him,' she smirked.

They chatted through the pulsating beat of the song

and, as it wound down Jack leant forward and ran his fingers over Abrielle's right hand which was stretched out in front of him, her new ruby ring glowing in the candlelight.

As the gentle piano intro to 'We've Got Tonight' began, Jack played out the notes with his fingers, tapping on Abrielle's hand, her fingers the white keys, her knuckles the black.

'You play the piano?' she asked.

'Only an imaginary one. I'm not bad, better at air guitar though!' Jack said as he took Abrielle's hand in his. 'Come on, this song was meant for lovers everywhere, we should treat it with respect and dance to it.'

Abrielle stood up, not letting go of Jack's hand, as she moved towards him. She put her left arm around his neck and, once that was firmly in place, let go of his hand and brought her other arm up to sit on his shoulder, clasping her hands behind his neck.

Jack placed a hand on either side of her body, a small gap between the two of them, their faces only a few inches apart, looking into each other's eyes. A routine so familiar to them now, but one that brought with it something new each time. They gently leant forwards until their foreheads met, their eyes too close to focus.

'Tonight has been lovely, Jack,' Abrielle whispered. 'I've really enjoyed myself, despite the political lecture at the beginning!'

'I've enjoyed most of it too,' said Jack.

'Only most?' said Abrielle, a hurt look on her face.

'Burnt fingers!' Jack responded, grimacing. 'Not much fun.'

'Oh, of course. Not very clever, was it? Here, let me see them.'

Jack raised his hand and Abrielle brought his fingers up to her face, inspected them for a few seconds, then said, 'You know what they need?'

'No, what?' said Jack.

In reply Abrielle gently took the index finger of his right hand and lightly kissed it, then each finger in turn, before working her way back to the beginning. She then took his index finger into her mouth and gently sucked upon it, before paying equal devotion to each of his other sore fingers. She closed her eyes and looked to be thoroughly enjoying herself, although Jack doubted she quite realised the effect it was having on him.

'There, that should help,' she said with a wicked smile.

'Thank you,' said Jack, slightly out of breath.

Abrielle looked up at him, Jack back at her, into each other's gaze. They slowly moved towards each other, their noses touching first, rubbing together, before their lips met, gently at first, kissing lightly. Jack pulled her closer, his hands tightening together at the small of her back, their bodies more together, contact increasing as Abrielle opened her mouth letting Jack's tongue enter. A heaven-sent taste, he thought, her taste, so special, so unique. Their tongues gently exploring, their bodies pushing against each other. Jack could feel her breasts against his chest, his groin against hers, his hands roaming her back, down to her backside, pulling her closer, her hands in his hair, fingers running through his locks, their kissing reaching a new level of intensity as their tongues squirmed and jousted. Jack felt his heart beating, beating loudly, his breath short, he pulled back and looked into her eyes.

'Abrielle,' he said looking at her seriously. 'I love you.' A pang of regret as the words left his mouth. He'd wanted to keep it to himself, but the words had just forced themselves out. He knew it had just been a matter of time, and now the deed was done ... but what would be the reaction?

Her smile disappeared and Jack's heart fell. 'Oh, Jack,

117

you shouldn't have said that!' Her face turning away from his, her disappointment impossible to hide.

Jack felt miserable. A minute earlier he was the happiest man alive; now he'd gone and ruined it.

'Jack, as soon as you're back in London, I'll bet you'll forget me in an instant. You'll be looking for another innocent girl to corrupt ... and that's if you haven't already got one waiting!' She smiled as she tried to defuse the tension.

'Hey, that's unfair,' said Jack defensively. 'I meant what I said. I'll never forget you, Abrielle. I'm sorry, I thought you might have felt the same way.' His sad face looked despondent.

She lifted her head slowly and looked up at him with tearful eyes. 'I do Jack, but it scares me, it scares me so much.'

'You do?' exclaimed Jack, stunned at the revelation.

'Oh of course I do! I've never met a boy who made me feel like you do,' she said almost reluctantly. 'Whose presence can make me weak at the knees, who's so sexy!'

It was all coming out now and Jack was finding it hard to take it all in. 'Me, sexy?' he exclaimed, beginning to think he must be having an incredibly vivid dream.

Abrielle looked all coy for a second. 'Yeah, you're lovely!' She regained her composure and smiled that beautiful smile.

'I don't think anyone's ever called me sexy before,' said Jack, gradually recovering from the shock. 'Why are you scared of telling me you love me?' he asked.

Abrielle looked into his eyes before responding. 'Jack, in three weeks, we'll be hundreds of miles away from each other. I hate it when I'm not with you now; what's it going to be like when we won't be able to see each other at all?'

'But what difference does that make to whether or not

118

we tell each other that we love each other?' asked Jack, slightly confused.

'All the difference, Jack, now we know,' she said, shaking her head. 'It'll only make it harder.'

'Perhaps,' said Jack, 'but I'd prefer to know, and I want you to know as well.'

Abrielle smiled at him. 'Well we've done it now, haven't we? We can't go back!'

They kissed passionately, Jack's hands pulling her tight against him. Emboldened by her reluctant declaration of love, he knew where his wandering hands were taking him, no matter how he tried to behave. He explored her back, gently raking his nails down her soft skin, before turning his palms flat and gradually bringing his left hand round to her flat stomach before it began on its upward trajectory towards her breasts. Abrielle made no pretence at resistance and thrust her mouth harder against his as Jack's hand reached its goal. She wasn't wearing a bra. Jack caressed her right breast gently, gradually moving towards its centre, before closing in on her nipple and taking it between his thumb and forefinger. He squeezed it and Abrielle let out a little gasp. He lovingly kissed her mouth, her nose, her eyes, her forehead, her hair as if he might never get the chance again.

Now Jack felt Abrielle's left hand reach up to his shirt and deftly undo each button... Where was this going? Lust, though accompanied by love, had taken over and their passion for each other was breaking into new territory. The music had finished, but the tape rolled on in silence, which was probably what saved them from considerable embarrassment, as Jack heard the sound of footsteps on the stairs.

'Jesus!' he muttered. 'Quick!' He broke away from Abrielle and did up the buttons on his shirt while she rearranged her top to show an acceptable level of decency.

Abrielle looked at her watch. '*Merde!* It's after ten, I'm going to be in so much trouble if they're back!'

'Look, say your hellos and goodbyes quickly and then get home. Say you couldn't sleep and went out for a walk or something,' Jack suggested.

Jack picked up the dessert plates and turned to a slightly dishevelled Abrielle. 'Can you grab the glasses, please?'

The front door opened and in trooped the Webers, led by Peter who sported a ridiculously large smirk on his face. Jack had hoped there would be no trace of Abrielle by the time they arrived home. Instead she was still there as was the mess he'd created in the kitchen. Still, much better to be caught in the act of clearing up than what they had been up to a minute earlier!

'Hey, how was your evening?' asked Peter. The insinuating smile said it all.

Jack turned to him with a smile and responded as nonchalantly as he could manage. 'Very nice, thanks, Peter. How was the restaurant?'.

'Good actually. Simone and her mother were there as well.' Abrielle looked at him concerned. 'In fact...' He paused momentarily. '... As we left, they were arguing with the waiter about whether or not the bread should be included on the bill.' He glanced at Abrielle. 'Probably be home in a few minutes.'

The relief on Abrielle's face was evident. 'I'd better go now.' She flashed big friendly smiles at Mr and Mrs Weber. 'Good night, Heike,' she said as she walked quickly past her.

Jack followed her to the front door. 'Hey, how about one last kiss goodnight?' he asked.

She turned and put her arms around Jack's neck, pulling him towards her, and kissing him firmly on the lips. 'Bonsoir, mon chèrie,' she whispered and with that she was off, racing down the stairs, leaving Jack feeling full of warmth and love.

Jack returned to the lounge where the Webers were now seated in silence, Peter at the drinks cabinet, a bottle of scotch in his hand. 'Fancy one, Jack?' he asked, motioning to the bottle.

Jack smiled. 'No thanks. I've got a bit of clearing up to do.'

As he stood perched over the sink, hands immersed in hot soapy water, Jack reflected on the night's events. She'd told him she loved him, really loved him – what beautiful music that had been to his ears. Heike came into the kitchen. She was smiling, but there was a hint of disapproval. 'Is this some new fashion you're trying to start, Jack?'

'Sorry?' said Jack, not understanding the question.

'A new fashion, the shirt,' she said, nodding towards Jack's shirt.

Jack lowered his head to look at his shirt, and realised his mistake: each button was perfectly misaligned with its respective hole. He felt himself blushing.

'Whoops!' was all he could manage in reply.

Chapter 16

I sat there happily listening to her talk about her meeting with Hariri, watching her animated face as she described his charm, the way he carefully chose his words when he expressed an opinion. Abrielle believed she had found him in a revealing mood.

'Enough of me, how was your day? How was Baalbek?' she suddenly asked, bringing me out of my trance-like state.

Her eyes sparkled, lighting up her face as she asked the question, making me stop for a second before responding. That feeling, that sense was slowly but surely coming back to me, that realisation of the way that her mere presence made me feel so alive. I wondered why, if she had this effect on me, it hadn't happened with someone else, why she hadn't found love and happiness. There was an answer out there, but at the moment she was keeping it to herself.

'It was really interesting actually. You know the wine we were drinking last night, the Ksara?' She nodded. 'We visited the vineyard, saw the caves where they store the wine, sampled a few bottles, then we went off to Baalbek, into Hezbollah country.'

'Hezbollah country, what do you mean?' she asked, looking slightly concerned.

I smiled, but I hadn't been so relaxed when I was told first thing that morning. 'Much of the Bekaa, particularly the south, is controlled by Hezbollah, not officially, but the government hasn't got much power there. You know how all over Beirut, there are pictures of Lahoud and Assad, both Assads actually; well, there are none down there. As you enter each town, there are pictures of local Hezbollah leaders, all dark beards, unsmiling, slightly menacing-looking. One town even had a picture of Ayatollah Khomeini, and he's been dead for fifteen years!'

'This is Hezbollah, the terrorist group we are talking about, the ones who kidnapped all the westerners in Beirut?' Abrielle asked, looking slightly incredulous.

I nodded 'Yup, that would be them, same Hezbollah.' I smiled, feeling rather pleased with myself, as if I was a brave warrior who had returned from battle, rather than a tourist who hadn't been in the slightest danger all day.

'But what was it like? Were there militiamen with guns looking for wealthy tourists to kidnap?' she asked, only half-jokingly.

'No, it's not like that at all. I didn't see a single gun. Hezbollah, apparently, are much more than a bunch of terrorists; a lot of their work is charitable and helping Shia communities.' I was doing it again, trying to sound knowledgeable, as if I was well versed in the politics and life in the Bekaa, when all I had learnt had been picked up that day.

'Baalbek is impressive, worth a visit. It's a huge complex. It took over three hundred years to build, you know.'

Abrielle nodded. 'And what about the pillars? Were they as spectacular as you hoped?' she asked, looking genuinely interested.

'There are six of them, two point two metres in diameter, fifty metres above the ground. They're stunning. You stand next to them, and they're huge, and you think how the hell did they manage to build these two thousand years ago. It's an incredible sight,' I enthused.

Abrielle gave me one of her lovely smiles as she listened

and I felt a now familiar stirring inside. Don't go there, Jack, you can't, you mustn't!

'The pillars were part of the Temple of Jupiter, and there's not much of it left now, but the Temple of Bacchus is still standing. Part of the cornice had fallen from the roof. The décor is so intricate, tiny details, lion heads, dancing girls, bacchantes I think they're called... No wonder it took so long to build!'

Abrielle smiled again. 'What's Baalbek itself like?' she asked.

'It looked a bit of a dump really, tacky and cheap. Lots of Coke and Pepsi signs, Kodak too, all vying for space, fake artefacts, specially inflated prices for the gullible tourists. As soon as we got off the coach, we were surrounded by boys, men, young and old, trying to get us to buy books, maps, strings of postcards. It was rather desperate actually, a bit sad. They all looked like they needed a good meal to fill them up.'

'OK, time to change the subject,' Abrielle announced. 'If we keep talking about poverty, we won't feel like a meal, and I'm getting hungry!'

'All right, shall we eat?' I suggested.

We walked through the lounge to the Japanese restaurant. I had been hoping for a romantic candlelit table, but instead we were seated next to each other around a steel counter, with the kitchen area behind. The chef turned out to be more like a cocktail waiter than a cook, throwing large plastic salt and pepper pots over his head, round his back, catching them in his oversized bright-red chef's hat.

It was a simple chicken noodle dish we both opted for, but it was the cooking performance that made it special. A small dash of oil on the hob, a flash of fire leaping tiger-like into the darkness, the chef throwing his head back as the flame roared, like a boxer on the receiving

124

end of a knock-out punch, only to bounce back unscathed. But the pièce de résistance was the egg, a simple egg, but skilfully thrown around, before being flicked into the air. It sailed gracefully upwards before gravity took over and it plummeted back towards the hob. I caught the concentration in the chef's eyes as, with perfect timing, he turned the metal spatula through ninety degrees and the egg landed on its edge, the thin blade cutting through the shell and the contents landing on the hot hob. For a moment the empty eggshell sat on the side of the spatula before being unceremoniously flicked into the air and landing in the chef's hat.

We gave him a gentle round of applause. He smiled; he knew it had been a good performance. Another minute's cooking and the food was served, along with another bottle of the Ksara, which we were both getting rather fond of.

We both went for the salt at the same time, our hands touching accidentally, a little current of electricity flowing between us. It was then that I saw it, amongst a number of rings she wore, on her little finger on her right hand, a thin gold band, a slightly faded ruby, smaller than I remembered, but still unmistakable. I held onto her hand for a second, before looking up into her eyes. She realised I'd recognised it and surprisingly looked slightly sheepish, as if embarrassed.

'You kept it all these years?' I asked, amazed that she still had it, let alone still wore it.

'I kind of liked it,' she said, hesitating, choosing her words carefully before adding, 'it reminds me of one of the happiest times in my life, some very special days, shared with someone very special.' She never took her eyes off mine as she spoke, watching for the reaction, waiting to see how I would respond. I wasn't quite sure what to say. I hadn't expected such honesty, let alone such a revelation.

'Jack, you meant an awful lot to me. I'd prefer to forget about the last two days of our time in Spain, but the few weeks before that...' She paused thoughtfully again. '...They were some of the best I've ever had. I've worn this ring ever since the day you gave it to me, I've never taken it off.'

I was stunned. I knew how much she'd meant to me, how I'd never forgotten about her, but it had never occurred to me to think she might have felt the same. After we'd gone our separate ways, I thought she must hate me.

'But that's history,' she said. 'You're happily married now; I have a successful career. Life goes on and it was a long time ago.'

'But what about you? You never married, why not?' I wasn't sure why I was pushing. She'd already answered the same question last night, but she seemed more open now and perhaps the truth would come out.

She gave me one of those looks, but she still chose to answer.

'I'm not sure why, Jack. Perhaps I was scared of the commitment. There have been a couple of serious boyfriends. There was Robert. He was an artist, quite a good one actually. We were together for five years and we even talked about marriage, but something was missing. I'm not even sure what it was, but it just wasn't meant to be,' she said, shaking her head. Her face took on a sad expression but she shook it off with a smile.

'You're lucky, Jack – you have your wife, your two boys – that's nice. You never tried for a girl?'

I was caught out by the question. I hadn't expected it, a perfectly innocent question. After all, she didn't know, couldn't have known. I wasn't quite sure how to respond, it wasn't something I ever talked about, but equally there was no reason to lie.

I could see the sudden confusion on her face. No doubt

my face had looked pained as memories came flooding back, memories that I had to a certain extent put behind me but which now I had to face again.

'Sorry, Jack, was that a bad question?'

I tried to smile. 'Susan always wanted a little girl,' I began. 'She had problems after Paul was born, postnatal depression, but we got through that and decided to try again. She had a couple of miscarriages. We should have stopped, should have realised that it wasn't meant to be. I could see the damage it was doing to her, but it just made her more desperate. Then, about four years ago, she got pregnant again. It wasn't the easiest of pregnancies. She had high blood pressure, had to rest a lot, but she got through to nine months. In the end it was a straightforward birth and we had a little girl, Eleanor – Ellie. She was beautiful, a gorgeous little thing. Her brothers doted on her.' I sensed a small smile escape as I remembered. 'She was eight weeks, had just started to sleep through the night. Susan had breast-fed the boys, but with Ellie, it just didn't work, so I'd given her a feed at ten and put her down in her cot in the nursery. She had a bit of a cold, but nothing serious. I was woken about six the following morning by a piercing scream, a scream so intense, so haunting, that it just cut straight through me, a scream full of anguish, full of pain. I jumped out of bed and ran to the nursery, but I already knew what had happened, not how or why, but the scream said everything. I found Susan sobbing, sitting on the floor, holding this lifeless child, her face a deathly blue, a child that used to be our daughter.'

It's funny how you can put the memories to one side, keep them in check, keep them in the past, but suddenly talking about it again, they all came flooding back, as if it was only yesterday it happened, and you have to go through the pain all over again.

127

Abrielle picked up her napkin and gently wiped a tear from my face, which I hadn't even realised had crept out.

'I'm sorry, Jack, I'm really sorry. No parent should ever have to bury their own child; it must be the worst thing in the world.' She took hold of my hand and gave me a reassuring grasp, squeezing it tightly. A warm feeling flowed through me, one of someone who cared how I felt; it seemed alien but nice.

'Sorry, I didn't mean to cry, it's not the sort of thing I usually do in public...'

She put her finger on my lips to stop me. 'Don't apologise, Jack. Tears are a good thing, they let some of the pain out.'

I regained my composure. 'It just brought it all back to me. A cot death – it makes it even worse not to know why a child has died. We did everything right, kept her on her back ... she wasn't too hot or too cold ... but still she died, and to be honest Susan died with her. It's over three years and she still hasn't got over it, I'm not allowed to change the nursery; it's more like a shrine to Ellie these days. Pictures of her pretty face everywhere, her cuddly animals, even dried flowers from her funeral.' I sighed.

'It can't be easy for her, Jack; it sometimes takes a long time to heal the pain.' I looked at her. She seemed like she was speaking from experience.

'I know it does, but you have to move on, get on with life, continuing to mourn for a child that isn't going to come back isn't doing her any good. She still blames herself, thinks that if she persevered with breast feeding that Ellie would still be alive today.' I looked into Abrielle's eyes. 'Do you know, I don't think she's ever going to get over it.' As the words came out, they hit me really hard.

'It was the worst few weeks of my life, trying to deal with it, trying to understand something that no one could explain, trying to keep Susan from going over the edge, stop myself too, but in the end it came down to a simple choice. Give up or try to pick up the pieces of a shattered family and try and rebuild it, which, for the sake of Susan and the boys, I had to do. Gradually as weeks turned into months and then months into years, a sense of normality returned, at least for me and the boys, but not for Susan. For Susan, every day still revolves around the memory of Ellie. She drops the boys off at school, takes them to football, helps them with their homework, cooks for them, but she's just going through the motions. She still spends hours in the nursery, trying to remember, crying, talking to Ellie as if she's still there, fast asleep in her cot. She even changes the cot linen every couple of weeks.'

Abrielle was a good listener and I didn't feel like I was betraying Susan revealing her problems. It was the first time I had spoken to anybody about them and it was probably something I needed to get off my chest.

'You've had it tough, Jack, but you seem to have come through; your marriage still seems intact,' she said, a warm smile of empathy on her face.

I gave her a slightly ironic smile back. 'No, it's not,' I said, shaking my head. 'The marriage died when Ellie died. I'm sorry to say it's just a façade. We don't talk any more. When we do we argue, and when we argue, it's always about the same thing. I want to get rid of the nursery, try and erase the daily reminders of pain, but Susan won't hear of it, she doesn't want to move on. I'm tempted just to throw everything out, except a few pictures, paint the room in bright colours, turn it into a playroom for the boys, and see what happens. It may drag her out of her stupor, but I'm scared it might tip her over the edge. I don't know what to do.' I sighed and paused, before continuing. 'Come on, let's change the subject, something happier, anything!'

Abrielle smiled. 'That'll teach me to ask nosy questions.'

'Tell me more about your day, your other interviews?' I asked, wanting to hear the sweet sound of her voice again, rather than my depressing monologues. I could see her eyes light up immediately I asked the question.

'Well, apart from Hariri, first thing this morning I met an official from the Ministry of the Interior who gave me the official pro-Syrian view – that they were welcome here, and so on. When I challenged him on this, given some of the comments from the anti-Syrian politicians, he just went into denial. He wasn't even very convincing; I'm not sure he believed it himself.'

'I also met a Druze MP. I was due to meet him for lunch tomorrow but he had to change it to today. He was very forthright in his anti-Syrian views, although that's nothing new, but he did feel that the winds of change have begun to blow, especially if the UN does get this vote through. And then I met Hariri, and well, as I said, that was just incredible. Not only were his comments revealing, but he has this huge presence, he was fascinating to listen to, very astute too. He has bided his time with the Syrians, and now I get the impression that he's going to make his move, although that's going to upset them.'

I decided to broach an idea that had been mulling around my head all day.

'You said you were flying back tomorrow afternoon?' I asked unnecessarily. She nodded, no doubt wondering where I was going with this.

'You couldn't delay your departure twenty-four hours, could you? I've found someone willing to give us a personal tour of Beirut's delights, and if you can afford the time, well...' I hesitated, knowing I shouldn't be going down this route, but I'd started and had to finish. 'It would be nice to spend a bit more time catching up.'

Abrielle smiled. Was she thinking about it, or was she

130

about to launch into a tirade of how I was always thinking of myself and how selfish I was.

'I'd love to, Jack, but I can't. Friday morning I have a meeting and unfortunately it's not one I can miss.'

Unless I was mistaken, she looked slightly disappointed. Time for plan B. 'What time is your meeting? There's a 6 a.m. flight, which will have you back in Paris by ten.'

I watched her take this in and I could see she was thinking about it. I decided to go for the kill. 'Come on, we could see the Jeita grotto, go on the cable car to Harissa and see the statue of Our Lady. Apparently there are fantastic views over the Bay of Jounie and Beirut. Then we can walk along the Corniche in the evening sun.'

She gave me one of those mischievous looks of hers, which I couldn't interpret.

'You have planned this, haven't you?' She seemed to think about it a bit longer, making me wait, then smiled. 'The meeting's not until twelve so I guess I could delay my return a little. OK then, sounds like fun, but I expect a first-class tour.' My heart did a little jig – tonight would not after all be our last night together.

'So who exactly is our guide?' she asked curiously.

'His name is Faris, but that's all I'm saying.'

'OK, I can wait, but I'll need to check I can change my ticket first – the flight might be full.'

'I can do that for you if you want. There's no problem with the flight, there's lots of availability.'

'Really, how do you know that?' She was a little annoyed, I think, at my thoroughness.

'I booked up the same flight first thing this morning and it's not even half-full.' I pre-empted the next question. 'It's easier for me to go through Paris than straight to London because of the timing of the flights.' I felt slightly guilty; it was stretching the truth a long way.

She seemed to accept what I said, but I could see she was mulling over something; I wasn't sure if that was good or bad.

'What time is your onward flight to London?' she asked, an impish grin lighting up her face.

'It's midday, but it's easy enough to change, why?' I asked, wondering what she was up to.

'If you can delay it until late afternoon, then there is something I'd like to show you, something I think you would find interesting.'

'Really, what's that?' I asked slightly perturbed.

'Patience never was one of your strong points was it, Jack? You'll just have to wait and see.'

'What about the meeting though?' I asked, wondering how I fitted in.

'Don't worry about that! I'm not going to leave you hanging around for hours by yourself, just trust me!'

I had little choice, but I didn't mind. It seemed that I was prepared to take whatever opportunities were presented to me to spend a few extra hours in her company.

'Come on, Jack, time for bed; it's getting late, it's gone one.'

She'd said exactly the same the previous night and it made me smile again. No double entendre intended, but it sounded so much like an invitation. I'm glad it wasn't, I don't know if I'd have had the will power to resist.

As we walked out of the restaurant to the lifts, two large and loud American businessmen stood in our way. As they made no attempt to move, we were forced to walk around them to get to the lifts. When they spotted Abrielle, their conversation ceased instantly and I could sense them leering at her, drooling pathetically, no doubt mentally undressing her as well. As the lift door closed behind us, I just caught the words 'lucky bastard!' Not so lucky, I thought, but then they didn't know that.

Abrielle heard them too. 'I hate men like that, who just stare, it makes me feel horrible. And it's invariably the ugly and really obese ones who are the worst, the ones that no woman would give a second look to.'

I pressed the ninth-floor button and changed the subject. 'Have you got time to meet for breakfast tomorrow?' I asked as nonchalantly as I could.

Her smiling face returned. 'Yeah, OK. I have to leave at 8.30, so is 7.45 OK for you?'

'7.45 is fine.' If I was honest with myself, any time would have been fine.

We reached the ninth floor and she looked at me suspiciously.

'My mother always brought me up to be chivalrous, to always see a lady home, so I have to see you to your door.' I knew it sounded corny, I just didn't want the evening to end.

'Jack, I'm a big girl, I can look after myself, especially from the lift to my bedroom door.'

'I know you can, but with unsavoury grotesque Americans lurking around, better to be safe than sorry.' I smiled my most sincere smile as I said it.

It was pathetic and we both knew it, but she smiled. 'If you insist.'

I was surprised to find that the ninth floor was remarkably different from the eighth, with the lift opening onto a glass window rather than more bedrooms. A swipe of a key card and her door was open. Abrielle turned to me. 'I enjoyed tonight, Jack.'

I smiled. 'Me to!'

There was no uncertainty about how to say goodnight tonight. Abrielle took control, putting her arms around my neck and pulling my head next to hers in a firm hug. I kissed her on the forehead and resisted the urge to lower my lips and kiss hers. Hesitatingly, I let go, and

133

sensed her reluctance as well. But if I kissed her, she might kiss me back, and then, and then...

'Breakfast at 7.45 then,' I said, turning away before it was too late.

'It's a date. Sweet dreams!' she whispered back and closed the door behind her.

A date – that sounded a little strange. I called the lift – it seemed a little extravagant just to go down one floor. As I entered, I saw my reflection. I studied it, a deeply frowned look. Where was I going with this? I'd delayed my return home, now I'd persuaded her to delay hers. What was I hoping for, to start off a relationship that had ended in a different lifetime when things weren't so complicated? Was this my mid-life crisis, or was it my way of dealing with a marriage that had died? As much as my brain tried to rationalise and take the sensible, well-lit road, my heart preferred the dark narrow path, lingering with dangers at every turn, ready and waiting for that false step, that one step too many that I suspected I'd live to regret, should my heart win.

Chapter 17

The night following the meal in the Webers' apartment, Jack and Abrielle ate out together in a restaurant in Rosas. Later, as they walked back home along the front, they watched the spectacular blood-red sky as the sun dipped beneath the horizon. By the time they reached the path and began the coastal walk, the moon was up and a gentle breeze was blowing in from the sea. They reached the entrance to the rocky path down to the secluded beach and Abrielle pulled Jack towards it. 'Come on, this way!'

'What, in the dark? We won't be able to see where we're going,' Jack pointed out.

'Yes, we will, there's enough moonlight, and if we keep our hands against the walls, we'll be fine.'

Abrielle led the way and Jack reluctantly followed. They made it to the bottom, not without a couple of minor mishaps, but both in one piece.

The beach was lit up by the moonlight, but it looked very different at night. The sand looked ghostly white and large dark shadows stretched out from the rocks. Jack was wondering what might be lurking there, ready to pounce, when Abrielle suddenly turned and put her arms around his shoulders and brought her lips up to meet his. Her tongue instantly worked its way into his mouth, as he wrapped his hands around her back and pulled her tightly against him.

Abrielle pulled him tighter, kissing his face passionately, as his hands reached under her T-shirt, caressing her back, working their way slowly around to her stomach.

135

She stopped him. 'Wait a second, I've got some towels.'

'Towels, where?' said Jack bemused. She only had a small shoulder bag.

'Over here, I came down earlier and left them here,' she said as she walked into one of the shadows and returned with two large beach towels.

'What are they for?' asked Jack. 'Are we going skinny-dipping?'

Abrielle looked up. 'Skinny-dipping, what's that?'

Jack began to regret his comment. 'Well, it's when you...' he hesitated. '...You take all your clothes off and go for a swim at night.'

Abrielle laid the towels out on the moonlit sand and beckoned him to lie down next to her. 'It sounds exciting, but I have a better version. Why don't we just take all our clothes off, but rather than get all wet, why don't we make love instead?'

Jack was completely taken aback. While he might have dreamt of making love to her, he wasn't expecting it so soon, nor Abrielle to be quite so forward. He hadn't planned this; he was used to being in control but, with Abrielle, he found he rarely was. Perhaps that was why he found her so fascinating, so different from any previous girlfriends.

'Is that OK, Jack? You don't seem too sure; if you don't want to, we don't have to.'

Jack smiled, replying quickly before she changed her mind. 'Oh I do, I just wasn't expecting it. I didn't know if you were ready?'

'I am Jack, it's time I became a woman, and I want you to make me that woman.'

Jack suddenly realised that he had no condoms on him; they weren't something he had a habit of carrying around with him. 'Abrielle,' he said softly, 'we can't make love.' He saw the look of disappointment on her face.

'Why not?' she asked slightly uncertain.

'I didn't know you had planned this. I haven't got any condoms and we can't make love without protection.'

A big smile lit up her face. 'Simone gave me a little something earlier. You don't get off that easily.'

Abrielle gently pushed Jack onto his back and kissed him on the forehead, her right hand running over his chest. Her lips traced their path around his face, with special kisses for his eyes, his nose, until she reached his mouth and forced her tongue inside. Without taking her mouth off his, she moved astride him, sitting on his groin, her denim skirt riding up her thighs. There was enough pressure in his jeans already, Jack thought, without the added pressure of her on top, but he wouldn't have changed it for the world. This was heaven, he thought to himself, as she undid the buttons of his shirt and roamed her hands freely over his chest.

She stopped for a second and sat up, then in one swoop removed her T-shirt to reveal her beautiful naked breasts. Jack stared for a second, but he could wait no longer. His hands moved swiftly up her stomach until they reached their respective targets, closing in on a breast each, pushing firmly, grappling forcefully as she leant forward again and reached for his mouth, their tongues entwining once more.

'Jack!' Abrielle whispered, 'Be gentle with me ... this is my first time.'

But it was Abrielle who controlled everything as they made love under the moonlight, stars twinkling in a clear sky above and the water lapping gently at their feet.

Chapter 18

I watched the pink LED display change to 2.00 a.m. and wondered if I was destined to stay awake all night. My mind was racing. I was confused and I didn't feel like sleeping. Abrielle had revealed a lot tonight. I wasn't sure if she intended to or if it had just been the alcohol that loosened her tongue a bit too much. And the ring! She still wore that ruby ring that I'd bought her. Bloody hell, it seemed as if she had been affected as much by it all as I had been. And she'd never got married. What did that mean? That she had never met anyone quite like me? Surely not ... but then I'd never met anyone quite like her...

I tried to think about something else, about the tour I'd planned for the next day. I'd got talking to Faris, the guide-cum-bus driver on the Baalbek trip, about where he would take a young lady if he was trying to impress her. He made a number of suggestions, before offering his services as personal guide and driver.

Faris was a very large but very friendly Lebanese Christian who loved telling stories, as all Arabs do, and I hoped he'd make the perfect guide. He certainly wouldn't be boring, but I hoped he would choose his moments carefully, knowing when to leave us alone and when to regale us with his embellished tales.

Outside I could still hear the occasional hoot of a car horn, but Hamra was quiet. The clock now showed 2:25 and I'd set the alarm for 7.00. I had to get to sleep otherwise I was going to be like a zombie tomorrow.

I tried to think of pleasant thoughts, remembering back to Rosas, and the time we spent together, when we first met. My mind was drifting through the warm sand, lying on a golden beach, the sun beating down, her body close to mine, when I heard a gentle knock on the door. Quiet but distinct. My heart began to race. There was only one person who would be knocking on my door in the middle of the night.

I turned on a sidelight and jumped out of bed, racing to the door, pulling back the security catch and then opening it. There she stood in a white full-length silk dressing gown, looking like an angel, just arrived from heaven. She raised an index finger to her lips and walked past me into the bedroom. I wasn't sure what to say, what to do. I closed the door behind me and followed her into the bedroom. I went to speak, although I'm not sure what I was going to say, but she put her finger on my lips to stop me.

I realised that I was wearing nothing but a pair of boxer shorts, but that didn't matter. What did was why was she here, in the middle of the night. What did she need to discuss that couldn't wait a few hours 'til breakfast?

I looked into her eyes, to look for clues, but there were none there. In the subdued lighting, they had none of their daytime sparkle, but a different kind of resonance, a darker more mysterious ocean-blue.

She raised her hands and then placed fingers over both of my eyes, bringing the lids down, until they were closed. I stood there wondering what to do, when I felt her lips on mine. A sensation that brought it all back to me. A kiss that I hadn't tasted in nearly eighteen years, but a kiss that I recognised as if it had been only yesterday.

I tried not to respond, but her lips gently probed away at mine, pushing gently, licking enticingly, gradually eroding my resistance until I could fight the urge no longer. I

139

succumbed, allowing her tongue to enter my mouth and all hope was lost as I responded in kind. Our tongues touched once more and the taste was as intoxicating as it had been all those years ago, the sensation as electric as I remembered. I felt my whole body come alive, as we pulled each other closer and closer until our bodies were moulded to each other as if one.

I kept my eyes closed, but my hands found the tie on her dressing gown and I pulled at it. I sensed it slacken, allowing me to slip my hands inside and feel her skin – she was naked underneath. Our bodies touched once more, skin against skin; it had been such a long time, but that didn't matter any more – we were together again, at last making love once more.

Chapter 19

The sun crept through a chink in the curtains and gradually a single shaft of light made its way up the bed and towards Jack's face. He'd watched its slow progress, wondering how long it would take to get to his eyes. When it eventually arrived, momentarily blinding him, he rolled onto his back, out of its path, and clasped his hands behind his head looking up at the ceiling and thinking back to last night.

Abrielle had taken him, literally, completely by surprise. It was she who had decided they were going to make love on the beach, and had carefully planned it, right down to her decision to go on top. She, not him, was the one in control. Together they had reached an intensity that was new to him, to both of them. Their bodies combining as if fused, coming together, impossible to part. They'd lain holding each other for a long time afterwards, watching shooting stars flash across the night sky. It was something he would never forget.

After a couple of espressos, Jack made his way down to the pool and, not for the first time, found himself its sole occupant. He took a deep breath and dived in, but as he rose towards the surface, he began to find himself short of breath and, as the far wall appeared, realised he was never going to make it. He surfaced and took in some air, slightly mystified at his failure. Complacency? He didn't think so. Perhaps making love to Abrielle had used up more energy than he thought. Jack tried not to be superstitious but, every now and again, he would succumb. What did this failure herald for him and Abrielle?

Jack jumped out of the pool, grabbed his towel and dried himself. It wasn't as hot as usual; white clouds had rolled in overnight and, although they were beginning to break up, there was still considerably more cloud than blue sky. Jack sat down, his towel wrapped around him to keep warm, looking out to sea. A couple of speed boats, waterskiers in tow, criss-crossed through the blue waters, creating streaks of white wake as they went. A large bright-yellow sail in the distance headed towards L'Escala, but from this far away Jack couldn't tell if it was a small dinghy or a windsurfer who had strayed a little too far from land.

The lack of blue skies meant a slow start for the sun worshippers, and it was nearly eleven before Peter and Heike showed up, with the twins arriving a few minutes later. Jack realised he'd spent hardly any time with them in the last few days. In fact, with the sole exception of Abrielle, he'd hardly spent any time with anyone, not even his hosts. It probably bordered on rudeness and perhaps, he thought, he should make a little more effort.

Simone and Abrielle sauntered down at around 11.30; nearly lunchtime, thought Jack, it was hardly worth it. Simone gave Peter a big sloppy kiss, but Jack sensed that their relationship was on the wane; there was no sparkle and Peter seemed to be getting restless. Abrielle, far less demonstrative than Simone, sat down beside Jack, and gave him a little peck on the cheek.

'Morning, how are you?' she asked. Her voice was flat and Jack immediately sensed something was wrong.

'I'm great,' he said, hiding his concern. 'Fantastic actually, it's not every day you wake up having made love to the most beautiful girl in the world.'

'Shush, Jack, it's not something to broadcast,' she said reproachfully.

'Sorry, I didn't mean to embarrass you,' he said

apologetically 'but it's not something to be ashamed of either.'

'I'm not ashamed, but it's something between you and me, no one else,' Abrielle replied tetchily.

'OK, point made,' Jack said. 'Do you want to come in the pool for a dip?'

'No, I'm just going to sunbathe, if that's all right. Could you put some cream on my back?'

'Of course I can!'

Abrielle rolled onto her front, and Jack poured some Piz Buin factor 2 onto her back. The swimsuit had made a re-appearance so there wasn't much back visible. Jack rubbed the cream gently over her golden-coloured skin, massaging it into her shoulders. He wondered what was wrong with her.

'Do you want some on your legs too?' he asked, not wanting to make any presumptions; in her mood, she might bite his head off.

'Please,' she said quietly.

Jack moved up her legs very slowly, spreading the cream delicately onto the back of her thighs. The cream had disappeared into a clear greasy moisturiser and Jack slowly rubbed his hand up and down the back of her thighs, each stroke getting slightly further round her leg, slightly higher up her thighs. He realised this was turning him on and he was breathing more heavily. There wasn't far to go to complete the job, but he was now approaching out-of-bounds territory as he brought his hand up along the inside of Abrielle's thighs, right up to her costume. She squirmed slightly but didn't protest, and Jack realised that it was turning her on as well. One more sweep up along the inside of her thighs, his fingers probing a little more than necessary, and the job was done.

'There you are, all done!' Jack said nonchalantly.

'Thank you,' she whispered, and then added even more quietly, 'that was nice.'

Jack lay down on his front as well, facing her, but she kept her eyes closed and eventually his started to shut as well. The temperature was heating up as the clouds were burnt off, and the sun's warmth radiated through him, sending him off to sleep.

Jack was woken with a gentle kiss on his cheek. He opened his eyes to see Abrielle kneeling next to him. 'I'm going back for lunch. I'll probably see you later. OK?' she said quietly.

'Yeah, fine, I'll be here,' Jack replied, unsure of what she meant by 'probably'.

At lunch, Peter told Jack that they, that is he and Heike, were going over to the twins' place for a poker evening and asked him along too. Jack jumped at the opportunity. He needed to be a better guest and, with Abrielle in a strange mood, he thought it was a good idea.

Jack delayed his return to the pool in the afternoon, wanting Abrielle to turn up first, but by three thirty she still wasn't there. Eventually he went down and swam a few lengths, but there were too many kids around to get into a smooth motion and both Magnus and his sister were hovering dangerously close to the diving board.

As Jack got out, he saw Abrielle sitting on the grass, with Peter and Simone, but she didn't seem to be part of their conversation. He wondered if she, too, had been waiting for him to return before making an appearance; if she had, then she'd won the mind-game battle.

Jack walked over and knelt down next to Abrielle. 'Hi, you OK?' he asked in as friendly a manner as he could.

She looked up at him unsmiling. 'Yes, why shouldn't I be?'

Jack was tempted to respond with a 'Well, you were a miserable cow this morning,' but opted for the more diplomatic 'No reason, just asking.'

Jack sat down on his towel and looked out across the

144

bay. It was much busier now, crowded with sailing boats, windsurfers and speed boats pulling waterskiers, even one towing a parachutist.

'I hear you're going out tonight,' Abrielle said coolly.

It was a statement rather than a question, but it still demanded a response and Jack decided to play it in as detached a manner as he could muster up. 'That's right, we've been invited to a poker night. I haven't spent much time with my hosts recently, so I thought it might be a good idea to go along, before they think I'm taking advantage of their hospitality.'

'Oh I see, and is that my fault?' was the stony response from Abrielle.

'Your fault?' Jack replied. 'Of course not! Why would it be your fault?'

'It sounded like you were implying that the reason you weren't spending time with them was because you were with me,' Abrielle said defensively.

'Well, I wasn't implying that,' Jack stated firmly, conscious of the rising tension. 'I've spent a lot of time with you, but that's not your fault; that has been my decision and therefore *my* problem.'

Abrielle didn't respond at first. Jack wanted to hold her, cuddle her, find out what was wrong, tell her he loved her, but her responses didn't provide that opportunity.

'So I'm a problem now, am I?' she retorted.

Jack smiled, determined not to get drawn into a stupid argument. 'Abrielle, don't be silly. I just need to show a little more courtesy to my hosts, that's all. End of discussion.' He said it as firmly as he could, without being aggressive.

Abrielle pointedly picked up a book and fell silent again. Jack decided there was little point in trying to have a conversation; she clearly wasn't in the mood for it and they'd only end up arguing. He picked up Joseph Conrad's *Heart of Darkness*, a book he'd been struggling with, on

145

and off, all summer. At least its dark theme seemed appropriate.

As the sun began its downward trajectory, its beams stretching across the sea from L'Escala in the west towards them, Jack wondered exactly what had gone wrong in the last twenty-four hours. They'd gone from the happiest couple in the world to being enemies who couldn't speak to each other without raising their voices. He didn't think he'd done anything wrong, but then he knew he was often oblivious to upsetting people. Perhaps his failure to swim a length underwater this morning had set the free feathers of fate floating away from him.

'Come on, Jack, we need to go!' shouted Peter, bringing him back to reality.

Jack picked up his towel, but then knelt down in front of Abrielle, feeling the need to do or say something to bring them at least one step closer together.

'How do you fancy a walk down to the beach first thing tomorrow morning, before it gets hot?' Jack said in his softest, friendliest voice.

'Why?' was the monosyllabic reply.

Jack wasn't going to take the bait. 'Why?' he said softly. 'Because I think we need to talk. We've hardly spoken today and you don't seem too happy, which after a wonderful night last night, I don't quite understand.'

'Well, if you weren't going out tonight, we could discuss it this evening,' she replied almost caustically.

'But I am going out tonight, so we can't. It will also give you a little more time to think about today,' Jack suggested, wondering if it was the smartest thing to have said.

'I'll see. I might be here, I might not,' Abrielle said, her resistance beginning to break down.

'Fine,' Jack said gently. 'I'll be going for a walk at 9 o'clock tomorrow morning. I hope you'll decide to join me.'

Abrielle didn't respond and Jack had no intention of waiting; he felt he'd done as much as he could.

As the evening wore on, Jack began to regret not being with her. Despite never playing poker before, he discovered he was rather good at it, or was it just beginner's luck? More likely, his lack of interest and dispassionate approach meant that he was good at bluffing, simply because he didn't care. He tried to forget about Abrielle and concentrate on his increasingly large pile of winnings. Even the numerous San Miguels seemed to have little effect on him.

By midnight everyone was ready to call it a night, with Jack the undisputed poker champion, a huge pile of matches in front of him. Shame it wasn't for money, he thought.

Chapter 20

Jack walked down the steps and out into the early-morning sun, dressed in jeans and a T-shirt. He regretted not putting on a jumper, as it was still quite cool. As he walked towards the pool, he glanced at his watch. Nine o'clock exactly, but no sign of Abrielle. How long do I give her? he thought. Two minutes, no longer. Jack walked around the pool, admiring the view over the bay. The clear blue seas were empty and peaceful-looking.

The two minutes were up and, as much as he wanted to give her more time, he wasn't going to be dictated to. He turned away from the apartments and walked down the steps onto the path. One last look back, but there was no sign of her. Jack sighed. He'd thought about this a lot, planned what to say, how to say it, and now she had decided not to come; he wasn't happy. Why hadn't she turned up?

Jack felt miserable, confused, depressed, then as he rounded the first turn, his heart missed a beat and he felt his spirit suddenly lifted. There, sitting on the rocks looking straight back at him, was Abrielle. As he approached, she got up and took a step towards him, her face as unsmiling as yesterday, but different – a look of determination in her eyes, which were sparkling once more. Jack stopped in front of her, she took a step even closer and, as Jack went to speak, she raised a finger to his lips to stop him. Then she slowly let her finger drop and raised her lips to his and kissed him tenderly, putting her arms around his head. Jack, not for the first time, was caught completely off guard, but it didn't take him long to respond in kind.

Abrielle pulled back and then whispered into his ear. 'I love you Jack, I love you so much.' Then she added softly, 'I'm sorry about yesterday.'

Jack leant back and brushed her hair away from her face. There were tears running down her cheeks, which he wiped away gently with the back of his hand. 'Hey, what's the matter? Why are you crying?' he asked, rather confused.

'Don't know,' she muttered. 'I'm crying and I don't even know why…' There was a hint of laughter coming through the sobs. 'Oh Jack, I'm all confused.'

'Why are you confused?'

'Oh I don't know, I just am,' Abrielle responded. 'I just feel strange. I thought that making love to you would make me feel like a woman, complete, that it would cement our relationship, but instead it just seems to have left me feeling slightly empty and unsure of myself.'

'Sorry, it left me feeling fantastic, I'm sorry if you regret it,' Jack replied, slightly hurt.

Abrielle lifted Jack's chin up. 'Jack, look at me. I don't regret it, not one bit. Making love to you was a fantastic experience. I didn't know I could have feelings like that, it was incredible, OK? It's just that when I woke up yesterday morning, I felt different. I don't know quite what I expected, but I felt that something was missing. Perhaps it's that I'm no longer a virgin, I don't know.'

Jack stood there feeling hopeless. He hadn't a clue what to say; he'd never quite understood women and he certainly couldn't comprehend how a woman would feel about losing her virginity.

Abrielle rescued him by continuing. 'The other thing that's bothering me is that in just over two weeks, you're going and I don't know if I'm ever going to see you again, and I find that really scary.'

149

Jack felt on much safer ground now. 'I know, it scares me as well, being without you, but I promise you right now, we *will* see each other again. We'll plan it before I go, all right?'

'OK, I'll hold you to that promise. Now, are we going for that walk or not?' There was a smile on her face again. Nice to see, thought Jack.

Jack took hold of Abrielle's hand and they walked off towards Rosas beach, gradually descending through the rocks towards the narrow stretch just before the 'Diving Board'. As they rounded the corner, they heard a mother shouting at a child, who was obviously ignoring her.

'Francesc, Francesc!'

As they came into view, Jack felt a shiver run through him. The mother was pushing a baby in a buggy, while young Francesc, who looked no more than two or three, was running ahead, oblivious to her cries of anguish, unsteady on the rocky path. He was approaching the gap in the rocks on the narrow stretch. Abrielle tightened her grip, as they both realised what was about to happen.

Francesc lost his footing, tripped, then lurched forward, falling to the ground, before rolling towards the edge, and then, almost in slow motion, as his mother shrieked in horror, he toppled over the edge and disappeared from view.

'Jesus!' muttered Jack as both he and Abrielle ran forward. There was the sound of a splash as Francesc hit the water below. The toddler's mother was still grappling with the buggy, as Jack and Abrielle reached the cliff edge. They could see no sign of the young boy in the sea ten feet below. Jack flicked off his shoes and jumped in, hoping he wouldn't land on top of him. He knew the water was only three or four feet deep, but he was still caught out by how quickly his feet hit the bottom. Fortunately

150

it was sand not rock, and as he stood up he saw a mop of blond hair under the surface just to his right. One stride and Jack grabbed at young Francesc and lifted him out of the water.

He had a look of total surprise on his face. One second he'd been running along minding his own business; the next he'd been pulled from the water by a total stranger. Not an everyday occurrence for a toddler, thought Jack, but hopefully he'd learnt his lesson.

Jack held onto the boy tightly as he forced his way through the water until he reached some low-lying rocks, where he handed Francesc up to Abrielle, who pulled him up and gave him back to his hysterical mother. She burst into tears of relief, prompting Francesc to let go as well; perhaps the realisation of what had just happened to him had finally hit home.

'*Gracias, muchos gracias!*' said his mother, turning to Jack, adding much more besides, none of which he understood. Nor did he understand the torrent of abuse that she then gave her son, as she held onto him tightly. It would be a while before he tried that trick again.

As mother and children disappeared, Francesc holding his mother's hand tightly – or perhaps it was the other way round – Jack stood their drenched and cold.

Abrielle laughed. 'My hero!' she said teasingly.

'Hardly,' replied Jack. 'I'm sure you would have done exactly the same.'

'*Non*, I've just done my hair,' she quipped.

'Why don't you take your jeans and shirt off and let them dry in the sun? It's beginning to warm up now,' Abrielle suggested.

'Bad idea,' replied Jack, removing his shirt with a slightly embarrassed smile.

'Why?' laughed Abrielle. 'Don't you have anything on underneath?'

'Err, no!' Jack answered. Only he wasn't joking.

'Really!' smirked Abrielle. 'Why not?'

'I'm not sure actually. I guess I couldn't be bothered. I thought I'd be putting on trunks fairly soon and I wasn't expecting to be found out.'

'Come on, Jack, we can't have you catching pneumonia,' Abrielle teased, as she tried to undo his jeans.

'Oi, behave!' shouted Jack as he wrestled with Abrielle's hands amidst their laughter. Eventually he managed to get hold of a wrist in each hand and lifted them away from his jeans, even though she fought back. Jack forced her hands higher until they were above her, then he pulled them back down around the back of his head. He pushed them together, and only then let go, as he put his arms behind her back and pulled her towards him, kissing her firmly on the lips, holding her tightly.

As they walked back up the path, Abrielle asked Jack if he fancied dinner in Rosas that evening, followed by a romantic moonlit walk. Then, if he behaved, she might arrange a little surprise later. Jack thought about it for a minute; he already knew the answer, but it was more fun to tease her a little.

'Well, I had planned to wash my hair, but I guess I could delay that.' He received a punch in the arm for his troubles.

They decided to eat at the Matador Restaurant, where Heike's parents had eaten the night before. Jack was dubious about any recommendation given by the Webers, but Abrielle insisted they give it a try. At that point, however, Sebastian made an unexpected visit to the pool and was mortified when he heard that Jack and Abrielle were going to the Matador.

'Oh, you can't go there!' he said forcefully.

'Why not?' Abrielle asked. 'It's been recommended.'

'Oh you just can't! It's ... just awful; the service is lousy,

152

the food is bland, always overcooked; it just caters for German and English tourists who just want to be fed... Please, please don't go!'

No wonder Heike's parents thought it was good; it sounded perfect for them, thought Jack, but kept his thoughts to himself.

'Well, where do you suggest then?' Jack asked Seb. 'We're always on the look-out for a good restaurant.'

'Why don't you try Viva Espana on Sant Pere Boix street, just off the front?' he suggested.

Jack smiled. 'Is it really called Viva Espana?' he asked.

'It is ... I know it's got a silly name, but the food is good; simple but good.'

Jack was far from convinced, but it still sounded better than the Matador.

'So what's new with you then, Seb?' Jack asked.

'Oh not a lot. I seem to spend most of my time writing, sometimes at home, sometimes down in a café in Rosas,' Seb answered vaguely.

Jack studied Sebastian as he spoke. He couldn't quite fathom him out. Why was he spending so much of his time on his thesis in the summer holidays? He'd already said it didn't need to be in for another nine months. And then there was Heike, just waiting for him, and he liked her – no doubt about it. There was something he wasn't telling; Jack was sure of it.

As they walked down the coastal path into Rosas, Jack and Abrielle continued to debate their destination. Jack favoured Viva Espana, despite its name, but Abrielle was determined to give the Matador a chance. Against his better judgement Jack eventually gave in.

They walked along the front and then turned right up Riera Ginjolers, until they reached Sant Sebastia, before turning right again, and there was the Matador Restaurant. As Jack walked in, he knew it just wasn't for him, and he sensed the disappointment in Abrielle as well, but she wasn't ready to accept that she was wrong yet.

They were given a table immediately, but it was ten minutes before a waiter returned to provide them with a menu and order drinks. Jack was already getting frustrated and he could see that Abrielle was as well. Ten minutes later Abrielle had decided enough was enough as well.

'Come on, let's go,' she said firmly, but with perfect timing the drinks arrived.

'Come on, we might as well stay now,' Jack suggested.

'No, I've had enough. I'm going!' She stated firmly.

'Is there a problem?' asked the Spanish waitress in strongly accented English.

'Yes!' Abrielle shouted, much more loudly than necessary. 'We've been here twenty minutes and we've only just got our drinks, yet alone ordered!'

He'd never seen her so angry, but rather than try and pacify her the waitress decided to fight back. 'We're very busy tonight, OK!' It was said much too aggressively and Jack knew it wasn't the smartest move.

'No, you're not!' shouted Abrielle. 'You've only got five tables in so far!' And she was right, busy they were not, and the waitress belatedly realised that Abrielle was the wrong person to take on.

'Jack, we're off!' It wasn't a suggestion, but a clear instruction and Jack had no intention of arguing.

'You'll still have to pay for your drinks!' the waitress said as a passing shot, but there was resignation in her voice; she knew she'd been beaten. Abrielle turned as she walked out and gave her a glare to die for.

'Jesus!' muttered Abrielle as they walked out of the restaurant, 'What a stupid bitch!'

'Hey!' shouted a voice.

Jack turned to see a rather large gentleman, presumably the owner, sweat running down his forehead, moving quickly towards them, his bloated stomach bouncing up and down in excitement.

'You have to pay for the drinks!' a strong Spanish accent.

Abrielle turned and stared him down. 'No we don't!' she screamed, stopping him in his tracks. 'Crap service, crap restaurant! I don't pay for shit!'

As surprised as Jack was at her anger, the Matador owner was completely caught out, and meekly turned around and went back into his restaurant, muttering under his breath.

As they walked down Sant Antonio, back towards the front, Jack, with a hint of trepidation, asked if she was OK. Abrielle turned and gave him a huge smile. 'Can't let these idiots get away with it, you know!' she said, calm as anything.

Before Jack had time to respond, they found themselves face to face with Sebastian walking towards them, even though he seemed oblivious to their presence.

Whether Sebastian had seen them or not, Jack wasn't sure, but he certainly kept his head down, as if trying to remain anonymous. They'd both seen him, but Sebastian was doing his best not to be noticed. As he walked past them, Jack stopped. 'Hey, Seb!' he shouted.

'Oh, oh hello,' Sebastian said, looking slightly embarrassed. 'What are you doing down here?'

Jack hesitated for a second. Bizarre question, he thought. 'We're looking for the restaurant you recommended,' Jack said. 'We tried the other, and you were right – it was crap!'

Sebastian regained his composure. 'Told you,' he said. 'Oh well, have a nice meal! It's just down there, first right, and then it's up on the right-hand side. See you later.' Sebastian tried to go, but Jack was intrigued and wasn't going to let him get away with it that easily.

'Hey, Seb, what are you doing here, especially when

Heike is back up there?' It was a slightly loaded question and Jack knew he wasn't being entirely fair, but he couldn't quite fathom what Seb was playing at.

'I'm ... I'm ...' hesitated Seb. Fatal, thought Jack, whatever you're doing, you're lying about it.

'What is it, Seb? Do you have some secret date you've been keeping quiet about?' asked Abrielle mischievously.

Sebastian looked sheepish. 'Just a local Catalan girl, no one you know,' he responded, almost under his breath.

'OK, see you later, Seb.' Jack stated, bringing the matter to a sudden conclusion.

As they walked off, Abrielle turned to Jack. 'Hey, I was enjoying that. Why did you have to end it?' she asked.

'He seemed to be getting embarrassed; I thought it time,' Jack responded.

'Oh Jack, you're too sensitive. He was fine,' Abrielle teased.

They found Viva Espana, and it was acceptable, not fantastic, but the food wasn't overcooked, the service was good, and there was a bit of an atmosphere as well.

At the end of the meal Jack raised his glass. 'To Seb! He was right; Heike's parents were wrong ... I wonder why he didn't choose here as well, if he's trying to impress some girl?'

'*Merde*, I've left my bag at that stupid restaurant,' Abrielle interrupted suddenly.

'You go and get it; I'll pay the bill here,' Jack suggested. 'I'll meet you there.'

Jack watched her leave and watched heads turn. Jesus Christ, he thought, not for the first time, what is that stunning girl doing with me? He smiled – he'd never felt happier.

Jack called for the bill, when the first sound of sirens, lots of them, shattered his thoughts. Nervous glances went around the restaurant. The noise eventually got to Jack as well and he began to wonder what the hell was going on. The bill took ages and Jack began to feel uneasy. It eventually arrived and he threw in more than enough notes to cope with a generous tip. Then he quickly got up and walked out, not bothering to wait for the change.

When he got outside, the place was bristling with police, running around, shouting at people, but Jack couldn't work out what was going on – everybody seemed confused. As he turned the corner, back towards the Matador Restaurant, people were being ushered away from the area, down the side streets, into alleyways, anywhere but Sant Sebastia it appeared. A policeman ran past him, shouting and pointing him away, but Jack ignored him, the sense of unease rising inside him.

Jack fought his way through the oncoming crowd, before at last he could see the Matador fifty yards away. At last! he thought, feeling a slight respite from the tension. But the momentary sense of relief was shattered, when suddenly the Matador Restaurant disappeared into a ball of flame. There was a fierce flash and a mixture of glowing oranges and roaring reds lit up the street. There was a haunting beauty to it as the flames leapt into the sky, a momentary awestruck silence, before the sound of a terrific explosion hit his ears, followed by the sound of shattering glass.

Jack felt the pressure wave hit him and took an involuntary step backwards, followed by a blast of heat that warmed his face. Shards of glass and crockery flew past him as charred pieces of plastic seat fell from the sky and burning embers of napkin floated down through the poisoned air.

For a second everybody froze, not quite knowing what to do, before the real panic set in. A little girl in front of him screamed, and a woman, her hair bedraggled, pulled at the girl's hand, running past Jack, mascara-stained tears running down her face. Jack was momentarily paralysed before he started to think the worst. God, please

157

no, please, don't let this happen, he prayed. He tried to make his way forward towards the Matador, but he was fighting against the tide – people covered in blood pushing past him, shock written all over their faces; people looking for their loved ones, shouting, screaming, others in tears.

As Jack got closer to the restaurant, the police were trying to force people to move away and most were happy to oblige, except those who had lost someone, those who shouted out names, usually in vain. Flames spat out of what used to be the Matador. Plastic tables were melting in the heat. No one in there stood a chance, thought Jack, trying to come to terms with the surreal scene before him. A tall policeman barred Jack's path, shouting at him, and pointing behind, but Jack was desperate, pleading with him. Now wasn't the time for diplomacy, and Jack felt the policeman's large hands on either shoulder spin him around and then forcefully push him away.

Jack lurched forward and stumbled away from the restaurant before regaining his balance and turning around. Golden flames continued to pour out, a gentle wind fanning them, but the air was now dominated by a thick black smoke, an acrid pungent smell soured by the sickly stench of charred human flesh. Jack could feel the nausea rising in his throat and turned away, trying to take in some fresh air, but there was none to be had. The urge to vomit was becoming overwhelming, but he didn't really care... Where was Abrielle? It must have been no more than five minutes between them leaving the restaurant. She must have been in there still; otherwise where was she?

Jack sank to his knees, trying to take slow deep breaths, but he could feel the rising dread, that sense of disbelief, despair and helplessness increasing. What do I do? he thought. I've got to find her. He knew what he had to do; if she was in there, he was going to find her. He didn't care about the police. He had to find Abrielle.

158

As he stood up, having resisted the urge to retch, Jack tried to work out how he was going to get past the loose police cordon that now surrounded the restaurant and was slowly being widened. Jack stood staring at the police, trying to think, trying to concentrate, but macabre thoughts kept flashing across his mind. Her dead body lying there, disfigured, charred, unrecognisable amongst the ruins, or was she lying there still alive but burnt, choking for breath, flames licking at her maimed body, unable to move? Either way some misguided bastard's pointless fight had just destroyed the most wonderful thing in his life. And all because she forgot her bag. How did that make sense? Jack wanted to scream out, why, God? but he didn't have the breath in his lungs.

The deep sickening feeling in his stomach rose as he realised that there was no way she could have survived the inferno. He was oblivious to the people still running past him, bumping and pushing as they struggled to get away, away from a desperate scene of death and carnage, and all for what?

Someone gripped his arm and he ignored it at first, until he realised that they had linked their arm in his. He didn't need to look. The sweet-scented perfume contrasted with the putrid smells around him, and the relief was immense, the world lifted from his aching shoulders. A silent prayer of thanks, before he turned to his right, and the shell-shocked eyes that met his told him she was OK. Ashen-faced, bewildered, but in one piece.

Jack put his arm around Abrielle and pulled her round to face him, before putting his arms behind her and pulling her tightly against him, tighter than he had ever held anyone before, so tight so that no one could break the grip. He felt her start to cry, tears of relief, and he just squeezed harder, wanting to hold her as close as possible, like a mother protecting her child.

159

'Jack,' she whispered, 'Jack, please, you're hurting me!'

'Sorry, I just wanted to hold you.'

'It's OK. Let's get out of here,' she said softly.

It was mayhem. The police weren't sure what to do. People were crying, screaming, dazed, looking for their loved ones, their friends, amidst the continuous wailing of sirens. Confused faces, many blackened, covered in blood, haunted faces, children who ten minutes ago were enjoying their summer holidays, now with tears running down their shocked faces, having witnessed death and destruction, the innocence of childhood shattered in one brief but deadly instant.

Jack saw the owner of the restaurant, the idiot they had argued with; he had some sympathy with him now. He was covered in blood. A miracle he'd survived, Jack thought. But the man was shouting at a policeman, pointing, screaming, probably not making any sense. An uneasy feeling flitted through Jack's mind as the owner pointed in their direction.

'Let's go, Jack! Down here.' Abrielle pulled his hand and they ran down a side street, little more than an alleyway, that led back to the front, the beach and then the way back home. Jack breathed a sigh of relief. Their nightmare was over.

As they reached the end of the street a police car screamed to a halt in front of them. Four gun-toting police jumped out, raised their guns and pointed them directly at them, shouting and screaming. Jack had no idea what they were saying, but it wasn't hard to work out that it wasn't particularly friendly. Jack slowed and then stopped, the closest policeman pointing a gun straight at his head, screaming something at him. It was then that he heard above the clamour Abrielle's soft but eerily calm voice next to him.

'Jack, just put up your hands.'

Chapter 21

The sirens continued wailing into the night, a never-ending cacophany of high-pitched screams. Jack couldn't differentiate between them – the police, ambulance and fire service, all of whom must have been called upon. It hadn't been a pretty sight, the aftermath of such a huge explosion. How many dead? he wondered.

Jack winced as he felt his swollen lips, running his fingers over the dried blood, a crust beginning to form where they'd been split. His nose was throbbing, but he didn't think it was broken, just badly bruised; his eyes, too, were sore and it was debatable whether he'd get away with one black eye or two. He'd yet to have the pleasure of looking in a mirror to see the damage inflicted by the less than friendly welcome he'd received at the hands of the police. He just hoped Abrielle had fared better; surely they wouldn't have hit her too.

After being arrested at gunpoint, they had been thrown in separate cars and Jack hadn't seen her since. In the back of the police car two burly Spanish policemen had taken it in turns to abuse him, shout at him, slap him, before a few fists to the stomach and face had stopped him protesting.

Jack was dazed by the time they had arrived at Rosas police station where, after having his personal belongings removed, he was thrown into an empty cell. A solitary bulb lit up the room so brightly that, even with his eyes firmly closed, it still felt like the sun was shining down on him. It was anything but. The cell was sparse – a stone bench, a metal bucket and a wooden chair, damp creeping up the windowless walls. The stench of urine was overpowering at first, but gradually he had become used to it. He wondered what the hell was going on. Presumably their arrest had something to do with the explosion, but quite why, he didn't know.

The police had taken Jack's watch away, but he knew they'd arrived around ten; he reckoned that was a couple of hours ago. He lay on the bench, eyes closed, wondering how long he was to be left alone in the stinking cell when he heard the metallic clink of a bolt being undone. It sent a jolt of nervous energy flooding through his body, slight relief that something was happening, tempered by the fear of the unknown. The metal door was thrown violently open, hitting the wall with a loud clank that reverberated around the cell. No doubt the aggression was meant to scare him and it certainly had the desired affect. Jack felt a slight loosening of his bowels – it didn't look like he was about to be offered a cup of tea.

In walked the tall policeman who had earlier stopped Jack from getting back to the Matador. Jack thought he saw a flicker of recognition, but it was the anger on his face which got his attention. He shouted at Jack as he strode across the cell towards him, spittle flying from his mouth, but Jack's lack of Spanish meant he had no idea what he was saying.

Jack scrambled off the bench, retreating backwards, but the policeman kept on coming. As Jack found himself backed into the corner, he put his arms across his face to protect himself from what he thought would be another beating, but, in doing so, only left his stomach unprotected. He realised his mistake, but it was too late; the fist hit him hard in the stomach and he doubled up in pain, expecting another as he went down. As his legs started to crumble, his head facing down, a huge hand appeared

162

under his chin, grabbing him by the neck and pulling him upright again.

Jack struggled for breath as he felt his neck being slowly constricted, the policeman dragging him upwards until Jack was virtually on tiptoe, face to face with the brute. Jack could smell the alcohol on his breath, a disgusting odour and eyes so wide he must have been as high as a kite. Shit, I'm in serious trouble now, thought Jack. The bastard's stoned as well as drunk. For a second he thought about fighting back – he could easily get a couple of blows to his stomach from here – but he hadn't the breath or the energy to offer anything more than token resistance and this guy was immensely strong; it would have been David and Goliath, just without the sling.

The policeman's face was contorted with hatred, his eyes ready to pop out, the spittle covering Jack as he screamed at him, only a few inches between their faces. Jack tried to breathe in, but his windpipe was now being squeezed so tightly that nothing would come. His head started to go fuzzy, dizzy, nausea rising; he could sense he was starting to lose consciousness. Memories of him and Abrielle making love on the sand, holding hands as they lay side by side near the pool, the sun warming their bodies, in their own little private world; the flash of the explosion when he thought he'd lost her, before the temporary respite, and now ... this! Is this it? Are these the flashbacks one sees before death? Is this really it? Surely not. I'm too young ... I can't die yet, can I?

As the realisation hit him that he was on the way to meet his maker, Jack summoned up all his energy; he couldn't go without some kind of struggle. Putting as much force as he could into it, he flung his right fist into the policeman's stomach. There was a momentary flinch, before he let go of Jack, who promptly slumped to the floor. Jack found himself lying in a heap, breathing in the foul-smelling air, but it was better than nothing. He took a few gulps. His throat ached, but he was breathing again, heavily, but breathing, refilling his willing lungs with oxygen. He crawled into a ball to make himself as small as possible and waited for the kicking, but it never came.

After a couple of minutes Jack had enough energy to push himself onto his knees, wondering how one pathetic punch had managed to save his life and finding the answer standing in front of him. The brute had disappeared and had been replaced by a much shorter man, in a smart white shirt, dark-blue flannels, shiny, well-polished black moccasins.

'I am Captain Gutierrez of the Policia Nacional,' he announced loudly, much more loudly than necessary, Jack thought; it was only the two of them in the cell. 'Can you get up?' His English was accented but otherwise good. A relief, thought Jack.

'I'm not sure. I think your friend was trying to kill me,' Jack managed throatily.

'He is very angry. We are all very angry. Innocent people have died tonight and someone is going to pay for that.'

'So what's that got to do with me?' Jack asked innocently, even though he already knew the answer, even if he didn't understand why.

'Very good, Mr Duggan, play the ignorant fool. We will get to the truth later, I assure you,' he said menacingly, before adding, 'We have reason to believe that you were involved in the bomb explosion.'

Jack slowly pulled himself to his feet and stood up. He was a few inches taller than Captain Gutierrez and enjoyed being able to look down on him. His jet-black shiny hair was brushed backwards and was caringly groomed by the looks of it. He had a matching black moustache, meticulously parted in the middle, waxed at either end.

'Captain, I am an English tourist on holiday. Why on

164

earth would I be involved in the bombing of a Spanish restaurant?' Jack said bemused.

'All in good time. We will interview you shortly and you will see there is a lot of evidence pointing at you.' His smile was sickly. It made Jack feel even more uneasy.

'Fine, but I'm not being interviewed until I have a lawyer. I've already been beaten up twice tonight by your thugs and I want someone here who doesn't assume I'm guilty already!' Jack spat out the last words, more aggressively than he intended, but perhaps it would have a beneficial effect; at least with a lawyer he'd find out what his rights were.

Captain Gutierrez let out a slow chuckle, his narrow dark eyes sparkling, seemingly amused by the whole situation, but his smile thinned as he spoke. 'This is not England. This is Spain. This is terrorism,' he said coldly. 'You do not get to see a lawyer.' His thin smile disappeared and he turned around, rapping on the door twice. It opened and out he went, closing it loudly behind him. The locking bolt sent a shudder through Jack.

He wondered how Abrielle was, how she was being treated. Why on earth did the police think they had anything to do with the bombing? Jack thought. It was preposterous, and what was this evidence? How could they have evidence when he knew they were innocent?

An hour later Jack found himself in another windowless room, but this one was much smaller, a table and chairs the only décor. Captain Gutierrez and another unnamed policeman faced him, partially silhouetted by the spotlight behind them which shone straight into Jack's eyes.

They'd sat there for five minutes and no one had said a word. It was surreal. If it wasn't for the fact that the situation was so serious, it would be rather comical. It brought a temporary smile to his face, but Captain Gutierrez's cold eyes staring back removed it instantly.

165

Gutierrez leant forward, elbows on table, hands clasped together, as if he was praying. 'Why don't you tell us about this evening, Mr Duggan?'

Jack paused before responding. 'Exactly what do you want to know? About how we were nearly killed by the explosion? How I was beaten up by a couple of Spanish policemen, or perhaps how another tried to kill me?' It was a dangerous response, but he'd been on the defensive for hours and he'd had enough.

The Captain took in a deep breath, began quietly, but gradually his voice grew in tempo. 'Don't mess with me, Mr Duggan, I am not in a good mood. You mess with me and you'll soon realise that what has happened so far is nothing. After we've finished with you, you'll wish you'd never been born!' He paused, smiled, then brought his fists crashing down on the table. 'Now you cooperate, OK?' he yelled.

It had the desired effect, Jack stared back, tried to look as nonchalant as he could, but inside his heart was racing. He felt his bowels weaken – perhaps cooperation wasn't such a bad idea after all.

'OK. We began the evening at the Matador. The service was very slow, so we left and went for a meal at Viva Espana instead. When we finished, Abrielle realised she'd left her bag at the Matador, so she went back while I paid the bill. It was then that the first sirens started. When I got to Sant Sebastia, I could see the police moving everyone away, and then suddenly bang, the place exploded. At first I couldn't find Abrielle. I thought she must be in there getting her bag when the bomb went off, but then she found me. We left and suddenly we're facing armed police, and the rest you know.' Jack paused. 'That's it. Why you think we had anything to do with it, I don't know.'

Captain Gutierrez smiled his thin unfriendly smile. 'Very good, Mr Duggan. I like it. A good liar always keeps very close to the truth, very close,' he said, twiddling his moustache, almost Poirot-like.

'Why would I lie? I have nothing to lie about.' Jack protested.

'But you have already lied to us!' shouted Gutierrez. 'You have repeatedly said you are English, when in fact you are Irish. You have an Irish passport! Do you think we are stupid?'

Jack sighed, shaking his head. 'I'm not Irish. I was born in England, I have lived all my life in England, I'm English. My Dad is Irish and I have an Irish passport because he wanted me to, OK? And even if I was Irish, what's wrong with that?'

'Where is your father from?' Gutierrez snapped back.

'What?' asked Jack. 'What's that got to do with anything?'

'It matters because I asked it!' he shouted. 'Just answer the question. I will decide which questions to ask!'

Jack took a breath. This was getting weirder and weirder. 'He was born in Dublin, brought up in Belfast,' he said softly.

'Has he ever been in prison? Has he ever been accused of terrorist offences?' persisted Gutierrez.

Jack resisted the temptation to give a caustic reply and kept up the quiet approach; it seemed to be working better. 'No, he's never been accused of anything in his life; he's a well-respected doctor.'

'Does he support the IRA?' Gutierrez asked, slightly deflated.

'No, he's a pacifist.'

'But he is a Catholic, isn't he? A Catholic from Belfast?'

'Yes, but that doesn't make him an IRA supporter, does it? Just because he would like to see a united Ireland doesn't mean he believes in murdering innocent people. There are other Nationalist parties who utilise peaceful means, you know!' Jack said firmly.

167

'What about you? Do you support the IRA? Are you a member of the IRA?' Gutierrez said, raising his voice. 'Are you a Volunteer?' he said, sneeringly, his eyes narrowing.

Jack stared back at Gutierrez and took a deep breath, again fighting the temptation to raise his voice or get sarcastic. 'No, I am not.'

'You see, there has been a lot of cooperation between the IRA and ETA in the last few years. They've trained together in Libya and in South Yemen. And in the last couple of weeks there's been a lot of coded communication between people in Ireland and Spain, particularly in this area. In fact, it seems to have been ever since you arrived. What a coincidence!' Gutierrez leant back to see the impact this had. None! Jack knew he was innocent and this hardly even qualified as circumstantial evidence.

'Well, that had nothing to do with me. I haven't made a single phone call since I arrived, except to tell my mother I'd got here safely!' Jack said smugly.

Gutierrez leant back, pulled out a packet of Marlboro, casually flicked open the top and in the same motion pushed a cigarette up a little, before raising the pack to his mouth and pulling it out between his lips, never taking his eyes off Jack. From the same shirt pocket came a slim silver lighter. The flint caught first time and a large gas-fuelled flame roared upwards. Gutierrez sucked in a deep breath of noxious smoke and continued to stare, before leaning forward and blowing the smoke into Jack's face.

'You want a smoke?' he growled.

Jack leant back trying to avoid the smoke. 'No,' he replied softly. 'If you ever let me out of here alive, I don't intend to die of something self-inflicted.'

Gutierrez just stared. His unfriendly gaze unnerved Jack, but it also got him wondering. Was he just beginning to realise that Jack perhaps wasn't guilty after all.

'Why did you run away when you were asked to stop?'

168

Jack put on his confused face. 'Run away? We didn't!'

'Don't lie, Mr Duggan,' Gutierrez said, raising his voice. 'Outside the restaurant, when the owner spotted you and pointed you out to one of my colleagues, you turned and ran. When he shouted after you, you ignored him. That is a crime in itself you know – to refuse to obey an order from a policeman.'

'Captain,' Jack said, more aggressively than he had intended, 'we did not run from the police. If you were there, you will know how horrific it was – the smell of burnt flesh, people crying. Anyway, we were being told to go. Once we had found each other, we just wanted to get out of there as quickly as we could.' Jack could feel his blood pumping round his body as his anger rose. 'If someone was shouting at us, with all that noise, the sirens, the yelling, people running and screaming, then it's hardly surprising that we didn't hear them, is it?' Jack thought he sounded convincing, but he was beginning to learn how stubborn Gutierrez could be.

'Oh come on, Mr Duggan. You saw the owner talking to the policeman, pointing at you. You knew he had recognised you, and you ran to try and avoid capture, but you failed!' he finished with a sarcastic smile.

'Sorry, Captain, but you've got it all wrong. We were just innocent bystanders who were in the wrong place at the wrong time.'

'Of course, we haven't discussed your accomplice yet, have we?' It was said with a leering sickly grin. 'The lovely Abrielle, so pretty, lovely soft skin, silky hair ... but then, of course, you would know that, wouldn't you?'

Jack's confidence which had been gradually rising over the last few minutes took a dive. The way Gutierrez was talking about Abrielle made his skin crawl. He sounded more like a child molester than a policeman.

'Such a pretty face!' he said softly. 'At least it *was*. Not so good now, of course.'

Jack leapt forward at Gutierrez without pausing to actually think about what he was doing and his hands went for the throat, but they never got there. The other policeman, the silent one, the one with no name, was up in an instant, grabbing Jack's wrists and pushing him firmly back into his seat.

'Don't be stupid, Mr Duggan, you are in so much trouble. Please don't make it worse,' said Gutierrez coldly.

'You touch her...' Jack shouted, but got no further.

'Yes?' screamed Gutierrez, violently shoving the table at Jack as he stood up. '... And just what are you going to do?'

Jack stared back at him, breathing deeply, he could feel the adrenalin pumping through his arteries. He shouldn't have taken the bait. That was all part of the plan and he'd fallen for it. He silently cursed himself.

'Now, your girlfriend, what do you know about her?'

Jack wasn't sure where Gutierrez was going with his line of questioning, but he didn't want to get into another trap. He said nothing, just glared.

'A fighter your girlfriend, isn't she? A real fighter. She doesn't look too good at the moment though, not much better than you. I hope her scars heal though; it would be such a shame if they didn't.'

Jack took a deep breath to try and contain his anger. Don't take the bait, he thought. He tried to put out of his mind the thought of Abrielle's pretty face looking anything like his own felt.

'What do you know about her, Mr Duggan? Do you really know who she is, who her parents are, what her background is?' Gutierrez asked, almost sympathetically.

'What are you getting at, Captain. Are you really suggesting that she had something to do with the explosion?'

Jack asked, shaking his head and smiling, thinking how ludicrous this was becoming.

'Where was Miss Dicharry born, Mr Duggan? Do you know?' Gutierrez asked softly, leaning forward, so close that Jack could see the lines stretched across his forehead. Bet he doesn't look as bad as me, thought Jack.

'She's from Paris. I think she said she was born there,' said Jack.

'Wrong!' shouted Gutierrez triumphantly. 'She was born in Biarritz. Do you know where that is?'

'Course I do,' said Jack, 'but so what?'

'She's Basque. Her mother is Basque, her father is Basque, the name Dicharry is Basque,' screamed Gutierrez, making Jack recoil.

'Do you know the name Areggi?' shouted Gutierrez.

Jack was nonplussed. He shook his head.

'Areggi is the name of one of the most wanted ETA terrorists.' Gutierrez spat out the name.

'So what has that got to do with Abrielle?' asked Jack, unable to follow the line of questioning, until Gutierrez made it clear for him.

'Areggi also happens to be the name of Mrs Dicharry before she was married.' Gutierrez let the idea sink in before continuing more softly. 'What is more, Areggi is believed to be living in hiding in Paris!'

'So?' asked Jack, unconvinced.

'I don't believe in coincidences.' Gutierrez's eyes narrowed to two tiny slits as he spoke. 'Your girlfriend, Mr Duggan, is a Basque terrorist. She has admitted it!'

'No!' shouted Jack. 'I don't believe you!'

'Mr Duggan, ask yourself, was it you or her who wanted to go to that restaurant? Was it you or her who wanted to leave after just a few minutes? Who suggested running from the police, you or her?'

A cold shiver ran through Jack. He knew the answers

171

to all the questions, but it wasn't that; it was the final words she had spoken to him. Her last words, said so calmly when they were surrounded by guns: 'Jack, just put up your hands.' It hadn't sounded quite right at the time, but now they were coming back to haunt him, those words. The girl he loved, could she really be a terrorist? Had she really admitted her involvement?

'Mr Duggan, have a think about it. It's very simple, really. We have the evidence; she will be prosecuted. The only question is, will you be too? Or, if you are innocent as you insist, will you be a witness against her?' Gutierrez didn't wait for Jack to look up; he jumped up and walked out of the room, leaving his silent companion staring at him.

Jack lay back in the chair, looked up at the ceiling and wondered just what he had got himself caught up in. Could she really be a terrorist? Just because she was Basque hardly made her a terrorist; surely there were millions of Basques and only a handful of them were terrorists. It was just like Ireland – a few murdering bastards, but the vast majority wanted peace. But those words, those words kept nagging away at him. Why?

After half an hour or so Gutierrez came back. The silent one hadn't moved, hadn't spoken, hadn't done anything but stare at Jack, but when Gutierrez sat down, he turned to him and rapidly reeled out something, softly spoken, and in Spanish, but whatever it was it brought a satisfied smile to the face of Gutierrez.

'So, Mr Duggan, are you ready to speak? Are you ready to look after yourself, rather than protect your murdering girlfriend?'

Jack stared back at the Captain, realising how much he had come to dislike this man, detest him in fact, in just a few hours.

'I've thought about what you said, and it's all very

172

interesting, and I have to say...' Jack paused for effect, he could see Gutierrez was expectant. '...I believe...' He paused again before smiling. '...I believe that you've been talking absolute bollocks!'

The smile on Gutierrez's face vanished.

'I don't think Abrielle has admitted anything. I don't believe a seventeen-year-old schoolgirl is a terrorist, and I think that the only thing you have on us is an unhappy restaurant owner looking for someone to blame. You are desperate to find someone responsible and we obviously made easy targets. Well, I suggest you prove it!' Jack finished firmly. His heart beat loudly, but his voice had remained calm, even if inside he didn't feel it.

Gutierrez pushed the table at Jack and turned to the silent one, shouting at him as he jumped up. Jack put his hands up to stop the table hitting him, but smiled to himself, feeling sure he was right, Gutierrez had nothing on them. The two policemen left the room arguing. That told Jack he was right. Surely it was just a matter of time now.

A few minutes later Jack was escorted back to his cell, where he lay down on the cold stone bench, feeling strangely contented. He had managed to stand up for himself, and more importantly for her.

Jack lay on his front, his face buried between his arms to try and keep out as much light as he could. It was uncomfortable, he was cold, but he was also exhausted and eventually sleep came to him. Strange dreams haunted him – people burning, flames spouting out of them, running towards him like zombies. He turned and ran into a group of children with empty dark sockets where their eyes should have been, shrivelled black stubs for noses. Burnt black arms tried to grab him, but he lashed out, hitting the arms and faces, and they crumpled around him, helpless. But the more he hit, the more they came,

173

until he was swamped by them, pulling him down, holding him down, sitting on him, suffocating him. He fought for breath, but the weight on his chest was too much. He had no breath left. This was it. This was the end.

The sound of a bolt being undone awoke Jack with a start. He opened his eyes and for a second wondered where he was, relieved he wasn't in his dream. Then the door opened and in walked Gutierrez – he remembered.

Gutierrez stared at him, an unfriendly gaze. 'Get up, time to go,' he said gruffly.

'Go where?' Jack asked, uncertain.

'Where?' repeated Gutierrez. 'I don't care where. Just go, get out of my police station!' he said angrily.

Jack got to his feet and looked at Gutierrez confused, not sure if it was another wind-up or not.

'So a few hours ago I was an IRA Volunteer, Abrielle an ETA terrorist. She had even confessed to blowing up a restaurant, and yet now I'm free to go!' Jack was still not convinced, but he saw the beaten look on Gutierrez's face. 'And Abrielle?'

'Yes, her as well. We found her bag. A little charred, but intact. It wasn't the source of the bomb.'

There was no apology, only disappointment written across his face, but Jack felt a surge of relief flow through him.

Chapter 22

A siren went off in the distance, a throbbing screech, pausing for a split-second before repeating itself, monotonously, repetitive and unrelenting. In my head, the noise seemed to be getting louder, gradually interfering with my subconscious, eventually becoming impossible to ignore. Reluctantly, my eyes opened, the clock said 7.00 and reality slowly dawned on me. I hit the snooze button. Even after the noise ceased, the throbbing in my head continued; a few glasses of wine too many last night I think. Jesus! Last night! It came back to me like an avalanche, hitting me full on – making love to Abrielle again.

It had been fantastic, not just the pure unadulterated sex – or should that be adulterated – but the intimacy, the closeness, that feeling of being joined together as one, that unique intensity that only making love to someone you deeply care for can create. It had been the physical and emotional release of eighteen years of pent-up frustration and *making love* was exactly what it was.

As the clock ticked on, the realisation of what we had done began to filter through to my conscience. It wasn't guilt, at least not at first, more an assessment of the implications. How did this change things: for me, for us, for her, for Susan? No longer were we ex-lovers who had just happened to bump into each other. Whereas previously we had skirted around the subject of our feelings for each other, now it was out in the open; we had consummated it as well and nothing we could do could change that.

Where did we go from here? Was it a one-off, just two consenting adults taking advantage of circumstances and each other? No, I didn't think so; it meant so much more than that. Was it one last goodbye forever? Or was it the start of something new? Was it what it should always have been – Jack and Abrielle, on temporary hold for eighteen years, but now back together for good?

Except it wasn't quite as simple as that, was it? We lived in different countries and we had eighteen years of baggage to deal with. And there was an awful lot of baggage, especially on my side; on Abrielle's I wasn't sure, she only told me what she wanted me to hear. Suddenly life seemed a lot more complicated than it had been twenty-four hours earlier.

What about Susan, I wondered, our marriage, my boys? A tinge of regret flickered through me, but only because I couldn't go on with Susan. Why were we being punished twice? Why was she? Surely losing a child in infancy was more than enough. It was tearing both of us apart and I had reached the point where I couldn't go on. I wondered if it had only been a matter of time, not until I betrayed her, but until I couldn't cope with living with her any more. I had tried, God knows I'd tried, but slowly she had been going downhill and she was trying to drag me down with her, down into her own abyss, but it was somewhere I wasn't prepared to go.

The alarm went off again, and again I hit the snooze button, but I was too awake now to worry about falling back to sleep. I turned over to look at the lovely Abrielle, as I felt now, the love of my life, and if I was honest with myself, always the love of my life, there had never been another. But the lovely Abrielle was nowhere to be seen, her side of the bed was empty.

Uncertainty crept through me. Why would she have left, why would she have gone without a kiss goodbye? I struggled into a sitting position and the headache hit me harder, a pain from the back of my head right to the fore, as if a hot poker was toying at my nerve endings. I closed my eyes, trying to shut out the pain.

I dragged my feet off the bed and pulled myself slowly up. My bones stiffened, tendons complained, muscles ached. As my body grudgingly made its way towards the bathroom, I sensed something wasn't quite right. I looked around. Nothing seemed out of place, but something was amiss. My eyes scanned the room, looking for something I couldn't pinpoint. Then it hit me, like a slap around the face, waking me from my stupor. It wasn't what was out of place; that was the point. There was nothing out of place, nothing, no sign of Abrielle, no sign of what we had done last night. Like a criminal meticulously removing all evidence from the scene of the crime, she had covered over her traces as if she had never been there. *She had never been there.*

I'm not sure if it was the disbelief or the alcohol that was still careering around my body, but my brain was working very slowly; at least that was what I convinced myself. Perhaps it was just that I didn't want to see the truth; it's never as good as the fantasy.

Still not convinced, my heart sought to prove otherwise, but as I looked at myself in the mirror, there it was for the world to see, the irrefutable evidence. A pair of boxers, not discarded on the floor as evidence of a steamy night of passion, but limply hanging off a pair of wiry pale legs.

But my brain refused to accept the overwhelming if not conclusive evidence. I rushed to the door, the security latch, I knew I opened it for her. The latch was firmly in place – locked. Unless she'd left via the window, she'd never been in the room.

The sound of a lavatory flushing raised my hopes

177

momentarily, and I ran, I actually ran across the bedroom, until I realised that fast movement and hangovers don't mix. I also saw the bathroom was empty and in darkness, and the sounds of the flushing lavatory faded back into the hotel walls from whence they had come.

I sat on the bed, my heart confused, my head confused. Had I really dreamt last night? How could I have? It was all so vivid, so real, the feelings I had felt, both physical and mental. Were they really nothing more than the result of an overactive subconscious?

I didn't know whether to laugh or cry. I spluttered out a chuckle; it was as much as I could manage, my brain mixed up by conflicting thoughts of relief and disappointment. I hadn't betrayed my wife, at least not literally, but I hadn't made love to Abrielle either. Perhaps the dream was a warning, a warning that I was now a long way down a treacherous path and if I went any further, I might never get back.

Chapter 23

When Jack and Abrielle were released early in the morning, they found both Heike and Simone's mother already at the police station. Sebastian had seen them arrested and gone back to the apartments to let the others know. Everybody had trooped down to the police station to complain and try and get them released, but needless to say the police weren't interested in their views. One by one they'd returned home to get some sleep, and by 7 a.m. only those two were left to greet them. Abrielle, thank God, had not been touched, despite Captain Gutierrez's comments.

Rosas had become a very sombre place. People were in shock that something so devastating could happen in such a tranquil town. Three people killed, many more wounded, children maimed, limbs lost, sight gone, lives destroyed for ever. Why? Jack wondered. Did the callous perpetrators of this atrocity really believe that it had furthered their cause? If they did, then they were as deluded as they were evil.

Jack slept for much of the day, but when he surfaced around mid-afternoon and went down to the pool to see the others, he learnt how more details about the bombing had slowly been filtering out, and they only got worse. The three dead were a Belgian family on the last night of their holiday, who had been too slow to get out of the restaurant when the police started to clear the area. Apparently, they'd been the last ones to leave and as they reached the exit they'd taken the full force of the explosion as the bomb detonated. Shortly after he arrived at the pool, the Spanish news, which the little TV at the bar had been tuned to all day, announced the names of the dead. It was what everyone had feared, but no one had voiced, just in case it tempted fate. But fate had already made its decision – Eric and his parents were dead.

There were tears, especially from the girls, except Heike who was made of sterner stuff, but it was too much for JP1 and JP2, they'd been friends with him. Jack felt guilty. He'd never liked Joe 90, couldn't stand him; he'd even wished him dead at times, particularly when the two of them had been vying over Abrielle's heart. But it's one thing to wish someone dead when it's merely hypothetical; it's very different when they're actually dead, having been blown to pieces, their only crime, to have been in the wrong place at the wrong time. Still, Jack felt like shit.

Abrielle arrived shortly afterwards. She'd seen the announcement on the TV in the apartment. Jack watched her walk down the steps towards them. The contrast with her usual demeanour was stark. Normally she held her head up high, slightly aloof, but now her head was bowed, shoulders slightly hunched, and when she arrived her red eyes betrayed that she'd been crying. Jack got up and walked towards her, and she came into his arms.

She seemed to have aged a few years in the last day, he thought. She wasn't just worn out; in some bizarre way he felt she had matured as well. Perhaps it was the interrogations she had gone through with Captain Gutierrez. He'd given her a hard time too, had told the same lies to her that he had to Jack – that he was an IRA member and had admitted to the bombing. She seemed to have handled it better than him though, never letting Gutierrez get to her, always fighting back, but without losing her temper.

The following day, Sunday, Simone's mother decided enough was enough and finally carried out her threat to take the girls off to Madrid. They left first thing that morning and Jack was left wondering how he was going to get through the next week without Abrielle. He now had less than two weeks left of his holiday in Spain, and he wanted the next week to go in an instant, but the following to go at a snail's pace, but he knew it was much more likely to be the other way round.

Down at the poolside Peter and Heike were chatting away, but Jack wasn't listening; his heart and mind were in Madrid. Jack saw a flicker of excitement flit across Heike's face before she regained her self-control, and before he even had time to think why, the answer arrived. Jack smiled to himself.

'Evening, all,' said Sebastian. Just like an English copper, Jack thought. 'Beers all round?'

'Please,' said Jack and Peter in unison.

'Hey, I'll help you,' said Heike, jumping up.

Jack watched her walk over to him. It was obvious she liked him. At least it was to Jack; Peter seemed oblivious to it. But Sebastian was a strange one. Sometimes he seemed keen on Heike, and you thought at last something was going to happen, but then he would become more distant, as if he was scared of getting too close. Jack hadn't told Heike about bumping into Sebastian the night of the bomb. If Seb had a local girlfriend, then that was his business and, unless he felt Heike needed to know, Jack couldn't see the point in telling her.

When they returned with the beers, talk inevitably turned to the bombing. It seemed impossible to get away from the subject at the moment and every snippet of information was repeated and recycled on the constant TV news. The latest, Sebastian stated, was that ETA hadn't claimed responsibility, but another group had.

'Who else is there?' enquired Heike.

'Terra Lliure they're called. They said that they planted

181

the bomb to try and dissuade tourists from holidaying in the occupied country of Catalonia.'

'Jesus!' exclaimed Jack. 'Occupied! When has Rosas ever been anything but Spanish?'

'Jack, you know we Catalans don't like to be called Spanish. We've always believed that we should be a separate country.' Sebastian was calm in his response, but Jack was riled.

'So are you saying you support this Terra Lliure?' Jack asked aggressively.

'Hey, Jack, that's unfair!' interrupted Heike.

'No, it's not Heike. All I'm hearing is some kind of a justification for murdering innocent people.'

'Well, start listening then because that's not what Seb said. He was trying to explain who they were, not justify it!' Heike's cheeks flushed red, whether it was annoyance with Jack or a realisation that she was fighting Seb's battles for him, he wasn't sure, but it was good to see some passion in her eyes.

Sebastian cleared his throat. Jack hoped this wouldn't herald another long speech on independence for Catalonia.

'Jack, Terra Lliure simply means "Free Land". Like ETA, they just want to be freed from Madrid's interference. The people of Catalonia are a very unique and independent people, and self-rule is important to us.'

'Seb, how can you sit there and talk about it so matter-of-fact, when a bomb has just gone off in your home town and killed someone you knew?' Jack asked, getting exasperated.

Sebastian paused before answering, taking in a slow breath. 'I'm just trying to explain why these people are so determined ... I was very sad to hear about Eric,' he added, dropping his head.

Jack wasn't convinced; he'd like to have seen a little more remorse and a little less flying-the-flag for Catalonia.

Jack was fed up with the conversation, fed up with the talk about the explosion. His mind drifted away. He'd been so pleased to see Abrielle when they were finally released yesterday morning. They hadn't said anything, hadn't needed to; they just held each other tightly. Their actions and touch of their bodies said everything that needed to be said.

During the following week Rosas was like a morgue; only now the dead bodies had gone. A dark cloud had settled over the town, leaving the remaining tourists fearful, and there was a sense of foreboding in the air. Would it happen again? Many had fled in the immediate aftermath of the bombing, and the normal weekly intake had been well down on the usual number. Some decided to brave it out, but the town was eerily quiet. Many of the restaurants were closed; those that were open were three-quarters empty.

The solemn mood in the town matched Jack's own. He couldn't quite fathom how the week was going so excruciatingly slowly. Every second seemed to tick louder, remind him that he wasn't with her, and as much as he tried not to think about her, there were constant reminders, whether it was a pretty, long-haired girl in the distance or the empty place next to him by the pool – somehow his brain managed to conjure up a reason to think about her and to think about what he was missing. And then, when he tried to be positive, thinking about seeing her again in a few days, his brain would rudely remind him that a week later, that was it, they would go there separate ways and only God knew if they would ever see each other again.

Even by the poolside the atmosphere had become desolate. Most of the group had now left Rosas, either because their holidays were up, or because they no longer felt safe. Sebastian was the only one still around, and yet he wasn't often seen, concentrating on his thesis – much, Jack suspected, to Heike's disappointment.

Towards the end of the week Jack finally tried his hand at waterskiing, but his heart wasn't in it and after numerous failures, somehow or other he'd ended up in the water without his trunks on. Afterwards he went to assuage his humiliation by downing a few beers by the pool. Peter and Heike kept him company. As Jack began what he thought was his sixth beer – he was losing count – he saw a smile light up on Heike's face as she looked past him. Seb, he thought.

'Hey, Seb!' boomed Peter. 'We never see you any more. Where've you been all day?'

Sebastian looked sheepish. 'Oh, you know, just doing some college work. I've got...' But he was interrupted by Peter who, fuelled by the considerable intake of beer, was in a boisterous mood.

'Seb, you're really missing out. Today on this very bay in Rosas...' – Jack squirmed, guessing that what was coming was at his expense – '...the world witnessed the greatest failure in the history of waterskiing!'

Peter paused for effect; Sebastian looked bemused. 'Jack here spent over two hours trying to ski, and yet the only thing he succeeded in was losing his trunks!' Peter roared with laughter, leaning back on his chair until he would have toppled backwards if Jack hadn't grabbed it.

'Perhaps I should have let you go,' Jack quipped as Peter rocked forward.

'I'm sure you weren't that bad, Jack?' remarked Sebastian generously.

'Oh he was!' interjected Heike, joining in the fun.

'Well,' announced Jack, slightly seriously, as if he was about to make a speech for the defence, 'I could try blaming my instructors, or the second-hand equipment, or even the poor water quality...' he paused. 'Or – and

184

it pains me to admit this – I could just agree that I was totally and utterly useless.'

Having pleaded guilty, the others left him alone and Jack found his thoughts drifting back towards Abrielle once more.

'Missing her, Jack?' Seb broke him out of his daydream. Jack looked up. It was a serious question, not a tease. Seb didn't really do humour, sarcastic or otherwise.

Jack smiled. 'Just a bit!' Let him interpret that how he wants, thought Jack.

'Only two days before she's back, though – not long now...' Seb mused. 'How long are they staying after that though? Are they still planning to stay till late August, or are they going back early after what's happened?'

'I presume they're staying on,' Jack said, but an unwelcome thought entered his head. What if Simone's mother *had* decided to go back to Paris early? He'd never considered it. Since the bombing he and Abrielle had spent so little time together, they'd not had time to discuss such a possibility – they'd both just assumed that, once she got back, they'd have one final week together. He tried to dismiss the thought but it kept on nagging away at him, all night long.

Chapter 24

I let the steaming-hot water pour over me, hoping it would rinse the hangover out of me and cleanse my mind of adulterous thoughts at the same time. I stood there for ages, the flowing water slowly reviving me and gradually soothing my throbbing head. I really needed to go slower on the wine. Would I never learn?

I arrived for breakfast on the dot of 7.45, but Abrielle was already tucking into a bland-looking fruit salad. I ordered a black coffee. I was desperately in need of some hardcore caffeine to counteract the alcohol that was still swirling around my bloodstream.

She looked radiant, as if she hadn't touched a drop of wine and had benefited from a full night's sleep. I looked at her closely, and she gave me a puzzled look back. 'Please tell me you don't feel as fantastic as you look?' I pleaded.

She screwed up her face and gave me a funny look. 'I *think* that's a compliment, albeit a rather strange one... But no, I don't feel fantastic, and that's your fault!'

'Mine!' I protested innocently.

'Yes, yours! You kept plying me with alcohol, and lots of it, and I've got work to do today, you know; I can't go back to bed like you can!'

Momentarily I thought of suggesting that she could if she wanted, and there was room in mine if she wanted to join me, but thankfully, for once, common sense ruled and I resisted the temptation to lower the tone.

'Not true,' I argued instead, 'I have work to do as well, you know.'

She raised an eyebrow, Roger Moore-like. 'Really, and what would that be?'

Good question, I thought. I had no idea, it had been one of those comments which is meant rhetorically and doesn't expect a response, but it had got one and now required an answer.

'Well, I can't really tell you,' I said, playing for time, 'except to say that I've got a fair bit of planning to do today.' It was a cop-out and we both knew it, but it brought an end to the questioning.

She smiled. 'OK, but don't forget you promised you'd sort out my flight change,' she said, passing the details across to me.

'And, Jack,' she added, looking intently into my eyes, 'now I've changed my plans just for you, you better make it worth my while!'

I smiled back, not quite sure exactly what she meant. I tried not to think of the possibilities. She was reeling me in once more. She knew it, I knew it, but neither of us could admit it; that wasn't the way the game was played. And it was a game, an unspoken game that was fun and scary, and much too serious to be considered merely a game because we were playing with people's lives.

Chapter 25

Jack woke to the sound of a loud bass drum beating slowly, rhythmically, monotonously. He turned over and buried his head under the pillow to deaden the sound, but he knew it would have no effect – the beat was coming from inside his own head. It had been a daily occurrence since Abrielle had been away, the result of drinking countless San Miguels every night in an attempt to numb the ache he felt at her absence. Today, though, was the day on which she was to return.

His excitement at the thought of seeing her again was tempered by the doubts that had been quietly feeding off his insecurity and which now began to creep from deep within his brain to the surface, where in the light of day they could feast on his growing anxiety. Would she still feel the same way about him, or would a week apart have cured her of this ridiculous love? Would she have come to her senses and realised that she didn't love him at all and that it had all been just a bit of fun?

Even if her feelings hadn't changed, what if the old dragon had decided Rosas was no longer safe and that she and the girls should make an early exit for Paris?

Jack had no idea what time they were due back, so he decided to hang around the pool all day. But with nothing to do but think, his imagination ran wild and his mood darkened as the sun arced further across the empty sky. Still no sign. What if they had gone directly home to Paris?

As the sun began its descent towards the horizon, Jack

looked at his watch – 6 p.m. Why weren't they back? Had there been an accident? Was she OK? Was she still coming back? He couldn't stand the uncertainty and decided to go for a walk, but before he'd got fifty yards he changed his mind. What if she got back and he wasn't there waiting? She'd think he didn't care for her any more. Jack climbed the rocks and turned to watch the cars coming up the hill from Rosas. His heart raced a little each time a large blue car emerged from the cliff's shadows, only to be disappointed when he realised it wasn't the battered old Citroen that Simone's mother drove.

Jack turned away from the road, away from the pool and looked out to the beautiful spectacle of Rosas Bay. He put on his Ray-Bans, and soaked up the sun, trying to pull himself together. Be positive, he thought, be positive! Everything will be fine. Please God, let everything be fine.

Jack stared out to sea and thought back to that first evening, that electric first moment when their eyes met, that moment when the world stopped, when his heart missed a beat... Without even realising it, a big smile crept across Jack's face as he reflected on what was perhaps one of the defining moments of his life.

As the sun gradually lost its heat, a gentle breeze came up and blew through Jack's hair. The wind picked up a solitary leaf and Jack watched it ride the warm currents of air rising high above him, before gently fluttering back down to earth, without a care in the world. As it disappeared behind him, he felt a tickle on the back of his neck. His first instinct was that it was the leaf, but leaves don't emit warmth, and as the feeling lingered he could feel the heat being transferred into him. An overwhelming sense of relief flooded through him as all his doubts disappeared in an instant. Jack offered up a silent prayer of thanks as he took in her smell, absorbed the aroma that was simply her.

189

He made no move and continued to stare out to sea. He felt Abrielle's legs slip around his as she sat behind him, her arms wrapping round his chest, pulling him tightly against her, as she continued to gently kiss the back of his neck. They were back together in their private world. 'I missed you so much,' she whispered.

Jack turned his head and was struck afresh by those stunning blue eyes. A week away and his memory had already begun to let him down.

'Did you miss me?' she asked, an inquisitive look on her face reflecting her uncertainty.

'No, not really,' he said with the straightest face he could manage, but he was unable to hold back the smile, and as the grin spread across his face, she started to playfully thump him in the ribs.

'OK, OK, I missed you!' Jack belatedly admitted, before adding quietly, 'Actually, I missed you very much. I've been a miserable git all week.'

'Git, what's a git?' asked Abrielle, stroking his hair.

'It's a pregnant camel, but it's also an expression used about an annoying person.'

'Really, and exactly why have you been a pregnant camel?' Abrielle asked with a smirk. As if she didn't know!

Jack grinned, and decided to tell the truth. 'Because I hated not being with you, not seeing you, not touching you, not even being able to talk to you. It was horrible and I've been feeling really sorry for myself!'

Abrielle pulled him closer. 'Well, I'm back now, so you can stop being a git.'

'What are we doing tonight?' Abrielle asked.

'Ah, sorry, I already have plans,' Jack replied instantly, but this time the straight face lasted less than a second and he was rewarded with a much harder punch than the first.

Jack twisted himself round and then leaned forward

and kissed her on the lips, 'I thought we might find somewhere quiet, secluded and watch the stars and then perhaps later...' He left the comment hanging there; he didn't want to appear presumptuous.

She gave him a big smile back. 'Sounds like a good idea!'

Abrielle took his head in her hands and kissed him on the lips. Jack had forgotten just how good the taste was, and suddenly they were filled with a fresh sense of urgency as their tongues, reunited once more, reawakened feelings that had lain dormant for a week.

Abrielle pulled back, breathing deeply. 'Not later, Jack, now! Let's go to the beach now!'

Jack jumped up, grabbing his towel with one hand, her hand with the other, and they made their way gingerly down the steep path to emerge on the sun-baked empty sands below.

Afterwards, they lay there in each other's arms, in silence except for the sounds of their heavy breathing. Abrielle's long hair blew gently to and fro across her bare breasts.

Abrielle lifted her head and turned to face him, a serious look on her face. 'Whatever did I do to deserve you?' she asked.

Jack smiled. 'It's a question I keep asking God about you,' he said. 'I can only presume I was a saint in a former life and you are my reward.'

The serious look on Abrielle's face dissipated and a smile appeared, before quickly being replaced with a look of concern. 'But what's going to happen to us, Jack? In a week you'll be gone. When will we see each other again?'

Jack pulled her close. 'Don't worry! What we have is something really special,' he whispered. 'It's not just going to end on Saturday. We can't let it, can we?'

Chapter 26

The following day it rained and Heike suggested a trip to the Dalí Theatre Museum in Figueres. Abrielle had already mentioned to Jack that she'd like to go, so with Peter and Simone having nothing better to do either, the five of them climbed into the dual-control, bright-orange Beetle and headed inland.

Figueres is not a large town and has little to offer, save for a few expensive shops and many overpriced restaurants, but the one thing tourists flock to see in Dalí's home town is his museum, which houses some of his most famous pieces. It was still raining when they arrived, and yet the queue stretched fifty yards back down the hill from the museum entrance, twisting through the windy streets.

After a bland lunch in a dark smoky restaurant, the rain had eased into a drizzle and the queue was down to thirty yards. While the others joined the queue, Jack and Abrielle walked around the museum's perimeter, where Dalí's eccentricity could be witnessed at first hand. Old television sets climbed up one wall, while another, painted in shocking-pink, was decorated with loaves of bread amongst the iron-barred windows. On top of the castle-like wall sat giant eggs guarding the ramparts like soldiers. Jack cuddled Abrielle, trying but failing to protect her from the incessant rain. He pulled her around to look into her eyes, her wet hair sticking to her face. He brushed it away so that he could see clearly into them. She smiled up at him, her gaze reflecting unspoken words that sent a shimmer of warmth through him.

'Smile lovebirds!' Simone's recognisable screech hit Jack's ears. A flash went off as they turned, catching the two of them off guard.

'Oh Simone, look at us! We're all wet. It's hardly going to make a great photo!' Abrielle protested.

Jack smiled. He didn't care how he looked in a photo. Then he suddenly realised that he hadn't even got a picture of Abrielle – something he would have to remedy in the next few days. He couldn't leave Spain without at least a picture of her. None of his friends would believe that he'd fallen in love with the most beautiful girl in the world – they would want to see the proof.

'Come on, we're nearly at the front of the queue,' Simone pleaded. Jack took Abrielle's hand and slowly they trudged back through the puddle-strewn streets to the entrance. Simone's definition of 'nearly there' was a generous exaggeration of the truth; it was another ten minutes before they made it to the entrance.

'Wow, look at that,' muttered Abrielle to herself as much as to any one else. 'It's rather weird.'

Jack followed her gaze to the strange-looking statue standing high above the railings that protected it. Half shrouded in a white sheet, it had an egg for a head and a sculpted frieze for a chest.

'That's what you call Surrealism, Abrielle,' said Heike, slightly patronisingly.

Abrielle shot her a look to kill. All day long Jack had noticed a simmering tension between the girls.

When they finally entered the courtyard, it was like stepping into a different world, a world where art took on a new interpretation, a new dimension. It was a completely new experience to Jack. He'd seen Gaudí's architecture, but Dalí's surrealism was in a different league.

As they walked into the Mae West room, Jack looked at the unusual pinky-orange sofa in the shape of a pair of lips and a larger-than-life nose, before ascending the stairs and looking through an antiquated-looking lens... And suddenly there she was, Mae West, as she'd never been seen before. Next they went into the enchantingly named Palace of the Wind. 'My God, look at that, Jack,' said Abrielle, in awestruck tones. Jack looked up to see two sets of huge feet, toes rounded and purposeful, either end of the ceiling, before they turned into rotund bodies in matching blue and red and then disappeared into the sky-blue heaven above.

'It's his version of Michaelangelo's Sistine Chapel.' Heike's knowledgeable voice brought a smile to Jack's face. What was she up to? he wondered. 'That's Dalí and Gala, his wife – she died a few years ago; she was quite a bit older than him,' Heike continued almost guide-like, her voice available to anyone who wanted to listen.

They walked through the rest of the museum, Jack holding tightly onto Abrielle's hand as they passed through the weird and the wonderful, as well as the downright perverse.

'Oh Jack, this is what I wanted to see. This is a portrait of his wife looking out to sea. It's so clever!' Abrielle said, her voice betraying her childlike excitement.

Jack looked at the picture of Gala and wondered quite what was so wonderfully original. 'OK, very nice, but what's so clever about it?' he asked, rather nonplussed and concerned that he wasn't appearing rather stupid.

'Walk away, Jack. Slowly! Keep looking.'

Jack could sense her excitement growing, but could not understand why, but as he retreated Gala slowly disappeared, to be replaced by the outline of a man's head. The further Jack walked, the clearer the character became ... until he recognised Abraham Lincoln.

'Jesus!' Jack muttered to himself. 'That's brilliant!'

'It's fantastic!' Abrielle squealed. 'He's so clever, isn't he?'

194

Jack looked at her. He'd never seen her quite so animated before. He smiled at her, took her face in his hands and pulled her close. 'Did I ever tell you how much I love you?' he asked spontaneously.

Abrielle smiled up at him, her warm smile telling him that he meant as much to her as she did to him, before her expression suddenly turned to one of pain and anguish.

Jack immediately knew something was wrong. 'What's the matter?'

'I'm not sure,' Abrielle responded, a confused look on her face. 'I'm getting sharp pains shooting across my stomach. Let me sit down for a second.' She moved over to a seat in the hallway. Jack wondered if it was a piece of Dalí's work. It looked old enough, but not weird enough, but clearly Abrielle needed to sit down, so he wasn't going to worry too much about protocol.

After a while the pains eased. 'Must have been the prawns I had for lunch,' Abrielle suggested. 'They didn't taste quite right.'

But the pain continued and when they got back to Rosas in the late afternoon, just as the sun was making its first appearance of the day, Abrielle decided that bed was the only option. Jack was disappointed, not because they wouldn't get to make love that night, but because every lost minute was time that they wouldn't spend together.

The evening was a strangely sober affair. Jack stuck to Coke, feeling a need to stay clear-headed, just in case. Just in case what? It was only a case of food poisoning after all, wasn't it?

Jack's mind wondered; it had always played the devil with him. Surely it wasn't anything else, nothing more serious. His head said no, but his heart, his heart which too often had been right, said different. It didn't say what; it just said, 'Beware! Beware of the unexpected!' An

195

uncomfortable shiver ran up his spine, reminding him that he didn't dictate play. That wasn't his privilege, that was fate's unpredictable role.

Chapter 27

I stared at the clocks behind reception, slowly tracking time in far-off places, watching the minute hands gradually eat up the distance to the hour. I looked at my watch – nearly one o'clock. It told me exactly the same thing – she was late, nearly half an hour late. Why? We'd agreed to meet at twelve thirty in the foyer. I'd definitely got that right, so where was she? Had something happened to her? Had there been an accident?

I took in a deep breath, trying to calm myself down. There could be a million perfectly good reasons why she wasn't here, but the only ones that resonated with me were either a change of mind, which common sense told me was wrong, or that something awful had happened, something which my foreboding thoughts had threatened – surely she was OK?

I watched the second hand slowly tick round to one o'clock. The plausible explanations were running out... Then in she walked and my whole being breathed a sigh of relief. The sun behind her shone through a white linen dress, showing off a perfect pair of legs. A distant memory stirred of my hands caressing them in the summer sun many years ago – smooth, tanned and sensuous.

She walked towards me and as I stood up I could see an enchanted look on her face, like a child who had just come top of her class. She was desperate to tell me her news.

'Jack, Jack, you'll never guess who I met!'

I smiled. 'You're right, I won't. You can't beat Hariri, so who else is there?'

'OK, I'll give you a clue. He's one of Lebanon's most fearless journalists – always stands up to the Syrians!' I'd never seen her face so animated, not even when she'd met the Prime Minister.

'Abrielle, I am sorry to admit this, but I have no idea. I don't know any Lebanese journalists.'

'Jack, I met Samir Kassir. You must know *him!*'

The name meant nothing to me, though I wish it had; she so wanted me to share in her excitement. 'Sorry, who is he?'

'Oh Jack!' The exasperation in her voice was impossible to disguise. 'He's one of the most outspoken journalists in Beirut. He writes for *An Nahar*. He's been brave enough to criticise Syria and the Lebanese intelligence services.'

'Sorry,' I muttered, shaking my head apologetically.

A huge smile appeared on Abrielle's face. 'I guess you wouldn't have heard of him, would you?' she said, realising that I lived in a different world to hers. 'He's a journalist I've admired for a long time. He speaks out against the Syrian presence, risking his own life by doing so. It was fascinating to listen to him. Just like Hariri, he feels that the winds of change have begun to blow.' Her face glowed with excitement and optimism.

'So a good trip, then?'

'It's been a fantastic trip, Jack. I've met Hariri and Kassir ... and I've bumped into you again – that's been nice.' I noticed her face redden a little; she was voicing what we both knew.

I decided to unfold my plans for the afternoon, a nervous anticipation running through me as I realised it felt like a date, a date to entice, a date to seduce, a date to persuade an innocent young woman to fall in love with me again. I wanted to remind her of what it was like, just the two of us, in our own little world, on our own private beach.

'OK, are you ready for this?' I smiled.

She smiled back, raising an eyebrow. 'Ready for what?'

'An afternoon of intrigue...' I tried to look mysterious, but probably only succeeded in looking an idiot. '...An afternoon of wonder and miracles.'

Abrielle stared at me. 'Is this to be a religious expedition or have you been drinking?'

I realised she was half-serious. 'No!' I smiled. 'Forgive the excitement, but, but...' I looked for the right words and decided to be dangerously honest. 'I just want to make it an afternoon that you won't forget, an afternoon when it's just about the two of us, no one else, just you and me. Just like it was eighteen years ago...'

She stared back and I knew I should have stopped there, but the words kept flowing.

'Back then we could face anything. Everything that is except the unpredictability of fate – that we couldn't fight, that was something we couldn't deal with – but that doesn't mean we can't now. Now we have the maturity, now we can defeat it, just the two of us.'

Abrielle stared at me as if I had gone mad. Perhaps I had. I had just delivered a speech so surreal that even Dalí would have been thrown by it.

'So, Jack,' she said, smiling, 'I take it this will be a day I won't forget?'

Her face lit up, almost childlike, and I felt my heart miss a beat, as I felt myself moving that one step nearer to the promised land. To the promised land of touching her again, of holding her tight, of holding her naked once more.

She moved closer, stood on tiptoes, and leaned forward, her lips touching mine. A single spark of electricity spun through me, travelling instantly around my body, touching every last nerve ending. It had been eighteen years, but in all honesty, it could have been only yesterday. It could

199

have merely been translated as a kiss of thanks, nothing more, except it was more, so much more – the taste electrified me as her lips lingered on mine, much more than was necessary. She took a step back, her eyes never leaving mine, her chest moving up and down, failing to disguise her heavy breathing. I felt it too, and like her, I was reluctant to admit it.

'Come on, I'm hungry... Where are we going for lunch?' She took my hand and pulled me along, before realising that perhaps that was a little too familiar, and let me go again. It *was* familiar – after all, we'd spent the best part of a month arm in arm, hand in hand, together as one.

We took a taxi downtown, driving through the striking contrasts that Beirut has become, brand-new buildings competing with bullet-ridden monoliths. We jumped out at Place de l'Etoile, Star Square or Nejmeh Square, depending on your naming convention – every place or road of importance has at least two, if not three, names, an Arab name, and either a French or English name or sometimes both. We walked up Exhibition Road, otherwise know as El Maarad Street, and I realised it was here, not Hamra, where the heartbeat of the city now resonated.

We opted for Scoozi, a restaurant offering an intriguing combination of Italian and Japanese cuisine. I wasn't quite sure what to expect – I didn't really care. We sat outside, a bright-red umbrella shielding us from the heat of the sun. They squeezed the tables in, tight up close, but that only meant we were forced into a not unpleasant intimacy, our knees bumping into each other on a regular basis. We both opted for the *tricolore* and the *escalopine de funghi*, not inspired choices, but I didn't care, the wine flowed, the sun shone and, if I was honest with myself, I was with the woman who inspired me in every sense, whom I had loved more than any other I had ever known, and whom I knew I was falling in love with all over again. And the really

200

scary thing was that, unless I was very much mistaken, she was falling in love with me all over again as well!

Abrielle reached for her glass, but as she picked it up she only succeeded in knocking her bag and the contents spilled onto the table. Something wavered on the edge before disappearing over the side. I leant over and picked up a picture, face down. I couldn't resist being nosey and turned it over. I sensed my body stop, and my mind froze. A surreal moment, apt given the subject of the picture.

At first all I saw was the pink walls, and the loaves of bread dotted symmetrically across them, but then the main characters came into focus – two drenched wretches, looking particularly stupid in summer clothes, soaked to the skin, but so close, a moment captured between a kiss.

I handed the picture to Abrielle, her eyes betraying a slight embarrassment. 'Why?' I asked intrigued.

She stared back at me. 'Why what?' I knew she was playing for time, and she knew I knew.

'Why, Abrielle?' I reiterated more firmly.

'Why not, Jack?' she retorted immediately, a flash of annoyance passing across her face, before her calm composed self returned. 'Why shouldn't I keep a picture of us? It was the happiest few weeks of my life and I will always treasure that!' Tears welled up in her eyes, but she fought them back. 'If you feel differently then good for you, I'm pleased! But for me, that was it, that was the moment I discovered what love really was, and, and...' Her voice trailed off, as if unsure or reluctant to say anything else.

It wasn't often she needed reassuring, but now was one of the moments. I took her hand, held it tight, and I looked into those sad deep-blue eyes. 'Me too, Abrielle. It was probably the happiest time of my life. The birth of my boys was special, different, but being with you – I still think about it every night ... every single night.'

201

She smiled back, the tears rolling slowly down her cheeks, and I just wanted to hold her, hold her tight,

On the dot of two thirty, I felt a vibration in my pocket. I pulled out my phone – it was Faris ready and waiting for us. We walked back down the street and there, standing outside a sleek silver Volvo, was a ridiculously large, beaming, good-looking Arab – my new friend Faris.

'You must be Miss Abrielle!' he boomed, taking her hand. 'I am Faris, at your service for the afternoon.'

There is something about an Arab's warmth that comes across as so sincere, so genuine, that you can't help but like him.

Abrielle moved across the black plush leather seats, her white linen dress rising high, revealing a flash of her beautiful legs. Faris noticed and gave me a sheepish guilty grin.

As we drove out of town down the Corniche towards Jeita, Faris pointed out the landmarks, new and old, those that had survived the Civil War and those that were spawned from it. As we left the suburbs, the red-and-white chimneys of the power station came into view – I wondered if they were the ones that the Israelis had damaged the last time I was here.

'I will meet you in one hour – but if you need more time, no problem. Jeita Grotto is special, you take your time, I will be waiting.' Faris flashed a toothy grin.

We bought our tickets and then headed for the train that would take us to the upper grotto. We sat side by side as it climbed the hill and I could sense our knees touching. Each time, a little burst of electricity flowed between us – reminding us of what might be, what might have been, what we had lost.

We entered a white-tiled, fluorescent-lit passageway and I felt my heart sink. This certainly wasn't what I'd bargained for. Perhaps it was a deliberate strategy, to lull the visitor

202

into a false sense of despondency, only to surprise him with the real thing. As we entered the upper chamber, we found ourselves at the top of a series of steps looking onto a myriad of stalagmites and stalactites. Great pale columns, which must have taken centuries to form, seemed to hold up the roof, like the pillars of a cathedral, while, high above, thousands upon thousands of crystals glistened like sharp, white teeth.

'My God, isn't it beautiful?' whispered Abrielle.

We walked through the first cavern, then, following the path, meandered into the next, not sure which way to look. Everything was a mixture of browns, greys and off-whites – no bright colours, only subdued ones that had never been exposed to daylight. The back lighting created a slightly spooky atmosphere, throwing long shadows that loomed up in front of us, only to retreat as we approached. We entered a tunnel, which finally opened up into a huge cavern, the walkway shrinking against the backdrop. A glimpse of blue water far below.

We walked on in silence, in awe, as the walkway came to an end and was replaced by steps that led higher and higher and deeper and deeper into the hillside. It felt as if we were alone, just the two of us – faced by the enormity and splendour of God's creation.

As we made our way back, we gradually emerged from the gloom into the light. It was as if we were being reborn, and soon we found ourselves side by side, on a little tram, very close, touching, feeling the warm breeze on our faces, and watching the sunshine filtering through the trees. We could have been any ordinary couple in love.

Faris was waiting for us, leaning on the bonnet of the Volvo. As he got up, the car visibly bounced with relief. 'What do you think, Miss Abrielle – isn't it beautiful?'

'It certainly is, Faris. I don't think I've ever seen anything like it before.'

'It's only been open a few years. During the Civil War, no visitors, no tourists, so they closed it down and it fell into an awful state, but they've restored it again. It's something for us to be proud of.'

I could see a sadness in Faris's eyes as he thought back to the Civil War. 'Were you born before the war started, Faris?' I asked. He looked early thirties so I guessed he had been no more than a child when it began.

Faris took a big gulp of air as if he was about to launch into a major speech. I wondered what I had started. 'I was born,' he announced in a booming voice, 'on Black Saturday, 6 December 1975 – the day the Civil War started!'

'Really!' exclaimed Abrielle. 'What a day to enter the world.'

'It was the day, Miss Abrielle, that the Phalangists set up road blocks on the ring road, and any poor Muslim who found himself in the wrong part of town was murdered in cold blood. Over three hundred and fifty of them!' He paused to let the words sink in. 'Before that, groups of Palestinians and Phalangists would shoot at each other, but that was the first major massacre, and it started a cycle of revenge and retaliation. Whatever one side did, the other would do something worse.'

'And you were born into that!' Abrielle exclaimed.

'My mother,' Faris went on with obvious pride, 'was taken to hospital not in an ambulance, but in a tank!' He chortled at the thought of it.

'How come?' I asked, beginning to feel slightly sceptical.

'My father was a major in the Lebanese Army and he organised it. Not only a tank; we were escorted by lots of army jeeps!' He sounded sincere, but I wondered if the story had become embellished over the years.

'OK, here we are. I drop you off here and meet you at the top. Forty-five minutes – I find you, OK?'

'Thanks, Faris – see you later,' I said, slamming the car door shut.

'Where are we?' asked Abrielle, distinctly unimpressed by the surroundings.

Looking around I could see why. It looked like a small American-style mall, just a few unkempt shops and a garage.

I took her hand. 'Trust me,' I smiled, dragging her towards the ticket office. 'There's not much to the place, except that this is where the cable car starts.'

Only the cable car didn't seem to be working – nothing was moving and there didn't seem to be anyone doing anything. I was beginning to wonder if perhaps this wasn't such a good idea after all, when a tiny Indian popped his head up from behind a large metal wheel.

'Five minutes, only five minutes. You wait, OK?' he said in a strong accent, a huge smile across his small face.

'Thanks, that's fine,' I said. Abrielle looked happier.

'It must have been horrific living through the Civil War,' she said, her voice quivering slightly as she reflected on it. 'Faris talked about Black Saturday, but that was only the first atrocity, much worse followed. This country used to be so integrated. There were Muslim and Christian areas, but many lived side by side... And then with the Civil War there were just the most appalling atrocities, massacres on both sides.'

'After that, the partitioning began. Muslims fled to the south, Christians to the north. In Beirut, the front line was Allenby Street – ever heard of it?' she asked.

'No, should I?' I asked.

'You have heard of it, but you probably know of it by its more infamous name – the Green Line! The road was abandoned and weeds sprung up and, with no one to remove them, they grew and grew. Green weeds all along Allenby Street and that was the beginning of the Green Line.'

There was a sudden whirring of wheels, the sound of metal on metal as the cable cars sprang into life. The little Indian reappeared and took our tickets, ushering us into a creaking, slightly rusty, red capsule. It reminded me of a gondola in a ski resort and it looked none too safe.

Abrielle went in first and as I followed, unsure whether to sit opposite or next to her, I saw a look of uncertainty on her face – it didn't seem the most robust form of transport. I decided to sit next to her. It meant squeezing up tight against her again, but we were getting used to that and I convinced myself that she would feel more secure that way.

The cable car jerked into life, climbing steeply, heading straight for two residential tower blocks, passing narrowly between them, so close that I imagined if I'd stuck out an arm I might have been able to touch one of them. Then, suddenly we were out into the open, heading for the mountain pines, skirting the tops of trees.

Abrielle turned to look back. 'Jack, look at that!' Her face a picture of delight and wonder. I turned and saw the Bay of Jounie below us, gradually widening as we climbed. Towards Beirut I could see the red-and-white towers of the power station, and the headland to our right covered in buildings, built up as Beirut sprawled into the suburbs.

'So this takes us to Harissa, does it?' Abrielle asked.

'It does, and this is where the locals believe that God intervened in the Civil War.'

'Really, and exactly how did He do that?' asked Abrielle, not trying to hide her cynicism.

'I'll show you when we get there. That way you can see it for yourself.'

When we reached the top, we were both relieved to get onto solid ground, only to discover we weren't actually at the top. We followed the exit signs, which led to a very short but steep funicular railway, which climbed the last fifty metres in an even less robust little carriage than the cable car.

It was so steep that I dared not look back for fear that the realisation of how steep it was, would encourage the brakes to give way. As we reached the last few metres, it slowed down to a crawl, so slow that I wondered if we were ever going to get there.

This time when we got off, we were there, and as we exited there before us stood the stunning Maronite Cathedral and next to it the beautiful statue of the Virgin of Lebanon.

'*C'est magnifique!*' exclaimed Abrielle.

'It's beautiful, isn't it?'

We climbed the stone steps circling the statue, round and round, until we reached Our Lady herself. At the top, the views over Jounie Bay were breathtaking, the blues and green of the Mediterranean contrasting with the white buildings with their red roofs that crept all the way to the sea.

'When this was built at the beginning of last century, it was built looking over the bay, but according to the local Christians, during the Civil War, the statue turned slightly to face Beirut in order to protect her people.'

Abrielle said nothing, but gave me one of those disdainful looks – I expected no less.

'Just don't tell Faris you don't believe it – he certainly does!'

We trekked back down the statue and made our way to the gardens that overlooked the bay. They were dotted with pines and cedars, bringing some much needed shade. Although we were 800 metres up, it was still quite hot. As we stared out at the bay, side by side, she rested her head against my shoulder.

'Thanks for organising today, Jack, it's been lovely,' she whispered into my ear. I put a protective arm around her and pulled her closer to me.

We stood there in silence, staring and wondering what the next step would be. I didn't want to break the moment. We couldn't go on for ever, but neither could we just let go. I moved around to face her, leant forward and kissed her lips, letting mine linger on hers. She didn't respond, but neither did she move away or try to stop me. I wasn't going to push her and reluctantly I pulled back.

'Jack,' she said quietly, 'we shouldn't be doing this; it's dangerous. Things are very different. We have responsibilities now,' I looked into her eyes and could see that her thoughts didn't carry the conviction of her words.

'I'm sure you're right, I just couldn't help myself,' I said apologetically, even though I didn't mean it.

'Come on, let's go and see the cathedral,' Abrielle said with sudden decisiveness.

She turned and walked away, grabbing my hand and pulling me along, with no intention of letting go.

When we left the church a few minutes later, Faris was waiting near the exit. 'Isn't it beautiful?' I wondered if he was referring to the statue or to us holding hands. 'Did you hear how the statue moved during the Civil War?'

Abrielle smiled. 'I did, Faris. It's a wonderful story.'

'No, no. It's not just a story, it really happened. It's a miracle!' His voice implored us to believe him.

He changed the subject. 'You see those cedars, over on Mount Lebanon, some of them are 6,000 years old and twelve metres wide. Did you know that they grow a centimetre every year?'

'Really?' I remarked as I did the maths in my head. If Faris's figures were correct, the trees would be sixty metres wide by now! I was pretty sure I'd read that some were 1,500 years old, but 6,000? It seemed a little far-fetched.

I smiled and saw Abrielle had worked it out as well. We shared another unspoken moment together.

On the way back to Beirut, Faris regaled us with his stories of life during the Civil War. How he'd dodged bullets and had nearly got killed by a car bomb driving around in his father's Mercedes at the age of fourteen. There was a tirade against the Syrians and Israelis, only brought to an end when he dropped us off on the Corniche.

We decided on an early-evening stroll beside the sea. The whole of Beirut seemed to be out and about, sauntering along the wide pavement, with its parade of tall palm trees, or chatting on one of the ugly concrete benches. Families, made up of three sometimes four generations, ambled along, the youngest running ahead and then retreating, while the elderly took it at their own pace, dictating to the rest. Young Arab men sat on the blue railings, looking out to sea, while below us fishermen balanced precariously on rocks as they cast their lines out into the azure waters. A sole bedraggled Lebanese flag fluttered in the breeze.

Before we reached Ras Beirut, where the Corniche takes a ninety-degree turn and starts to head uphill, I suggested we go and sit on the rocks. There was something special about the atmosphere and I didn't want to leave. We climbed through the railings and clambered down to the rocks. As we sat there, I realised how reminiscent it was of those days when we would sit on the rocks in Rosas, watching a setting sun disappear below the horizon. The only difference then was that one of us would normally sit behind the other, legs astride the other's body, pulling the other close. Abrielle must have remembered too, because she moved from my side to sit behind me, her legs wrapping me up as her arms moved around my chest. I felt her warm breath against my ear.

'Oh Jack, where are we going?' she asked quietly, fearfully. I leant back against her revelling in her touch, our closeness. I felt I was being given a second chance, a chance I knew that I mustn't blow.

'We go where fate takes us,' I said, not entirely sure what I meant. 'Last time, we were robbed of what we had. This time we mustn't make the same mistake. We must just accept what is and go with it.'

Abrielle smiled sadly. 'But, Jack, we can't just say everything's fine and then carry on where we left off. That's too easy! But then that always was you, wasn't it? Live for today, plan for tomorrow. Perhaps that's why I love you,' she added, before quickly correcting herself – 'loved you.' But the words were out. She was heading down the same dangerous path that I was...

I turned to face her.

'Abrielle, kiss me!'

It was the moment of crisis. We had reached the abyss, the moment of no return. But we were blissfully unaware.

Abrielle closed her eyes and then moved to meet my lips. This time there was no lingering; this time we both knew what we wanted. I felt her tongue inside my mouth and I responded in kind, my heart beating louder and louder.

I suddenly remembered where we were – in public in an Arab country, admittedly a relatively relaxed country, but still an Arab country, and a little decorum was required. I pulled away and Abrielle looked at me sheepishly.

'Come on, let's get a taxi back to the hotel,' I suggested.

We jumped into a taxi and as we climbed up the hill, passing Pigeon Rocks, I felt her hand on my thigh, running up and down my leg. I felt overwhelmed by lust, out of contol. If I looked at her, I knew I would be lost.

At the hotel, before the lift doors had even closed, Abrielle's arms were around my neck, her body pressing

210

up against mine as her tongue forced its way into my mouth, pushing me back against the lift mirror. Her hands pulled me tighter to her, as mine worked their way up her body, gradually working their way towards her breasts . . . Then a 'ping' as we reached the eighth floor and the door opened. We quickly untangled ourselves but there was no one there.

'Would you like to come in for a drink?' I asked, which clearly meant, 'Do you want to come in and make love?'

Abrielle pushed me out of the lift, smiling. 'Not yet! We mustn't rush this, Jack.' She had a slightly serious look on her face. 'You're so insatiable! Perhaps later.'

I thought she was teasing me, but as the lift doors began to close and she made no attempt to stop them, I realised she wasn't.

'Half an hour, seven o'clock in reception – don't be late!' The lift door snapped shut, leaving me horny as hell, all alone in the empty hotel corridor.

Chapter 28

The clear blue sky heralded the promise of a better day, at least weather wise, but it was mid-morning before Abrielle appeared, by which time Jack had retreated to the solitude of the rocks.

As the wind whipped up little white tops on the water below, he felt a warmth on his neck, which he knew wasn't the sun. The lingering kiss that Abrielle had now perfected sent an instant shiver down his spine and a glow to his heart.

Jack turned to see a tired-looking, but smiling face. 'Hey, how are you feeling?' he asked.

'Rough night. I didn't get to sleep until about five,' she grimaced, 'but a solid six hours after that and I don't feel bad. Dodgy prawns, I think!'

'You should stick to meat!' Jack teased. 'Much safer!' But she wasn't taking the bait.

'Can you get the keys to the car?' Abrielle asked. 'I fancy a proper coffee and they don't do them up here.'

'Yep, should be no problem – no one's using it. Most sane people wouldn't be seen dead in something quite so bright anyway!'

Rosas was still eerily quiet. Places that would normally have been teeming at this time of day were empty, as if winter had come early. Jack sipped enthusiastically at his double espresso, the caffeine working its way quickly into his bloodstream.

'So what did you get up to while I was away? I hope you behaved yourself.' Abrielle asked.

Jack lounged back nonchalantly. 'Normal thing, went out clubbing, drank too much, chatted a few English girls up...' A mock yawn as he watched Abrielle's eyes. No flicker of emotion, so he pushed further. 'You know what they're like – so demanding, they were all over me. Even had to sleep with a couple so they'd leave me alone! Not at the same time though, but there's an idea!'

Her face broke into a broad smile. 'Do you really think there's any other girl who'd be mad enough to want you? Now why was it I fell in love with you? I can't quite remember. Was it because of your great sense of humour. Oh no! That can't be right – you'd have to be funny, wouldn't you!'

Jack smiled. Somehow she'd managed to turn his tease against him. He decided it was time for a change in direction. 'In answer to your original question, I went waterskiing and, apart from the unscheduled falls, it was great fun.'

'Really! I'd love to have a go. Do you think it'd be possible?' Abrielle's face lit up at the thought of it.

'Don't see why not. I can take the boat out; I'm sure Peter wouldn't mind. Why not try this afternoon? As long as the wind doesn't pick up.'

'Really! Oh Jack, that would be great. I had a go a couple of years ago, and it seemed so much fun!' Her face became an animated picture of delight, as the thought sunk in.

Jack wondered how smart a move this was. As long as he stayed in the boat, he guessed he was safe. He just hoped she wouldn't be as incompetent as he was. On the other hand, did he really want her to be better at it than he was?

'Jack, have you noticed all the police around?' Abrielle suddenly asked.

Jack looked out to the front as another couple of armed

policemen walked past. He'd been vaguely conscious of an increased presence, but hadn't consciously thought about it. 'It was like this straight after the bomb, but it's got less over the last few days...' He paused momentarily. 'Until today, that is...'

'There's something going on, Jack! Come on, let's get out of here.'

As they walked back to the Beetle, a police car, siren whaling, screeched past them, tyres screaming as it took the corner too fast. She's right, time to get out of here, thought Jack.

'Are you serious?' asked Peter incredulously when they went to ask him about taking out the boat. 'You really want to go waterskiing with Jack?' The look of amazement on his face doing absolutely nothing for Jack's credibility.

'Well, I was the one going waterskiing, not Jack, but he can have a go if he wants, can't he?' asked Abrielle, somewhat puzzled by Peter's obvious mirth.

'Course he can!' laughed Peter. 'As long as you don't mind picking him out of the water every few seconds!'

Abrielle turned to Jack. 'Didn't you say you were quite good?'

'Good!' Peter exclaimed. 'He would win an award for the world's worst waterskier if they had one!'

'I don't believe I said I was good. What I said was that I enjoyed it – big difference! You can be useless at something, but still enjoy it, can't you?'

Abrielle, of course, turned out to be an excellent waterskier. She danced over the wake as if she'd been doing it all her life, and Jack sensed the conflicting emotions of pride and jealousy rearing their ugly heads inside him – but pride won the day. Keeping his hand on the throttle, he slowly became mesmerised by her graceful movements, skimming over the wake and turning side to side, creating mini waves as she changed direction.

214

Jack caught her eye and a big smile lit up her face. A warmth flooded through him. She's mine, he thought, no one else's but mine!

She took one hand off the tow bar and waved at him. Show-off! he thought. Suddenly everything changed. Her expression turned from delight to horror as she threw the tow bar into the air and put her empty hands up to her face.

A sixth sense told him to turn around. Ahead of them, no more than thirty yards away, loomed a group of craggy rocks, and for a second he thought this was it – a premature end to his young life, when he had so much ahead of him, at a time when he'd never been so happy! A picture flashed across his mind: his parents all dressed in black, his pale-faced younger brother staring down into a darkened hole with his coffin in it... The finality of the image spurred him into action. He fought hard with the steering wheel, pulling it round tightly, and the boat span round, sending him flying into the side, his shoulder taking the brunt of the collision before his head cracked against the side of the boat. Jack felt a shot of pain through his forehead as his body sank to the floor, his head swimming as he stared up at the blue sky. He breathed a sigh of relief.

Jack struggled gingerly to his feet as the boat bobbed up and down in the water, its engine having fortunately stalled. He looked back and could see Abrielle's skis sticking out of the water in the distance, her head bobbing behind a wave. Jack got the engine going and motored slowly over to her. He was in for a serious telling-off.

Abrielle pushed the skis into the boat and scrambled in without saying a word. She grabbed Jack and pulled him tightly against her, pushing the breath out of his lungs in the process – he hadn't realised she was quite so strong.

215

'If you ever do something so stupid again...' She paused to look him in the eye. '...I will kill you!' she shouted. 'Jesus! What were you thinking, Jack?' Then suddenly her demeanour changed once more. 'You're bleeding, Jack,' she said and gently brushed her fingers across the cut on his forehead.

'I think a little blood is a small price to pay,' Jack replied. 'Could have been a lot worse!' The shock of how close he'd been to killing himself was beginning to sink in and he was beginning to feel nauseous.

'Come on, let's go in – I'd like to get back on dry land.' It was an instruction rather than a suggestion, but Jack was only too happy to oblige. Somehow being on the boat didn't seem quite so much fun any more.

Jack's brush with death and the image of his parents at his funeral reminded him that he was meant to give them a call. That Saturday he was due to join them in Bayonne, where they had hired a villa for a couple of weeks. That evening, after dinner, Abrielle accompanied him to the phone booth at the top of the hill.

The sun had set and long dark shadows crept towards them through the eerie twilight. Jack felt like they were being watched and sensed Abrielle tighten her grip on his hand – she felt it too.

'So are you going to get up early to kiss me goodbye on Saturday morning?' he asked, trying to lighten the mood.

'Course I am! Nine o'clock isn't that early! What time do you get to Bayonne?'

'Not till about five. I've got an hour or so to hang around in Narbonne, before catching the train through the Pyrenees – I'm looking forward to that bit.' Jack tried to sound enthusiastic, but the charm of a mountain train journey paled beside the pain of leaving Abrielle.

As they approached the phone booth, Jack could see

216

someone inside. It was only when they got closer that he realised it was Seb. Sebastian saw them too, an odd look appearing on his face, as he hurriedly finished the call. He obviously wasn't happy to see them.

'You OK, Seb?' Jack asked, feeling a strange sense of unease. But before Sebastian could answer, all hell broke loose. From out of nowhere, they were surrounded by half a dozen policemen, all pointing guns at them, screaming in Spanish. Telling them not to move, Jack presumed.

'Put your hands up, Jack!' Abrielle said to him forcefully.

Jack did as he was told, but he could see the fear etched across Seb's face. A look of panic. Startled, petrified eyes. Then Seb started to run back down the hill. Jack watched in horror. Another order was screamed out, but Sebastian kept on running.

'Seb, stop it!' Jack screamed. 'What are you doing?'

Two more policemen appeared in front of Seb to block him off, guns aimed at his head. He hesitated, then slowed and stopped as he realised there was no escape. Jack saw his face, a haunted look, a look of fear and resignation. The police converged on him and threw him face down on the ground. Within seconds his hands were tied tightly behind his back.

It was that last look that Jack would always remember. It was the look of a man who already knew he was dead. It was the last time Jack would see Sebastian alive.

Jack recognised Captain Gutierrez, his interrogator. 'You can put your hands down now. Just don't go anywhere near that phone booth!' he barked.

'Why have you arrested Sebastian?' Abrielle asked, a confused and scared look on her face. Jack already sensed he knew the answer – the jigsaw pieces were gradually coming together, although he still found it hard to believe.

Captain Gutierrez could see the look of confusion on their faces. 'We have been watching your friend for a while, monitoring his calls, waiting for the call that would provide us with proof. Now we have it.'

'Proof of what?' Jack couldn't bring himself to believe that Seb was involved with the bombing, but Captain Gutierrez had no such qualms.

'He is a terrorist, your friend, a terrorist!' he shouted.

'I don't believe he planted that bomb!' said Abrielle.

'No, he didn't plant the bomb – that was someone else – but he did act as a lookout.' Gutierrez smiled sarcastically.

'But he couldn't!' Abrielle pleaded, turning to Jack. 'Tell me he wasn't involved, Jack?' She buried her head against his shoulder. Jack held her tightly as her body started to shake and the tears started to flow.

Over her shoulder Jack watched the police drag Sebastian into the back of an unmarked car. As the car drove away into the night, Seb didn't look up. His body, slumped awkwardly in the back seat, already seemed lifeless, like a puppet whose string had been cut.

'I'll call my parents tomorrow morning before they leave,' Jack whispered into Abrielle's ear. 'Come on, let's get out of here.'

As they made there way back to the bar, they could hear Peter's booming voice. Their arrival flattened the boisterous mood in an instant.

'Jesus, what's the matter? You look like you've seen a ghost,' Peter joked. Heike and Simone didn't laugh – they realised something was desperately wrong. Peter belatedly clicked and the smile dropped from his face.

Abrielle went to speak but the words wouldn't come out. All eyes turned expectantly to Jack.

Jack took a deep breath, but in the end all he could manage was, 'It's Seb!' He felt his voice catch as tears welled up in his eyes. 'He's been arrested,' he finally gulped.

'Jesus, I thought it was serious!' exclaimed Peter, smiling.

'I thought he was dead or something. What's he done, been caught drink-driving?' He laughed, but when no one else did, the smile disappeared from his face.

Jack looked over at Heike's sad expectant face; she seemed ready for the worst.

'The police think he was involved in the bombing,' Jack said as calmly as he could. There was an audible gasp and Heike's hands moved swiftly to her mouth, as if to stop the blood draining from her face. Even Peter looked shocked.

'No, I don't believe it!' shouted Simone. 'They must have made a mistake!'

Jack shook his head, still looking at Heike. 'I'm sorry, I don't think they have.'

'They must have!' Simone continued. 'We know they're a bunch of idiots. They arrested you two for heaven's sake!'

'I don't think so, Simone,' Jack said gently.

'Come on, Jack, you don't believe he's guilty!' Peter exclaimed. 'You know Seb wouldn't be involved in something like that.'

Jack looked away from Heike. 'I hope I'm wrong, but you didn't see the look in his eyes. It was haunting. It wasn't bewilderment; it wasn't "What the hell is going on here?" It was resignation, fear, a realisation that he'd been caught – he even tried to run away. Six policemen pointing guns at him and he tried to run!' Jack took a breath. 'You don't do that if you're innocent.'

Heike was silent, lost in her own thoughts, as Simone and Peter began to dissect Seb's words and actions, searching for clues that would reveal his guilt. His detailed knowledge of ETA; his thesis; his regular disappearances... But they didn't add up to much, did they? Not enough to transform Sebastian into a terrorist, surely?

Jack and Abrielle wandered down to their secluded

219

beach. They didn't want to make love. Instead, they went and sat on the rocks looking out onto a darkened sea, the horizon faintly outlined in the distance.

Abrielle sat behind Jack, her legs wrapped around his, her arms joined together around his neck, resting on his chest. He could feel her warm breath against his neck, wisps of her long hair tickled his face as a gentle wind blew. It would have been idyllic, but the evening's events had left them both in low sprits, neither quite able to believe that the Sebastian that they had thought was their friend had been involved in the terror and murder that had come to Rosas.

Chapter 29

I waited patiently, or at least as patiently as I could, in reception. I'd arrived at five to seven; it was now five past and once again the lift doors opened expectantly only to disappoint, as a large Arab businessman, threatening to burst out of his suit, bustled out and headed determinedly for the front desk.

I looked away and back to the three sets of lifts. I watched the red numbers above, and the one on the left stopped at nine – surely this must be her. I felt slightly nervous and then realised how ridiculous this was after the day we had spent together. In the half-hour apart I'd had time to calm myself down and, in her absence, my brain had tried to regain control over my heart, pointing out to me the folly of travelling this road – driving blindfolded, unable to see what was ahead, unable to anticipate the danger that clearly hid around every corner. Whether it was possible to navigate such a treacherous path, my brain knew not, but as the doors opened and out she walked, my heart knew that her presence gave it dominion once more and it would be my heart and not my brain that would dictate our destiny.

She was dressed in a dark, but not navy, blue flowing skirt, with a loose white blouse. Her hair cascaded down both shoulders and her blue eyes sparkled. She looked absolutely stunning and I felt a shudder pass through me and the smile she gave me seemed to lighten up the room. It was sexy, it was loving, it was friendship, it was acceptance, it was understanding, it was everything that a smile between two lovers should be. Except that at the moment, we weren't two lovers; we were still just getting to know each other again after an eighteen-year gap, neither quite sure of where we were going.

I smiled back, and she came up to me and kissed me softly on the lips, a gentle protracted kiss, for everyone to see. It seemed like she was making a statement, an announcement to the world that we were an item again; that she was mine and I was hers. Throughout the day her protective veil had gradually been lowered. At first I thought it was the wine at lunch, but it had continued long into the afternoon, long after any alcoholic influence had gone, and it culminated in this public demonstration of togetherness.

We walked out of the Meridien Commodore hand in hand, up the road to Hamra Street to try and get a taxi.

'So where is this day of delights going to end then?' Abrielle asked, innocently enough. My mind flirted with saying, 'By making love to each other once again', but I decided that perhaps this was too forward, so instead I deliberately hesitated for effect. It was too subtle for Abrielle.

'We are going to a highly recommended restaurant called Bonaparte's.'

Abrielle nodded. 'And who exactly recommended this restaurant?' she enquired.

'The concierge did, said it would be...' I hesitated. I was going to say romantic but, despite our closeness all afternoon, not to mention the episode in the lift, it still didn't sound quite right. '...he said that it was one of the best French restaurants in Beirut.'

'Really? Are you sure the concierge's brother doesn't just happen to work there?'

I smiled. 'You really are cynical aren't you?'

'It's helped keep me alive,' Abrielle said, a dark look passing across her face.

222

'Jesus, where did that come from?' I asked wondering what had provoked her comment.

The darkness passed and Abrielle smiled. 'Sorry, sometimes I am a bit too cynical, but I find it easier that way. You rarely get let down if you don't expect too much.'

Abrielle realised she'd dampened the mood and tried to do something about it, although her choice of subject was questionable. 'Do you remember the last time someone recommended a restaurant to us? ... We nearly got killed!'

It wasn't something either of us was ever likely to forget, nor the night that followed or the revelation after that. Memories like that might dull, but they are firmly entrenched in the recesses of the brain.

'Do you remember Sebastian, that night we discovered he was involved? It was horrible,' she said, shuddering as the ghosts of the past were awakened. 'I wonder whatever happened to him, how long he spent in jail? Perhaps he's still there.'

A taxi pulled up and in we jumped. 'Sursock please. Bonaparte's?'

I decided to tell her the truth; it seemed silly not to. 'He's not in jail,' I stated matter-of-factly. 'He committed suicide a few months after he was arrested.'

Abrielle raised her eyebrows. 'Really? What a waste of a young life,' she sighed.

'It was, wasn't it?' I reflected. 'He seemed such a nice guy; I could never quite understand that bit.'

'Come on, time to change the subject; I'd prefer not to talk about bombs and restaurants. Too many painful memories. So have you just gone on this one recommendation?' She said challengingly.

Fortunately I hadn't. I smiled politely, if a little patronisingly. 'I have also checked it out on a website and a guidebook I bought.' I tried to sound firm and authoritative; I didn't want her to pursue this line of questioning.

'And?' Abrielle asked impatiently.

'And what?' I delayed answering, playing for time.

'And what did they say?' Her turn to be patronising.

I was beaten; only the truth would suffice. 'Neither had heard of it!'

'Oh Jack, are you serious?' Abrielle asked incredulously.

'Abrielle' – I looked straight into her eyes – 'trust me, I promise you it will be good.' I trusted the concierge; he promised me the food was superb; he'd even warned me it was expensive, so surely it must be good?

She stared straight back, but with the hint of a smile. 'Jack, I only ask for two things – top-quality food and a bit of romance.'

There, I might have been afraid to say it, but she certainly wasn't.

The taxi pulled up and I handed over a $20 bill, US dollars being accepted as readily as Lebanese pounds. A little generous, I thought, but then why not? – it was that sort of evening.

Bonaparte's was on Sursock Street, on the corner of St Nicholas, a stepped street that stretched down to Gouraud Street below. It was one of the wealthiest parts of the city, where large houses hid behind high walls and security gates and sleek black Mercedes cruised the neighbourhood. It was the place where many countries chose to site their embassies and consulates.

From outside the restaurant looked a good choice. I just hoped the inside and food would live up to expectations.

'Hey, Jack, I think you've surpassed yourself – I take it all back,' Abrielle said, beaming.

I pushed the heavy wooden door open and ushered Abrielle in. It was dark inside. Little natural light crept in through the partly closed curtains and it took a few moments to adjust. Lit candles decorated the tables, flickering as the breath of wind crept in; subdued wall lights provided the only additional lighting. A smiling maître d' appeared out of the darkness.

I knew it was the right decision. The restaurant had that ambience about it, that sense of luxury and quality that I knew she appreciated and I myself had been hoping for. It wasn't going to be cheap, but I really didn't care.

We were shown to our table, a romantic corner position, where a waiter immediately presented us with complimentary glasses of pink champagne.

Abrielle smiled and raised a glass. 'To us, Jack, to you and me. I've no idea where this is going, but it's lovely to see you again.'

Her eyes sparkled in the candlelight and I smiled back. Will this be how I remember her, I thought, this sexy sultry look, or will I throw my life upside down, sacrifice everything to be with her? The one part of my brain that was still in the real world hadn't given up hope, but the tortuous battle going on between my head and heart had already been lost and won – I'd gone past the point of no return a long time ago.

Chapter 30

Torrential rain swept across the bay below and menacing dark clouds raced across the skies above. A flash of forked lightning momentarily broke the greyness, stretching all the way down to the choppy seas. Almost instantly after came a deafening crack of thunder that made the glass doors shudder. Jack took a step back as the rain lashed against the shaking panes.

The weather matched his melancholy mood. In three days he would be on a train out of Spain to France, away from Abrielle, and he wondered when he would see her again. He was still at a loss to understand how he had fallen so hopelessly in love with this girl. He'd always been in control before; his emotions were never the ones hurt. That was for others – *he* was made of sterner stuff. But not this time.

The rain began to ease around eleven and Jack made his way down to the bar with Peter and Heike. Surprisingly Abrielle and Simone were already there knocking back espressos. There was only one topic of conversation and that was Seb's arrest; none of them – particularly Peter and Heike who had known him for a number of years – could quite grasp that their friend had got himself involved in a terrorist plot; it just didn't seem to add up. Heike was very quiet. Jack felt for her; he knew she had a soft spot for Seb and, for her, the discovery must have been particularly hard.

'You OK?' he said to her quietly.

'I will be,' she sighed. 'I could never quite understand

him. There was always something mysterious about him that was both fascinating and frustrating. I guess that now the true Sebastian has been revealed – it's just not what I expected.'

Jack smiled back sympathetically. 'We were all fooled, Heike. We all thought, "nice guy, a bit serious, but nice guy".'

'But that makes it worse, Jack. If he seemed such a nice guy, how come he turned out not to be, how do you go from nice guy to terrorist?' Heike raised her voice as she vented her frustration.

'Perhaps we're not wrong. Perhaps the true Seb is the guy we thought he was, but somehow he got indoctrinated,' Jack suggested. 'Someone got to him, played on his vulnerabilities, persuaded him that if he really believed in what he wanted, then the ends justified the means...'

There was an audible groan of exasperation from Jack's right and he turned to see Abrielle staring at him, eyes on fire, fury written across her face. 'For God's sake, Jack, you're talking *merde*! We were just wrong, very wrong. He's an evil bastard, with no care for others, so *we* should stop caring about *him*!'

Abrielle had made her point vehemently enough, but Jack was never one to know when to back down.

'But it's not as easy as that, is it? He was our friend, a good friend, a nice guy, someone we cared about – so how did he end up doing what he did?'

'It doesn't really matter how or why – the fact is that we obviously didn't know the true Sebastian and he clearly wasn't a nice guy!' Abrielle's voice rose as her anger increased. 'If he thinks it's OK to kill people, to kill someone we knew, then trust me, Jack, he's *not* a nice guy!' She was breathing more heavily and her cheeks were reddening as she spoke. 'We spent a night in jail because of him, and the following day when we discovered Eric was dead, did he show any remorse? I don't think so!'

She was shouting now and Jack realised that he'd obviously touched a fairly raw nerve.

'That bomb killed three people. It maimed many others, including children!' her voice was moving towards a crescendo. 'If he's prepared to risk killing innocent children, babies, then he's not the sort of person...' She suddenly ended in mid-sentence as if something she'd said had distracted her.

Everyone stared at her waiting for her to finish, but her mind was elsewhere. Jack saw her eyes well up with tears, while she continued to stare at him; the fury disappeared, to be replaced by another emotion, one which Jack couldn't fathom. He was confused by the sudden change in her demeanour, something she had said or realised had triggered it, but he didn't know what. As the tears started to flow, she turned away and jumped up, and strode purposefully out of the bar and into the murky drizzle.

No one said anything for a few seconds; they just looked at each other, slightly discomforted by Abrielle's outburst. Eventually Jack stood up. 'I better go and see if she's OK,' he muttered.

'Better not, Jack, you'll probably only make things worse,' Simone stated firmly. 'I'll go! I think this needs a woman's understanding, not a man's!'

Jack was only too happy to leave it to Simone. Peter began talking to his sister in German and Jack got lost in thoughts about Abrielle – the seconds were ticking away and their last week together was not going the way he had planned. Perhaps a little more empathy with her feelings was required, and less thinking about his own – only it wasn't quite as straightforward as that because he didn't necessarily know, yet alone understand, what her feelings were.

Simone returned after a while. 'She's not feeling great, she's gone for a lie down.'

Jack watched her sit down opposite Peter; she could have sat next to him. Their relationship, never especially intense, certainly seemed to be cooling slightly. The girls were due to go back to Paris the following week, whereas Peter had until the very end of August in Rosas, so Jack guessed he'd be on the look-out for someone else.

The rain relented in the afternoon and a hazy sun made a welcome appearance, but there was little warmth and it was too cold to swim except for the bravest, who did not include Jack amongst their number. He sat in a pair of jeans and long-sleeved shirt reading and waiting, but Abrielle, unlike the sun, never made it out. Eventually, after dinner, she finally appeared and suggested to Jack that they go for a walk down the rocky path to the sea.

Jack started to apologise for upsetting her earlier in the day, but she stopped him. 'It's not your fault; it just suddenly all got to me – the realisation that someone I liked was a terrorist, that I don't know when I'm going to see you again. It was all a bit too much. I slept most of the afternoon and I'm feeling much better now.'

She finished with a smile, but her eyes lacked their customary sparkle. Jack wondered if anything else was wrong.

Their walk didn't last long and they ended up sitting on the rocks watching the sun go down against a perfect blue and pink sky, the clouds having long since disappeared. Abrielle sat with her knees pulled up to her chest, Jack behind her, legs astride her pulling her close and burying his head into the back of hers. He pushed her hair aside and kissed her gently on the nape of the neck, working his way slowly round either side, then back again. She squirmed slightly as the warm, slightly wet kisses kept on coming, but in this position there was little else they could do.

Jack was happy just to hold her, conflicting emotions ran through his mind as he wondered how he was going to cope without her, without being able to hold her like this every day, to kiss her, to get lost in her eyes. He tried not to think about it – because there wasn't an easy way.

'Right, we've got two days left. Let's make them two days that we'll never forget, so what would you like to do?' Jack asked.

'I really don't mind,' she said, turning to look into his eyes, 'as long as we're together.'

Abrielle continued to stare out to sea. After a time she manoeuvred her body round and lowered her head, resting it on Jack's chest. Before long he realised that she had fallen asleep. He held her for a long time, not wanting to disturb her and only waking her once it was dark.

Abrielle looked up at him disorientated. 'How long have I been asleep?'

'About half an hour –' Jack saw the tiredness in her eyes – 'I guess it's time for you to go to bed.'

'I do feel rather tired,' she mumbled.

Jack saw her back to her apartment block and then opted for an early night as well; he wanted to be fresh for whatever beckoned for tomorrow. He was determined to make the last two days memorable.

Chapter 31

I ordered a bottle of the '98 Château Musar, surprised at how cheap it was compared to buying it in an English restaurant. Its smooth velvety richness made it easy on the palate and much too easy to drink – I knew I had to be careful, or I would be in for the mother of all hangovers.

'So where do we go from here, Jack?' Abrielle asked abruptly, a serious look on her face.

I smiled. The question had been running around my head all day, but every route I went ended in a dead end.

'Do you know, Abrielle, I really don't know. I thought it was complicated last time around, but it's even more difficult this time!' I paused before adding, 'But I do know one thing, I'm not going to leave you in Paris tomorrow wondering if I'll ever see you again. I made that mistake once before, and now I've been given a second chance, it won't be happening again.'

The waiter interrupted the conversation with the first course; I'd opted for king scallops wrapped in bacon in a saffron sauce; while Abrielle had gone for a truffle and asparagus salad. Top marks for presentation and the taste turned out to be just as good.

'My apologies to the concierge,' smiled Abrielle. 'Excellent choice, Jack.'

I didn't want to revert back to a discussion on where we were going. There were clearly no easy answers and it was a difficult subject, particularly for me, as I was the one with the wife and children, although she clearly had her own ties to Paris.

'Tell me, are you still in contact with Simone?'

Abrielle's face lit up. 'Oh yes, she's still my closest friend, ever since we were kids. I'm godmother to her eldest, Jacqueline. She's got four kids, all girls, all red-headed!' she laughed. 'I feel sorry for Frank, her husband, five of them all talking at once, he never gets a look in.' She paused as a thought crossed her mind. 'She's a good friend; she's always been there for me, especially during the difficult times, when –' she hesitated momentarily – 'when my father died; other times as well. It hasn't always been easy, Jack – just like you, there have been bad as well as good times.'

As I listened to her, the candlelight flickered on her face and her cheeks seemed to glisten and her blue eyes to deepen. It hit me again, how she was just about the most beautiful woman I had ever met.

'What about Heike and Peter?' she asked, drawing me out of my reverie. 'Do you still see them?'

I shook my head. 'I kept in contact with Heike for a few years, but it was just Christmas cards and in the end we both gave up. I do remember asking Peter if he had Simone's details about a year later, so I could get in contact with you, but he'd never got them.'

Abrielle smiled softly. 'No, that ended with the holiday. Shame you lost contact with Heike; I liked her,' she said reflectively.

'Really?' I remarked, rather surprised. 'I'd always thought you were slightly jealous of my friendship with her.'

'No! Are you serious, Jack?' Abrielle asked incredulously.

'I am. I often felt that there was a bit of tension between the two of you.' I answered honestly, but sensed I was about to get a sharp rebuff.

'Oh Jack, you're so arrogant! You thought Heike fancied you?' The smirk on her face widened as she spoke.

I was beginning to feel slightly embarrassed – thank

God it was dark in here. But I wasn't going down without a fight.

'No, I didn't say that,' I said firmly. 'I just remember that there was sometimes a bit of friction between the two of you.'

'And you thought that was because of you!' she burst out.

'Well, yes, but not the way you're suggesting!' I knew I was struggling, always did – I'd have made an appalling politician.

A waiter saved me and appeared as if by magic and topped up our glasses, even though neither of us had managed more than a few sips.

We sat in silence as he delicately poured the wine, staring at each other, a big smile across her face as she felt she had made a point.

'Have you always had girls flocking over you, Jack?' Abrielle asked once the waiter had disappeared. The question was draped in sarcasm.

I knew I couldn't win this one, so I just smiled back and said, 'Only ever you.'

'Huh!' was the response. 'I don't remember throwing myself at you. In fact, I played quite hard to get, if I remember correctly!' Somehow I'd turned it and now she was on the defensive.

'Really? Who was it who made the first move on the rocks that first night, and who was it who couldn't stop staring at me all day long?'

Abrielle smiled. One-all, I felt.

'I thought it was you staring at me,' she countered. 'I guess it takes two – and you were quite cute!' She wrinkled her nose as she said it, almost coyly.

I smiled. 'Cute! You're the only woman who has ever called me cute. It's not the most masculine of descriptions you know.'

233

'Maybe not, but I always thought it was very apt, and it was meant as a compliment, not an insult – my cute Jack!' she laughed.

We had been the first in the restaurant to arrive, but it was beginning to fill up now. A large, sharply-dressed man – expensive suit, highly polished shoes, gleaming gold cufflinks, in his late fifties I guessed – accompanied by an equally adorned and elegant woman walked past us and sat in the corner opposite. They were ushered in by what looked like a couple of bodyguards, one tall and a little overweight, the other smaller, but well built – little and large.

I had my back to them now but Abrielle could see them clearly. 'Must be someone important,' I suggested.

'He is!' Abrielle whispered. 'He's a Sunni politician, one of Hariri's ministers, even more outspoken when it comes to the Syrians – and another who believes his life is at risk.'

'And is it?' I queried. 'I thought things were much quieter – safer – now.'

She smiled, slightly patronisingly I felt. 'It's true that since the Civil War ended there have been very few political killings, but that was because the Syrians kept a very tight control and I think for the Lebanese, they were just relieved to have peace. But now, politicians like Hariri are trying to reassert the Lebanese identity and are slowly pushing at the Syrians to try and dismantle their influence.'

She spoke authoritatively and passionately, and I felt another pang in my heart as I was reminded of another reason of why I had fallen in love with her all those years ago.

'The Syrians have some very nasty people working for them here who won't hesitate to kill if they feel their control is being threatened...'

'Dangerous place to be a politician, I guess,' I suggested.

'That's where Hariri is being clever. I'm sure he's partly behind the proposed UN resolution, but that way the debate gets played out on the world stage, rather than just here, and that makes it harder for the Syrians.'

I took a generous sip of the Château Musar and watched her animated face flicker with emotion and intelligence. Here was a woman who came alive when she started talking about something close to her heart. I wondered what it would have been like if I hadn't screwed things up in 1986; if our relationship had continued. Perhaps I'd have moved to Paris and watched the girl I loved turn into a professional journalist. I would have been there for her when she really needed me.

Chapter 32

Abrielle sat staring at her coffee. Her face looked drawn and she was very quiet, and Jack wondered if it was his imminent departure or something else that was responsible. She held onto his hand, but was lost in her own thoughts, as the others talked about the inclement weather which had become rather mixed after weeks of glorious sunshine – it certainly beat talking about Seb and terrorists, Jack thought.

Abrielle turned to Jack. 'I'm going into Rosas with Simone – I'll be back later, OK?'

'Why?' asked Jack, failing to hide his annoyance. 'couldn't I come too? We haven't got that long left, you know.' The words came out much more strongly than he intended and immediately he regretted it, especially once he saw the irritation in her eyes.

'You don't own me, Jack!' she said angrily. 'I'm not your property! I have to go into Rosas, and I'm going with Simone. OK!'

'Sorry,' he muttered, 'just feeling a bit sorry for myself.'

Abrielle stood up and gave him a peck on the cheek. 'Just remember who's in charge,' she whispered with a little smile – the first he had seen all day.

'Come on, Simone, let's go,' she said, walking out of the bar, without looking back.

Jack returned to the bar after lunch, where he and Peter whiled away the time playing a variety of card games waiting for the girls' return.

As the sun came out for the first time that day, Abrielle

and Simone walked in, unsmiling. This just wasn't going the way he had expected. Their last two days were meant to be fun together, but she seemed constantly lost in her own world.

'Come on, Jack, let's go for a walk,' Abrielle suggested.

Jack jumped up, only too eager to be with her and no one else. She took his hand and they walked silently towards the rocks. The clouds had started to break up and a hazy sunshine filtered through them.

'What's going to happen, Jack, to us I mean?' Abrielle asked softly, sounding unsure of herself.

Jack tried to smile reassuringly. 'I don't know. We can't just give up and say nice holiday romance, and move on, can we? But how the hell do we carry on a relationship from two different countries?'

'You mean you don't want to at least try?' she said looking hurt.

Jack put an arm round her and pulled her close. 'Of course I do! I'm not going to give up the most gorgeous girl in the world; I'm just saying it's not going to be easy. You can't give up school and I can't give up college, so we'll have to see each other when we can.'

'You mean you'll come over to Paris and see me then?' she said it almost pleadingly as if she dared not hope too much.

'Course I will,' Jack said confidently, but he had no idea how he was going to be able to afford it and wondered how often he would actually manage it.

The sun had dried out the rocks and they sat looking out onto the bay in a place that had become their own. There was a breeze that blew Abrielle's hair around and she kept on having to push it out of her face. They sat in silence watching a couple of windsurfers skimming across the waves below. A lone speed boat crossed the bay at high speed, jumping across the water.

237

'Jack, there is something else I need to talk to you about,' Abrielle said quietly, but Jack had already been thinking ahead.

'You know I don't go back to university until the end of September, I could probably get across to Paris in the middle of the month. I'm sure I could persuade my dad to lend me the money – it can't be that much if I went by coach...'

'Jack,' Abrielle tried to interrupt, but he was getting carried away at the thought of seeing her again so soon

'And then we have a mid-term break at the beginning of November. I'll have my grant by then, so I can use some of that to pay for it. I might have to starve for a week, but it'll be worth it,' he said excitedly.

'Jack!' Abrielle tried again, this time raising her voice, but it was in vain – Jack had hit a rich seam of ideas and wasn't going to be stopped easily.

'Perhaps you could come across at Christmas... My parents are pretty laid back – I'm sure they wouldn't mind... You could spend the New Year with me in London.'

'Jack. Shut up!' Abrielle shouted loudly, finally getting his attention. Then more quietly she added: 'I'm pregnant!'

Chapter 33

Little and Large seemed slightly edgy, their eyes constantly darting around the restaurant nervously; every newcomer was carefully scrutinised; even the waiters were watched intensely.

I ordered another bottle of the Château Musar, the first one having gone down far too easily, although in my defence I would have to say Abrielle had matched me glass for glass. We'd both opted for the chateaubriand, accompanied by chargrilled peppers, creamy spinach and dauphinois potatoes, all of which were delicious. After we had gorged ourselves on these gastronomic delights, there was little room for anything else – at least food wise.

As the alcohol began to loosen our tongues, I decided to bring the subject back to us.

'It's a strange thing fate, isn't it?' I asked rhetorically, looking into those delightful blue eyes. 'It deals you blows, then gives you unexpected opportunities, second chances. Why did fate decide for me to miss my flight? Was it just so that we could bump into each other?'

She smiled. 'Do you really believe in fate, Jack. Isn't everything just random?' She paused, a quizzical look on her face. 'I think it was just by chance that you missed your flight and chance that we met again.'

'No!' I exclaimed. 'You don't believe in fate at all?' I was surprised, even slightly disappointed. I'd always thought it a rather romantic notion and I wanted her to believe in it as well.

She stared into my eyes before responding. 'Sometimes,'

she said, 'but not usually.' The smile returned. 'Perhaps we were meant to meet again, perhaps there is a little room for fate, but if it was meant to be – where to now?' Her smile changed into a slightly fearful look as she too faced the question of our future.

'If I remember correctly, a long time ago we had a very similar conversation,' I said, my mind wondering back to those evenings on the rocks. We were as uncertain then as we were now. Except then it was just confusion and naivety; now we carried baggage as well.

'Do we just catch our flight to Paris and say goodbye, never to see each other again?' I could see in her eyes that she didn't want that any more than I did. 'Or do we make plans to meet again?' I suggested.

'You seem to be forgetting that you have a wife and two children and I have...' She hesitated. 'I have... It doesn't matter,' she said, shaking her head. 'I have my own life as well.' Her head dropped. She stared at her empty plate and I wondered what it was that she didn't want to say.

'Life seems to be a lot more complicated now I suppose,' I suggested. Abrielle looked up at me. A sad look.

'Really?' She raised her eyebrows. 'If I remember, it wasn't that straightforward eighteen years ago either.'

'No, I guess it wasn't,' I said, realising that we had managed to make it particularly complicated. Perhaps time had softened the impact, but the painful memory was still there – it hadn't been easy.

'I wonder what would have happened to us if things had turned out differently?' Abrielle asked. I assumed she was being rhetorical, but she, in fact, seemed to be looking for an answer.

It was dangerous ground we were stepping on, but the wine had freed up our inhibitions and natural caution, but I was still sober enough to know that I needed to go carefully.

240

'I could have moved to Paris, studied there, except I'd have to have learnt French first. Which would have meant getting a job, not the easiest thing to do at the time when you don't speak the language. I'd have probably ended up working in some crappy McDonalds!' I said, trying to lighten the discussion.

'No, you wouldn't!' Abrielle said firmly, a little smile lighting up her face. 'Remember, I was a veggie then; I wouldn't have let you!'

'Perhaps a street cleaner then?' I suggested, wanting to keep on the lighter side of this topic.

'No way!' Abrielle exclaimed. 'You think I'd have stayed with you if you weren't a little more ambitious than that?'

'You snob!' I retorted teasingly. 'It's not such a bad job – lots of fresh air, helps the community, good hours.'

'You'd have come home all sweaty and stinking; my parents wouldn't have let you into the house!' she said, laughing.

'You mean we'd have lived with your parents?' I asked, slightly taken aback.

Her smile dipped but didn't disappear. 'I think in the circumstances, they'd have wanted the best for me, for us, and I think they'd have probably agreed to it.'

Which circumstances were they? I wondered. Did 'us' mean a family, the three of us? Or was I just interpreting the words in the way I wanted to hear them?

Chapter 34

The blood drained from Jack's face and the tan that he had been working on for nearly a month disappeared in an instant, his jaw dropping as the words reverberated around his head. He wondered if it was a sick joke, but the fear in Abrielle's eyes told him otherwise.

'Close your mouth, Jack – you look stupid,' It wasn't said unkindly, but neither was it said with much affection either. She sounded like a mother already.

'But how?' was all he eventually managed, confusion etched across his forehead.

Abrielle raised her eyes scornfully. 'You mean you don't remember? You were there!' She didn't try and hide her annoyance.

'I know I was... I mean I remember.' Jack stumbled, unsure what were the right words and still not quite able to accept what she'd said. 'But when? We've always used condoms?'

'No, we haven't! Not that first time!' Abrielle said abruptly.

'But we used something, that spermicide cream?' Jack said, almost pleadingly.

'Well, obviously it didn't work!' Abrielle said exasperated. 'Because one of those little bastards got through and now I'm pregnant!' There was no humour in her voice.

Jack was confused; it didn't seem to make sense; it all seemed to have happened so quickly.

'But how do you know you're pregnant? It was only a couple of weeks ago that we had sex for the first time?'

' "Sex" is it now?' Abrielle shouted, her eyes lighting up in anger. 'You used to call it "making love", but now I'm pregnant you're already trying to distance yourself... Now it's only sex!' Jack could see a single tear emerge from her right eye and roll slowly down her cheek.

'I didn't mean anything by that,' he said softly. 'I'm just surprised that as we only made love for the first time two weeks ago that you could know you're pregnant so soon?'

Her pretty face contorted in anger. 'What are you suggesting, Jack?' – she spat out the words – 'Do you think I'm some slut who slept with someone else before meeting you and now I'm trying to blame you for getting me pregnant?'

The tears multiplied and Jack pulled her towards him. She didn't resist, laying her head against his chest.

'No, I'm not. Just like you, I'm in shock, but it hasn't changed the way I feel about you,' he whispered, 'so please don't twist my words.' Jack held her tight and could feel the tears flow as they seeped through his shirt.

'I presume you are definite about this?' Jack asked as delicately as he could manage.

'I am,' she said quietly. 'I've been feeling so tired over the last couple of days, and when my period was late, I thought I should just check, even though I didn't think I could be. That's why Simone and I went to Rosas, to get a pregnancy test, and well, it said I was pregnant!' She laughed, but it wasn't meant to be funny; it was said through tears, slightly hysterically.

Jack looked out to sea. The sun was beginning its descent, creating a path of light across the water. The clouds had disappeared, the sky was a deep blue and a gentle wind blew across his face. And here he was with the girl he had fallen so much in love with. It should have been the perfect romantic scene, but the fact that he was to become a father, at such a young age, had left him in a state of shock, unable to appreciate all the natural beauty around him as well as that beside him.

Jack's brain slowly began to accept the truth and he started to think about the future.

'Don't worry, babe,' he said softly into her hair. 'I'll look after you.' He pulled a protective arm around her. Babe! He'd never called her that before.

'I'll get a job to earn some money ... I can go to night classes to learn to speak French properly, and come and visit you, and then in a few months' time, once my French is good enough, I'll move to Paris, get a job there, and...' Jack hesitated as the fullness of the words hit him. '... And then I'll be there for the birth of our child.'

Abrielle removed her head from its resting place on Jack's chest, her tear-stained eyes adding years to her young face, and gave Jack an incredulous look.

'Jack, get real!' she said, shaking her head. 'You think it's all about you? What about me? I have a life as well.'

'We can do this together, Abrielle,' he said, trying to put his arm around her.

She brushed it away. 'Unfortunately, Jack, I live in the real world. You're being totally impractical! How can you come to Paris, get a job and look after us? You're a student, for God's sake; you wouldn't have a clue what to do!'

'So what if I'm only a student? Eventually students stop being students and have to get jobs, so what if I have to do that earlier than planned. I'm not going to leave you to do this all on your own you know.'

'Jack, please, think about it,' pleaded Abrielle. 'It wouldn't work, you'd never earn enough money to look after three of us. We'd just end up in an even worse situation.'

'I think you should give me a bit more credit, Abrielle,' Jack said firmly. 'I can be very determined. I promise I will look after you ... *and* the baby.'

244

'Sorry, Jack, it's just not going to work,' Abrielle said sadly.

'Well, what are you going to do then?' asked Jack, confused. 'Are you really going to be able to bring the baby up with just your parents' help?'

Abrielle said nothing, but looked coldly back at Jack. 'There is only one choice, Jack.' She eventually muttered.

'What do you mean, "one choice"?' Jack asked. 'I'm coming to Paris, there's no way you are going to go through this without me.'

Her face remained almost expressionless, and suddenly Jack felt the cold hit him as a shiver ran down his spine as he belatedly realised what she meant. He felt like someone had whipped him across the face, the sting cutting deep, all the way to his soul, before ripping it out.

'No! You can't!' he exclaimed as panic set in. 'You can't do that!'

Abrielle looked away. 'I have to, Jack, I'm seventeen years old, what do I know about being a mother?'

Jack looked stunned and bewildered. 'But Abrielle, you can't! It's...' He struggled for the right words, any words. '....It's our child, our love created it,' he implored.

'Jack, it's not our child, it's a tiny little blob that you can hardly see.' Jack could see the determination in her face, but he sensed an element of doubt as well.

'It's for the best,' she said softly.

'*Best!*' Jack exclaimed in a raised voice. 'Whose best would that be? Certainly not mine, and certainly not the baby's!'

'It's *not* a baby, Jack - get that into your head!' Abrielle shouted back.

'It is! It might be very small, but that blob as you call it will turn into a baby and a human being - one that we created -' Jack paused, trying to lower his voice - 'You're talking about our child, Abrielle!'

245

'Jack, please don't make this any harder; it hasn't been an easy decision,' Abrielle pleaded quietly, the tears trickling down her cheeks, her eyes bloodshot.

'Decision!' Jack shouted. 'So why don't I get a say in this decision? I thought I had something to do with this!'

Abrielle lowered her head and said nothing. Jack took in deep breaths, trying to calm himself down.

Abrielle finally managed to speak. 'I thought you'd understand,' she said quietly, 'not necessarily agree, but I thought you'd understand...' She raised her head and looked into Jack's eyes. 'Guess I don't know you at all.'

Her eyes betrayed her profound sadness and Jack realised that he needed to calm down; losing his temper wasn't helping either of them. Her words cut deep and Jack felt that they took away something of what they had between them – surely she didn't mean it?

'I'm sorry,' he muttered. 'I didn't mean to get angry, it's just...' but he couldn't find the right words and could sense tears welling up inside. He closed his eyes and never even tried to finish the sentence.

'Jack, I need you to help me through this. I know it's not easy, but it's even worse for me you know.'

She spoke with the voice of reason and calm, but Jack couldn't accept it. He fundamentally disagreed with everything she said, and then, scarily, he wondered if she was right after all – perhaps they didn't really know each other?

'Why can't we try and do this together, be a family? Perhaps that's the way it was meant to be,' Jack pleaded hopefully.

'Please, Jack, don't make it harder for me. I've thought about that – it just wouldn't work.'

'What do you mean, "thought about it"?' Jack responded, his voice rising again. 'You've only known you were pregnant for a few hours; that's hardly time to think it through!'

'It's long enough, Jack,' Abrielle said firmly, determination in her eyes. The doubt had disappeared. Jack felt a cold hardness in her, one he'd not seen before, and realised that he was fighting a losing battle.

'How pregnant do you have to be before you can have an abortion?' Jack asked, hopeful that however long there was before the operation would give him time to try and persuade her to change her mind.

Abrielle looked up at him curiously, her suspicions roused, wondering why he had changed his approach. 'It's not an abortion in the normal way because it's so early; they can do it with a couple of pills and that brings it on naturally.' She spoke quietly, but knowledgably. 'I have a month to do it this way.'

A month, Jack thought, up to a month to get her to change her mind, although, of course, she might not wait that long. Jack wondered how he was going to do this. He had to look like he was accepting her decision, but at the same time come up with a plan. He felt slightly guilty. There was an element of betrayal, but his machiavellian streak won through, and if they ended up a happy family then all would be justified.

Chapter 35

As I looked into those sultry eyes, I realised there was no kidding myself any more. Whether I had wanted to or not, I had fallen in love with her again. There was no denying it now – it wasn't just lust, it was love as well. It was clear to me now – I had to be with her. I didn't know what or how I was going to do it, but we'd been destined for each other and no one could take that away from us now.

Suddenly a man appeared at the table with a bunch of red roses.

'A rose for the lady?'

It wasn't something I would normally accede to, but in my mood and our situation it seemed perfect timing.

'How much?'

'For this beautiful woman? Just ten thousand pounds for a single rose, or fifty thousand for six?' he said with a big smile.

I handed over a 10,000 note and as I converted it in my head into sterling, I realised how cheap that was, even for Beirut – less than a fiver. Normally these guys are out to rip you off, not offer you a bargain – perhaps it was just my lucky night! A sign of things to come I hoped.

I handed the rose to Abrielle as Large appeared from the table behind and aggressively moved the flower seller on and out, escorting him all the way to the door, the two of them arguing in Arabic as they went.

Abrielle laughed at the commotion, her eyes lighting up as she smelt the rose. 'Thank you, Jack, it's beautiful.'

'Just like its owner,' I said, smiling back. It was a little corny I knew, but I didn't care. I felt so happy; I was loving every moment I spent with her.

Abrielle raised her eyes. 'Really, I knew you were arrogant, Jack,' she said smiling, 'but I never thought you'd call yourself beautiful!'

I smiled back. 'You don't think so?' I said playing along with her.

She stared into my eyes. 'I do actually... In a manly way of course – I've always thought you were lovely-looking.'

I wasn't quite sure how to respond; I wasn't used to that type of comment. I was happy to just keep looking into those all-consuming blue eyes, but eventually I decided to raise a toast. 'To a most beautiful couple,' I said sardonically, but it was the word 'couple' that clearly resonated with her. That warm smile sent little shudders through me every time.

We stared into each other's eyes for a while, a game that neither of us had forgotten, before Abrielle eventually spoke.

'You know that flower seller, he was an Arab' a little frown appeared on her face. 'That's unusual; they're almost always Asians...'

'Perhaps he was Syrian. They do most of the menial jobs here, don't they?' I suggested, but not really bothered. I wanted to get back to the subject of us, but Abrielle had a different subject in mind and I suspected it was done deliberately, to remind me of where my responsibilities lay.

'Tell me about your boys, Jack. What are their names?' she asked innocently enough.

'Liam and Paul – named after two of Arsenal's best left-footed players of the 70s and 80s,' I said and immediately felt stupid. Perhaps it was the condescending look she gave me, or perhaps it was because it was just one of those things that I should have kept to myself.

She raised her eyebrows. 'You named your sons after two footballers?' she asked incredulously.

'Not just two footballers,' I said defensively, 'but two great footballers, Liam Brady and Paul Davis – they were my heroes growing up. Why wouldn't I name my kids after them?' I could see by the look on her face that she wasn't impressed.

'Because it's stupid, Jack. Didn't your wife mind?'

'Well…' I hesitated. 'I never actually mentioned the reason for my choice of name, and she didn't mind, so I guess she doesn't actually know.' The more I spoke, the sillier I felt.

Abrielle shook her head. 'That's awful, Jack. You chose names for a stupid reason and didn't even tell your wife! You should choose names that mean something, not after some silly footballer.'

'What do you mean by "mean something"?' I asked, trying to get out of the hole I had dug myself. Best to let her do the talking.

Abrielle's sarcastic look turned into a warmer smile. 'Well, something more personal, a family name, or the name of someone close to you or even your partner – it just means so much more.'

'So how would that work then?' I asked, wanting to distance myself from my revelation, which seemed rather ridiculous now. 'If you had a son, what would you call him?'

'I'm not sure. Depends on his father's name,' she suggested.

I'm sure if I hadn't downed a bottle of wine, I wouldn't have risked it, and I had sufficient time to think about it, but somehow the subject was heading that way anyway – perhaps it was fate, but it came out all the same.

'What if his name was Jack?' I paused momentarily. 'What if we had a son, what would you call him?'

The warmth disappeared from her face in an instant and she looked hurt. 'That's not nice, Jack,' she said softly.

I took her hand, realising that she'd taken it the wrong way. 'I'm not talking about the past, Abrielle,' I smiled reassuringly, 'I'm talking about the future. What if we had a son, what would we call him?' I closed my hand on top of hers, stretched out on the table between us and held it tightly to assure her that I wasn't about to bring up the most painful aspect of our history.

'That's silly talk, Jack – not the sort of thing we should joke about.'

'Go on! It's a bit of harmless fun; it's only hypothetical. What would you call him, Jack or Jacques?'

Abrielle smiled thoughtfully. 'No, I think I would call him Jean.'

'Jean! Why Jean?' I asked confused.

'Didn't you always tell me that Jack was often another name for John?' Abrielle asked.

I smiled back. 'I did, it is. Sorry, brain's a bit slow – must be the wine.' Poor excuse, but probably correct. 'Jean it is then.'

'What do you mean?' asked Abrielle uncertainly.

I knew it was the wine speaking now. I'd have never had the bravado otherwise.

'In case things get out of hand later, at least there'll be no arguments over names in nine months' time!'

'Jack!' Abrielle burst out, but I could see the smile on her face; she didn't mind the comment. 'Don't be so naughty,' she whispered. 'Anyway it might be a girl!' she added, laughing.

'A girl, I hadn't thought of that. Jeanette?' I suggested.

Abrielle nodded reflectively. 'I think that would be nice.'

Chapter 36

Jack sat on the red-tiled balcony floor, knees pulled up to his chest, arms folded across them, and his chin resting on top. He stared through the iron railings at the empty car park below. The sun shone down from its highest point in a clear blue sky and the heat was uncomfortable, even though he'd managed to find the only piece of shade available. It was siesta time and the poolside and bar were deserted, save for a small bird perched on the back of a bar stool taking stock of its surroundings.

It probably didn't have a care in the world, Jack thought. With a single beat of its wings, it could fly up and away to somewhere new, somewhere happier – anywhere but here. Jack wondered quite how things had gone from being so wonderful to so miserable in the space of just a few days. He didn't want to be in Rosas any more; suddenly everything had become very complicated and depressing. Their last few days together, which he had thought would be so special, had gone to the other extreme. Now it was their last day and she had disappeared. Why on earth had she done that? Jack wondered, especially when they still had so much to discuss.

Peter interrupted his private thoughts. 'Hey, Jack, you want another beer?'

Jack would have loved one, but he'd already downed three San Miguels over lunch and he wanted to be sober when he finally spoke to Abrielle. 'No, I'm fine thanks.'

'You OK – you look shit?' Peter asked, seeming genuinely concerned.

Jack smiled reluctantly. 'Wasn't quite how I'd planned my last day here – that's all.'

'I'm sure they'll be back soon. I'm not quite sure what's going on with those two girls at the moment.'

Jack hadn't told Peter or Heike quite why he was so miserable and, as much as he would like to have confided in Heike, he felt too confused and didn't even know where to start.

'About bloody time!' Peter exclaimed as Simone's mother's car pulled up.

Jack jumped up a little too enthusiastically and rushed through the flat, bounding down the stairs two at a time – it wasn't the smartest thing to do after a few beers. He managed to avoid running into the wall at the bottom of the steps and slowed down to a walking pace. He wasn't quite sure why he was running; he just knew he wanted to be with Abrielle.

As she appeared, he could see how drawn she was looking. Not the fresh-faced girl he had met a few weeks ago, but tired, slightly older-looking, with the worries of the world on her shoulders – but still as beautiful. Simone gave him an icy stare as she walked past him and Jack wondered if she blamed him for everything.

'Hey, how are you?' Jack asked softly.

'Let's go for a walk, Jack,' Abrielle said abruptly, ignoring his question.

Jack immediately felt slightly uneasy. There was something in her voice that unnerved him, but she took his hand and squeezed it reassuringly as they walked down to the rocks. Jack wanted to know where the girls had been all morning but, given his penchant for upsetting her recently, he thought it best to let her speak first. Except she didn't. They walked in silence and gradually a sense of foreboding rose as Jack assumed that she wanted to say something, but wasn't quite sure how to.

Eventually it got to him. 'What have you been up to?' he asked. It was meant to come out nonchalantly, but there was a hint of an accusation.

Abrielle stopped and looked at him. 'Jack!' she responded indignantly, 'I don't need your permission to go somewhere!'

Jack was already on the back foot and tried to ease the tension. 'I know you don't! I'm sorry – it's just that it's our last day together and I was hoping we might spend all of it together. We do have something to discuss after all.'

'Discuss! What is there to discuss?' Abrielle responded angrily. 'We discussed it yesterday!'

'Yes, but I thought after you'd slept on it, had time to think about...' Jack couldn't think of the right words; this wasn't going the way he wanted.

'What? That I might change my mind?' Abrielle shouted.

I've done it again, thought Jack, managed to upset her.

'Abrielle, I'm sorry – I'm not very good with words sometimes. I'm just worried about you, I wondered where you were.' Jack said softly, trying to calm things down, but his words had the opposite effect.

'You really want to know where I was?' Abrielle asked, her voice wavering with emotion. 'I went to the clinic in Figueras!'

Jack felt like he'd been stabbed, the pain going right through him as the realisation of her words struck home.

'Why?' he asked as calmly as he could, but inside he could feel a torrent of anger building up.

'Why? Jack,' Abrielle said spitefully. 'Why do you think?' She spat the words out, staring with wild, scary eyes.

'You've killed our child!' Jack screamed, his rage exploding like a volcano. 'Jesus Christ, Abrielle, I really don't understand you... You won't eat a fucking chicken because it's too cruel but you're happy to murder our baby!'

'And you're a selfish bastard, Jack!' Abrielle retorted

254

aggressively, tears rolling down her cheeks. 'I needed you to understand, to be there for me, but all you could think of is yourself! Well, if that's how it's going to end, then that's fine by me!'

Abrielle spun round on her heels and stormed off back towards the apartments. Jack let her go. He knew that whatever he tried to say would end up making things worse – he needed to calm down first. He was furious with himself for losing his temper so quickly, but it had never dawned on him that she might have had the abortion so soon, and once he realised that she had ... well, it was the spark that lit the fire.

Jack sat on the rocks, in the same place that the two of them had spent so many happy moments. But this was not a happy moment; in fact, this was without doubt the worst moment of his life – he'd never felt quite so wretched. To lose the girl he loved so much, to lose a child, even if it had been no more than a tiny blob! It was because of what it represented that it hurt so much. Their love, which had been so strong, seemed to have evaporated in the space of a couple of days as if it had never existed at all.

After a long walk into Rosas, to the far end of the beach and back again, Jack had belatedly managed to start seeing the situation from Abrielle's point of view. The least he could do was apologise for what he'd said.

There was no one around the pool by the time he returned, which, he realised, left him with no choice but to knock on her door. Please let her answer, he prayed. He didn't fancy dealing with Simone's mother. Jack walked slowly up the stairs until he reached her door. He took in a deep breath, then knocked firmly twice. The sound reverberated around the hallway as he held his breath, his heart pounding.

But his prayers weren't answered. Simone's unsmiling

255

mother answered and her wizened face scowled when she saw it was Jack.

'Please can I see Abrielle?' Jack mumbled, hoping that she spoke sufficient English.

She stared back, looking Jack up and down disapprovingly, before eventually stating quite simply, 'No.'

It was said authoritatively, daring Jack to challenge her, but he knew he couldn't just walk away.

'Please! I need to see her.'

She stared back, seeming to enjoy his discomfort. 'You cannot see her. She is upset and not feeling well, and now she is sleeping. What is more, I do not believe that she wishes to see you. Goodbye.'

Jack was taken aback. She obviously knew more than he realised, although how much he didn't know. He also realised that there was no way he was going to get past this woman.

'OK, in that case' – he paused, wanting to make sure that the right words came out – 'please can you let her know I called and ... I just wanted to apologise.'

Chapter 37

'I never said I'm sorry, did I?'

'Sorry for what?' Abrielle asked, her beautiful eyes looking intrigued.

'Sorry for the way I reacted, the way I spoke to you.' I paused. Apologies never came easily to me, even eighteen years on. 'It took me a while to take it all in, to try and see your side, and even if I couldn't fully understand, I shouldn't have said what I said.' I lowered my eyes, unable to look into hers, despite the alcohol I had drunk. I still felt embarrassed – it wasn't the proudest episode in my life.

'Apology accepted, Jack. You did say some hurtful things, but it was rather an emotional time – I forgave you at the time, even if you didn't know it,' Abrielle said warmly.

'You know I did try and apologise that last night,' I said gingerly.

'I know, I got the message – I was quite surprised you were brave enough to come to the apartment and face Simone's mother!' she said smilingly.

'I was quite scared of her, you know; she looked a nasty piece of work.'

'She's OK, actually. I didn't really like her at first, but she helped me a lot after that holiday, seemed to understand what I was going through.' I could see a thought flicker across Abrielle's eyes, but she chose not to discuss it, so I let it go.

'I would have been there for you, you know, if things had worked out differently.' I hesitated before deciding to continue. It was a dangerous path I was following, but I needed to say what I had bottled up inside me for so long. 'I don't think you know quite how much I loved you.'

'It would probably have been a disaster, Jack. We were too young, we'd have argued, you'd have got bored with a baby to look after – it would never have worked.'

'You don't know that. We might have one big happy family now.' I realised it was the wrong thing to say as soon as the words came out.

'Jack, that's not fair. We can't change what happened, so don't go there.' It was said firmly. There was a flash of annoyance on her face before the warmth returned.

'Sorry, that was unfair,' I said quickly.

'Life might have been different if you hadn't overreacted, if you had spent a little more time listening, trying to understand, rather than just thinking of yourself.' It wasn't said aggressively; she just wanted to make the point.

'You know I never stopped loving you.' I sighed as I said the words, realising how true they were.

'A couple of years later I came so close to coming to Paris and finding you. I had train and ferry tickets all booked up.'

'Why didn't you?' Abrielle asked, a look of hope in her eyes.

'I was scared you wouldn't want to see me, that you'd still hate me.' I paused, thinking back to that moment when I came so close. 'I used the fear of rejection as an excuse for not going.' It hurt to still think back to what might have been.

'I'd have been happy to see you, very happy!' Abrielle said, and I could see a light in her eyes as the words had come from her heart. 'I forgave you a long time ago.'

'Really?' I asked, slightly surprised. 'You mean if I'd have found you, we could have ended up together, perhaps married, kids?'

Abrielle stared back at me. I could see uncertainty in her eyes, a flash of trepidation. Perhaps it was the realisation of what we had both missed out on, a lifetime together, but there was something else, something she was unsure about. She took in a deep breath.

'Jack...' she began but was interrupted by the unwelcome intrusion of a mobile phone. To my annoyance, I realised it was mine. I was tempted just to cancel the call, but when I saw the screen and saw 'HOME', I realised I shouldn't.

'Sorry,' I said, 'it's my wife. I probably ought to take this.'

Abrielle gave me a beautiful smile, one that I will never forget.

Chapter 38

'Come on, Jack, we need to go or you're gonna miss your train!' shouted Heike.

'Just give me five minutes; I need to speak to Abrielle,' Jack pleaded.

He had been desperately hoping to speak to her. He couldn't quite believe that he might leave Rosas without saying goodbye – after everything they'd gone through, it just seemed such a ridiculous ending to their relationship.

'OK, I'll be in the car waiting,' Heike replied.

Jack had said his goodbyes to her parents, thanked them for their hospitality, their generosity, especially on the alcohol front, but needless to say they didn't understand a word.

He had been keeping an eye on the poolside below since 8.30, expecting Abrielle to appear at any moment, but it was now 9.20 and there was still no sign of her. He realised that another trip to the flat was required, one that he knew he'd have to make, even if it meant facing that dragon again. As he climbed the stairs, he could feel his palms getting stickier and it was with some trepidation he knocked on the door.

To his partial relief, Simone answered the door. Better than her mother, but it was Abrielle he had been hoping for.

'I've got to see Abrielle, Simone. Please.' Jack asked as pleasantly as he could. Their relationship had cooled considerably in recent days.

'Sorry, Jack, she's not here,' she said sincerely. 'She

went out before eight this morning. I don't know where she is.' She looked genuinely sorry for him and Jack could see she was telling the truth, but it didn't help the way he felt, the despondency that took over, the horrible realisation that he wasn't going to get to say goodbye to her, to look at her beautiful face once more, or stare one final time into those mesmerising blue eyes.

'Simone, please tell her that I love her. I'll always love her, and I'm so sorry for what I said. Tell her I understand, promise me?' Jack pleaded.

'I will, Jack. I promise.'

Jack handed Simone a piece of paper. He'd intended to give it to Abrielle; now he'd just have to hope that Simone would pass it on. 'This has my number, my address – please ask her to call or write.'

Jack trudged wearily down the stairs and, as he came out into the light, looked one more time at the rocks where so many times they had sat so happily together. Suddenly they looked barren and unfriendly – without the two of them, they had lost their charm.

'Jack! Come on!' Peter shouted, pulling him out of his reverie. 'We have to go.'

Jack reluctantly climbed into the back of the Beetle and slumped deep in the seat, wondering quite where it had all gone so wrong. As they went through the deserted streets of Rosas, he looked out for Abrielle, but there was no sign of her. As they approached the edge of the town, in the far distance he could see a lone figure walking through the surf, where the headland reached out into the bay. He felt a pull inside and sensed it was her, but she was looking out to sea and out of hearing distance, even if he had managed to persuade the others to stop the car.

He wondered if he would ever see her again, a girl whom he had fallen so desperately in love with, who had

261

stirred feelings in him that he didn't know he possessed, who had literally thrown his life upside down and whom he would have done anything for. But what was their legacy? An abortion and betrayal. When she needed him most, he hadn't been there for her and he knew he would have to live with that for the rest of his life.

Chapter 39

The reception in the restaurant wasn't great and I didn't want to have a conversation with my wife in front of Abrielle – it just didn't seem right, so I decided to take the call outside. I pulled at the reluctant wooden door, a welcoming breeze hitting me as I stepped into the balmy Beirut evening.

It was dark outside, the solitary street light casting ominous shadows down Sursock Street.

Susan put the boys onto me first and I wondered if this was meant as a timely reminder from higher powers of the risks I was taking, of what I might destroy should I continue down the precarious path that I seemed determined to believe was my destiny.

It was nice to hear their voices. Liam had scored a goal in his school football match, while Paul had got full marks in his spelling test. Innocuous events in the greater scheme of things, but little things that mattered to them, that were part of a father–son relationship. It was these little things that I was threatening to destroy. Surely it would be them, the two most precious things in my life, who would suffer most.

Why? I thought. Why had fate presented me with a second chance with the only woman I had ever truly loved, but only at such cost?

My brain had reasserted temporary control over my heart but then Susan came on the phone and once more my fickle emotions switched sides. Her monotone conversation and the emotionless banality of her voice reminded me of why I needed to escape her. I had done as much as I could for her. I was mentally exhausted from the effort, but the light in our marriage had been switched out the day Ellie went to meet her maker. And now here I was, being given another chance with a woman who made me feel alive; who switched on senses that only she could inspire; with whom surely I was always meant to be with...

I was desperate to end the call as quickly as I could – all I wanted to do was return to Abrielle. The guilt diminished as Susan continued to tell me what she'd been up to – which was nothing! I knew I was betraying her, but I wasn't betraying the woman I married – I was betraying the woman who, through no fault of her own, she had become. I was listening but I wasn't. Nothing was really going in. I just wanted to get back to Abrielle, then get back to the hotel, then make love to the woman whom I had fallen so desperately in love with a lifetime ago one more time.

As I sensed the conversation coming to a natural end, I realised I had been pacing repeatedly up and down the road, from the front of Bonaparte's to the far side of St Nicholas, a distance of no more than ten metres.

As we said our goodbyes and meaningless 'love yous', I slowly became aware of the sound of a whining motorbike, its small engine pitch rising as it got louder and louder, nearer and nearer. I looked down the road, but could see nothing at first until, suddenly, it appeared only metres in front of me, lights off, out of the night, like a dark wraith escaping from the gates of Hades – both rider and passenger dressed all in black.

I jumped back, narrowly avoiding it, and turned as it screeched to a halt outside the restaurant, the stench of burning rubber hitting me as the tranquil Beirut evening was shattered by the sudden outburst of noise.

The passenger jumped off. No helmet, no light. What an idiot! Then he caught my eye and momentarily hesitated. There was a flash of recognition between us, but I couldn't place him. There was a scared look in his eyes, genuine fear, but then it hardened and was replaced by a cold ruthless determination that sent a chill down my spine.

He turned away from me and ran towards the open door of the restaurant, the door that I had left open. He put his hands together, then pulled them apart, discarding something as he did, before lobbing what he held through the open doorway and into the restaurant.

As he turned around, he glanced once more in my direction, grinning, a vicious smile on a cruel face, before he jumped onto the back of the bike. The flower seller! By the time I realised it was too late – the bike roared off, the tyres screamed into the night and I knew that something wasn't quite right.

I was confused, a detached observer, as everything appeared to happen in slow motion. I started to jog the few metres to the restaurant. I heard a scream from inside, a terrified scream. The warning bells in my head tolled away, yet I still couldn't fathom what was happening, only that something was desperately wrong.

As my jog turned into a run, my panic increased as the surreal scene unfolded before me. A flash of intense light, beautiful shades of orange and red flew through the open doorway, followed almost instantaneously by a deafening roar that screamed at my eardrums.

I sensed an agonising pain in my leg, as if a razor-sharp knife had been plunged deep into my thigh, as the force of the blast hit me, throwing me backwards into the road.

I lay there, my head thumping, as I stared up into the night sky: a glittering star filled panorama set against an ebony landscape; a crescent moon, with a couple silhouetted, perched on the point – the two of us sitting together on the rocks, Abrielle with her legs wrapped tightly round me, her arms around my chest, her head resting on mine, looking out onto Rosas Bay, as the glowing sun set on the horizon, leaving a blood red sky behind, as we planned our future together.

Epilogue

The queues of tourists snake back from Notre-Dame, taking in the warm spring sunshine, waiting patiently, noisily, happily. As I hobble past, I glance up to the Gothic towers, high up to the gargoyles that give the building so much of its character. It has been a long time since I have been up there; nor will it be today that I renew my acquaintance with those strange stone demons.

I walk to the rear of the cathedral until I find myself facing the Ile St-Louis, the smaller of the two islands on the Seine, the quieter one, not the one visited by millions of tourists. I cross the bridge between the islands and walk down rue St-Louis until I reach the church towards its end – St-Louis-en-l'Ile. The hands on the black-and-white clock face of its turret-shaped tower creep slowly towards midday as the sky above darkens. As I approach its dark-brown wooden doors, I hesitate; I don't really want to go in, but I know I have to. Reluctantly, I push at the heavy door and step over the threshold into the gloom inside. There is a musty smell, that familiar comforting smell of all old churches. I take a seat in an empty pew towards the back on the left-hand side, near the exit. Rectangular stone columns lead all the way up to the altar, each simply decorated with a cross or small picture. As I look around, I realise that the church is almost exclusively two colours – brown and gold – a combination of the drab and the beautiful.

Outside the sun breaks through the clouds and a ray of light lights up an arched stained-glass window; it is as if someone has flicked a switch and momentarily my spirits are lifted. Then out of the silence, comes the distant sound of a motorbike revving its engine and I am painfully reminded of why I am here.

After the blast I was dazed but managed to crawl into the destroyed wreckage of the restaurant, only to find a scene reminiscent of a war zone – broken tables and chairs, smashed crockery, and bloodied cutlery side by side with mutilated bodies, some stirring, some screaming, some lifeless.

I found Abrielle lying in a pool of blood close to where we had been sitting, her beautiful face looking pale and drained even in the darkened restaurant. Her face was untouched and momentarily I thought that the blood was someone else's and that she was unharmed, but as I reached her I could see the blood pouring from a wound in her left leg. I tried to stop it using my shirt as a tourniquet, but it did nothing to stem the relentless flow of bright-red blood.

I stared down at her beautiful face. She knew that she was dying and wore a calm look of acceptance. I knew it too, but it didn't stop me trying desperately to slow the bleeding.

'Jack!' she whispered. I cradled her, pulling her face close to mine. 'Jack' – she managed a small smile – 'I'm sorry – it wasn't meant to end this way.' She was struggling for breath. 'But I'm glad. I'd always wanted to tell you one more time that I loved you...' Her words were soft but clear, but her breathing was getting weaker. '... And now I have.' She smiled, her deep-blue eyes staring into mine, then the lids came down to herald the end of a young life that still had so much to offer.

I whispered my love into her ears, kissed her soft cheeks, but no amount of love could save her – she died before the paramedics arrived, lying in my arms while I held her tight, unwilling ever to let her go.

The hand grenade failed in its primary objective – assassination of the Sunni minister – but the collateral damage stood at four – Little and Large, the maître d' and Abrielle; innocent civilians caught up in somebody else's fight. So typical of Lebanese battles – it was always the innocent who had to suffer!

I spent a week in St George's Hospital in Achrafieh, recovering from the removal of a small piece of shrapnel that had embedded itself in my leg. I had nothing to do but reflect, to think, to question, to wonder why. Was it all fate, or was it just because it was? Twice, fate had intervened in our lives with devastating consequences, both times splitting us up, but this time it was for good. There would be no more chance meetings, no matter how hard I prayed...

Now the church is nearly full. I look at all the faces, faces that mean nothing to me. Faces that no doubt meant a lot to Abrielle – relations, friends, colleagues – but to me they mean nothing; they are all part of a life that I knew so little about, the other Abrielle, the everyday Abrielle that I would now never know.

Amongst the mourners, dressed exclusively in black, I notice the long red hair of a tall woman in the front row. Beside her, in descending order are four smaller versions, each with the flaming hair of their mother. Simone and her brood no doubt.

I can't follow the funeral Mass. I just go along with the flow, standing and sitting with everyone else. Someone, a man my age, makes a little speech, but frustratingly I can't pick up more than a few words. Does he mention her beautiful blue eyes that could entrap any man? What about her smile, her pretty enigmatic smile that could light up a room? He can't do justice to her; only I can do that; only I have seen her at her happiest; only I have seen her when she was in love.

As soon as it's over, I intend to leave quickly. I'm not

269

even sure I wanted to be here in the first place, but I feel Abrielle would have wanted me here. Unfortunately they carry out the coffin first with the mourners following and I get caught up in the throng.

Once outside, I gulped in some fresh air, a welcome change to the stale atmosphere inside the church. I decide to walk in the opposite direction to everyone else. I have done my bit, but now it is time to take my leave – I have said my final goodbye to my beloved Abrielle.

As I head away from the church, I breathe a sigh of relief. I don't like funerals at the best of times, but when it's for a love, a secret love, that no one else knows about, it makes it that much more difficult; there is no one to talk to, no one to understand.

'Jack, Jack!'

I sigh. It might have been eighteen years, but Simone's voice still has that slightly high-pitched edge to it. I try to ignore it, but she shouts louder and gets closer.

I turn and for the second time in a fortnight, I see an older version of a girl I haven't seen in eighteen years. She looks older than Abrielle, but then she's had four kids. Her red hair is being blown about in the breeze and she tries to keep it out of her face.

'Simone!' I grimace. 'I'd like to say nice to see you again, but in the circumstances...' I tail off, not quite knowing how to finish the sentence.

'Jack, I'm so sorry,' she said sincerely. 'It must have been horrific for you.'

'You knew I was there?' I ask, rather surprised and wondering how she could know.

'Abrielle called me the evening before you went out. She was so excited at seeing you again. She said you'd had a lovely afternoon and that you'd planned a romantic evening just for her.'

I nod smiling. 'We did have a nice time, everything

was going perfectly until –' I hesitated, but there were no right words – '...until the blast.' As the words come out, they suddenly hit home, bringing the bloody scene once more to the forefront of my mind.

'I felt so useless, Simone. All I could do was hold her and watch the blood drain away from her, watch her die. I tried to stop the blood, but there was so much of it.' I pause to catch my breath, but I know I have to finish. I've not spoken to anyone about it. The words have been trapped inside me for too long. 'Her face was untouched, you know, her beautiful face completely untouched. She looked completely at peace.'

I look into Simone's eyes and can see she's been crying. They are bloodshot and her mascara is smudged. It reminds me that I wasn't the only one suffering. Simone has lost her best friend and Abrielle's elderly mother has lost her only daughter.

'Jack, there is someone I'd like you to meet,' Simone says suddenly, interrupting my private thoughts.

This is the last thing I wanted, to meet her kids or husband, it's hardly a time for pleasantries.

'Sorry, Simone, I have to get back to the airport...' I begin, but as I speak, out of the shadows behind Simone, appears a young woman, a sad and scared look on her face. She is dressed all in black, her head cast down. Her sad eyes look up at me expectantly, searching for something. But what, I'm not sure.

Her long hair reminds me of a young Abrielle. A shiver runs through me as I realise that there is a lot about her that reminds me of Abrielle, high cheekbones, little button nose – a younger cousin perhaps? It is her eyes that are different, a grey-green colour, but why do they look up at me with so much expectation. As I look back, a feeling of familiarity comes over me. Something about those eyes...

271

Her sad face breaks into an embarrassed little smile, and instantly the look in her eyes changes. Suddenly I realise where I know those eyes from. I feel a shudder run throughout my body, sending shockwave after shockwave through me as the realisation of who is standing before me hits me. Those eyes ... but how can it be? Did she lie to me? They are eyes that I know so well, eyes that stare back at me every day, every time that I look in a mirror.

Simone breaks the silence. 'Jack, this is Jeanette.'

Acknowledgements

If I had known what I know now, I'm not sure if I would have had the patience, the energy or the determination to go through with this, but I'm glad I didn't know - it has been a learning experience, at times frustrating, at times infuriating, but ultimately an experience that I will never forget.

There are many people who have played their part, who have contributed in their own small way, some knowingly, many others obliviously, and there are those who encouraged me, when giving up on the dream seemed an easier option.

My first thanks must go to Tony Fraher, who in 1999, asked me to go and work in Bahrain and in doing so unleashed an unknown thirst for knowledge and understanding of the Middle East and a desire to travel and learn about my new neighbours.

It was in Bahrain I met Andre Roos, my first true critic, who asked all the uncomfortable and controversial questions that only the closest of friends dares to ask and through him, I believe I found my audience.

To Peter May and Janet Hally who gave me the guidance and belief that there was a story worth writing, and to all at The Book Guild: Carol, Joanna, Robert and Janet, who have all contributed to the completed novel.

But the most thanks must go to my wife and children, who have suffered for years: being dragged off to countries they would rather not go; visiting places they would rather not visit and for putting up with my absence when my desire to write took precedence. They have criticised, analysed and encouraged as appropriate, and without them, this novel would never have been completed.

A thank you also to my parents, not just for everything they have done for me throughout my life, but for their forensic and critical analysis of the proofs, which has been so important.

A final thanks must go to the people of Lebanon, a beautiful country that has suffered for decades, as others fight their battles from Beirut to the Bekaa, using the Lebanese as their excuse. The warmth, welcoming and forgiveness of the Muslims and Christians of Beirut begs the question of why people of different faiths, different creeds and different ethnicity can't live together. It must be God's wish, and *Inshallah*, one day it will become true.